BOOKISHLY
EVER AFTER

BOOKISHLY EVER AFTER

EVER AFTER · BOOK ONE

ISABEL BANDEIRA

Spencer Hill Press

Library of Congress Cataloging-in-Publication Data
available upon request

Published in the United States by Spencer Hill Press
www.SpencerHillPress.com

Distributed by Midpoint Trade Books
www.midpointtrade.com

This edition ISBN:
9781633920583 paperback
9781633920590 eBook
Printed in the United States of America

Design by Michael Short and Mark Karis
Cover by Jenny Zemanek

To all the teachers
and librarians who saw
a little girl who loved stories, fed
her love of books, and encouraged
her to write her own. With special
love to Mrs. Hubbard, Mrs. Beck,
Ms. Ponter, and Mrs. Leese.
Thank you for giving me
the gift of an endless
world of magic.

I rocked forward, balancing my book on my knees and tried to ignore the yelling and chatter around me. The edge of the cafeteria bench dug into my legs, practically cutting off my circulation, but I barely noticed.

Em elbowed me, leaning over to hiss in my ear, "Seriously, Feebs, put that down. You look like a freak."

"Uh-huh. Just one more page...it's getting good." I flipped the page. Maeve was about to be transported to the Otherland and the court.

"God, you *are* a freak." Em heaved a dramatic sigh and turned to talk to the rest of our tablemates.

Yes. This was it. It was like magic jumped off of the page and into my fingers, travelling straight to the pit of my stomach. *Aedan.*

The words rolled over me and the cafeteria faded away.

Aedan held out his hand, waiting, his gold-flecked eyes meeting hers, making it impossible to look away. Even though Maeve was dying to reach out and wrap her fingers around his, she hesitated. The whole situation was insane.

"Trust me..." I whispered along with him and my heart skipped a beat.

"What the *hell?*" Em broke into my thoughts and I jolted back to the cafeteria and caught sight of a guy a few tables over trying to stuff an entire hoagie into his mouth. God, reality sucked.

It took a second to focus and I closed *Golden* slowly, holding it so tight that the corners of the cover dug into my palms. Even on a reread, it was perfect. "Em, I think I'm in love."

"Just a tip, Phoebe," Em said as she none-too-gently pried the book from my hands and slipped it into my messenger bag, "Normal people don't read books during lunch, unless they have a test the next period."

My fingers itched to pull *Golden* back out of the bag. My brain was still on a book high, stuck on the Hill of Tara in Ireland with an incredibly swoon-worthy guardian. The contrast between that and a South Jersey high school cafeteria was jarring. "Normalcy is overrated."

"Normalcy is what keeps us afloat in this sea of teenage drama," Em said in her best authoritative voice with a dramatic toss of her short, dark curls. Without missing a beat, she managed to seamlessly pop back into her conversation with Grace and Alec.

We were like four legs on a wonky table. Em and me, the band geeks...I was the bookish one to balance her drama nerdery; Alec, the sciencelete; and Grace, our resident cheerleader. Most of us, like me, kinda flew somewhere below popular and above total nerddom. Grace, with her blown-out strawberry blonde hair and designer wardrobe, was a part of the glitterati but still deigned to sit with us nobodies. If she hadn't been a sciencelete with Alec before making the squad, she probably wouldn't even know our names. Instead, she was the voice of reason to balance Em's theatrics, Alec's geekiness, and my tendency to quote fictional characters. And Em and Alec, who had grown up next to each other, were the glue that held us all together.

I unpacked my sandwich and resigned myself to the fact that I'd gone from living in a world of ancient magic to lunchtime mundane.

"Can someone explain to me why we even need pep bands?" Em said, breaking into Alec and Grace's debate about football. "I'd do anything to get out of another Friday night of freezing our butts off in the stands and playing the stupid victory march over and over again."

Grace was still wearing her red and orange uniform from the pep rally that morning, and even her color coordinated, beribboned ponytail screamed school spirit. "That's assuming our team even manages a touchdown against Millbrook. Their offense has a spread-passing attack that dominates the field and their defense has given them five shutouts this season. I doubt you'll be playing any victory marches tonight." The words that came out of her mouth sounded like they made sentences, but I wasn't really sure what they meant.

Em elbowed me. "Did you understand anything she just said?" Grace sometimes forgot that Em and I routinely failed the football module in gym every year, which was kind of impressive considering we were forced to sit through all the home games for credit in band.

I took a bite of my sandwich, swallowed without chewing, and twisted my nose at Grace. "Total lack of athletic knowledge here, remember?"

Grace threw a carrot stick at me. "Says Miss Wannabe Olympian."

"Because archery is so much like football. If someone starts running at me, I don't try to jump on them. I shoot them." I anchored my hand alongside my chin and shot her with an imaginary arrow.

"Like that girl from that new movie." Alec said, "*Perfect Zombieism*. That was so awesome how she made a bow out of that tree branch and her shoelaces."

Not that scene again. The shoelace thing I could forgive even though it was a string made out of braided fishing line in the book, but the branch part was annoying. "That's so not possible. She'd never get enough force and distance out of the size stave they used in the movie. I read the books and they weren't that ridiculous. Hollywood messes up everything."

"But the movie is still really cool," Grace said with a shrug. "Even with its total lack of respect for the laws of physics."

"And biology," Alec added, which earned him another shrug from Grace. "What? All good zombie movies at least pretend there's some kind of biological reason for their zombies."

I pressed my hands flat to the table and sat forward.

"Okay, this is something that's been bugging me for a really long time. Did you notice that the people in *Zombieism* all have perfect vision? Totally not realistic."

Out of the corner of my eye, I saw Em mouth, "Here we go again," to Grace.

I continued. "Will someone please tell me why no one in dystopian or apocalyptic novels has bad vision? I'm so blind without my contacts that, if we ever have a nuclear or zombie apocalypse, I'm *screwed*. I won't even be able to get contact solution, and, if my glasses break, that will totally suck. If the world was ending and people were scrambling for their lives, you *know* there would be some people going 'Guys? Guys? I can't see where you are.'"

"Well, if the world is ending, we'll just leave you behind to fend for your half-blind self."

"Thanks, Em. Thanks so much."

"I'll blindly fight off the zombies with you." Came a voice from behind me. I looked up to find Dev standing over me with his lunch tray. He pointed at his eyes. "Contacts. We can stand back-to-back and just swing at whatever blurry things come our way."

I blinked dumbly at him. Dev usually sat on the other side of the lunchroom with some of the other theatre and band people, but this was the fifth time this month he had just showed up at our table.

"Um, I guess that might work."

Em scooted over to make room for him next to me. "What are you doing over here in misfit land again? I don't know if we can allow clarinets at our table. This is firmly flute territory."

"I'm working on breaking down barriers to musical diversity, one table at a time." He snorted at his own joke, then said, "Actually, I heard the word zombie and couldn't resist." Dev grinned at me. "Are you talking about *Perfect Zombieism?*"

"We were until Feebs started going off about glasses and stuff," Alec told him around a mouthful of hoagie.

"I was not going off."

"If the world were a book and my glasses were melted by a glittery dragon, I'd be screwed," Grace said in a high-pitched mock imitation of me.

I made a face at Grace and Em patted me on the back. "It's okay, we like the weird book-y world you live in. Makes the rest of our lives look a lot more normal."

"Normalcy is definitely overrated," Dev said, and I wondered if he had heard my earlier conversation with Em. Before I could ask, though, he looked past me and started a long, boring discussion about *Perfect Zombieism* and something about decapitation with Alec.

I let their voices blur together and thought about pulling the book back out of my bag when Kris passed our table. Kristopher Lambert. Junior class president and an exact match to the mental picture I had of Aedan from *Golden.* Well, if Aedan was real and not a creature out of Irish legend. Tall, aristocratic features, almost black hair that was always neatly combed into place, and golden brown eyes that I could look into forever. Time slowed and, for a second, only he and I existed. I let out a silent sigh, trying my hardest not to look like the girls who mooned over the football players.

Em reached around Dev to nudge me. "Not Kris again. What do you see in him?"

With an awful thud, time sped up again. "He's our class president and incredibly smart," I shot back at her, then dropped my chin into my hands and refocused on Kris, who had put on his campaigning expression and was talking to some of the guys from the football team.

Em stared at me like I had said I was going to run naked through the cafeteria. "Smart? He's a dumbass. How he even made it to junior year is beyond me." She poked me in the arm, a knowing grin spreading across her face. "You only like him because he looks like the guy in your book."

"I do not." At her look, I backed down a little. "Well, not entirely."

"You like Kris?" Dev asked. He took my silence for a yes and shook his head. "He's such a self-centered jerk. He only got class president because his family, like, founded this town and he's related to half the class."

I narrowed my eyes at Dev. "He's smart and ambitious…"

"… and looks like a fictional hottie." Em finished for me.

"What about real hotness? You know, like five foot ten of this?" Dev asked, pointing at himself and posing as if he were waiting for someone to take his picture. "My name *does* mean 'god' in Hindi," he added, winking a greenish-hazel eye at me. Between his athletic build, those eyes, and the straight black hair that kept threatening to fall into them, he definitely qualified as one of the cuter guys in our class. Half of the girls in the band and, if Em was to be believed, the drama club, were in love with him. But he was just so…Dev. He'd seen me freak out over the giant spider in the band room and geek out over the book fairs in middle school and I'd seen him in his ridiculous band uniform cleaning spit out of his clarinet reed one too many times.

I laughed at his goofy pose. "Don't worry, Dev. Fictional crushes pale in comparison to you. You're so hot, you're totally out of my league," I said, patting his cheek in mock consolation. "I'll just have to settle for boys in books."

He sat back, but not before tugging on my ponytail. "And yet again, my hotness works against me." Someone waved at him from across the room and he stood, gathering his things. "Sorry to deprive you all of this awesomeness, but my regular lunch table calls. See you in band."

Em watched him walk away for a few seconds, brows knit together, before turning her attention back to me. "So, the homecoming dance."

I picked at the crust on my sandwich. "What about it?"

"You're going, right? Now that they made it a masquerade, it's totally up your alley." She paused, then added, "Up *our* alley, because who doesn't love costumes?"

"You made me buy a ticket and talked my sister into making me a costume, so I doubt I have a choice anymore, do I?" The whole dancing in front of my classmates thing held no interest for me, even though a part of me thrilled at the idea of becoming someone I was not and maybe catching Kris' attention. But my friends didn't need to know about that.

"Actually, you do," Grace said before Em could answer back. "I'm skipping. Leia's really not into costumes."

Alec looked up from his hoagie in mock shock. "I thought Homecoming was one of those things cheerleaders *had* to do, along with pyramids and cartwheels."

"My girlfriend's discomfort trumps disappointing the squad. We're going to Marranos after the game, instead. You can come with us, Feebs."

"No, she can't. Jon's going." Em looked directly at me. "And you're going to look cute for him."

Eyes wide, I looked over at Grace and Alec who both shook their heads to show they weren't getting involved. With a dirty look at both of them, I tried not to groan. "Em—"

"What?" She stared me down in that intense no-excuses-Em way. "You need to get out more. Plus, I'm not letting you get stuck in this whole only wanting to crush on guys who fit descriptions of guys in books thing. He's hot. I get that you've got Kris on a pedestal, but Jon's in Junior ROTC. Hello, pushups and uniform." Em fanned herself dramatically.

A cough came from across the table. Alec raised his hand. "Remember, guy at the table."

Em grinned at him. "Sorry, forgot you were there."

"I really need to find a table with more testosterone."

I slumped in my seat, pulled out my book, and prayed for the bell to ring.

2

Family meals at the Martins house were like the compulsories at the Olympics. If you wanted to keep living in the house, you showed up on time and made it through dinner. Even if the entire place was on fire, we'd still sit at the table until Mom gave us the signal to start cleaning up. Mom and Dad were firm believers in the bonding power of food.

I shoveled mashed potatoes in my mouth while flipping to the next page in my book.

"Phoebe, are you listening?"

Food and conversation, even though Dad was just as bad as me about bringing scholarly journals or books to the table, and I'd seen Mom sneak her own books under the table, too. I scrunched my nose and stuck my napkin in my book to hold my place. "Yes, Dad?"

"We're heading up to Massachusetts this weekend."

"Aunt Terry," Mom said the name as if it tasted bad, "*finally* decided she was going to throw your grandmother a birthday party and invited us. And I know it's only two days' notice, but we shouldn't miss it." She plopped another scoop of mashed potatoes onto Dad's plate with a little more force than necessary.

"Ok-ay," I said slowly, waiting for the 'you should go even though this is insanely last minute' guilt trip to start.

"Grandmom Clara isn't going to be here forever, you know," Dad said, echoing mom's tone. Oh, boy. Even he was getting in on the guilt piling.

I shifted in my seat, pretending to focus on my book. "I know, but— the dance and work—I promised Cassandra I'd teach this weekend…" I heard the front door open and popped out of my chair. Saved by the big sister. Trixie would talk them out of making me go. "Trixie!"

Rushing into the foyer, I grabbed Trixie and swung her around, heedless of all of the bags in her arms. She was about my height, but her frame was so small that she looked delicate, as if she were going to collapse under the weight of her bags and momentum of my spin. "Save me from Massachusetts," I whispered.

"I'll try," she whispered back, conspiratorially, and added an exaggerated wink. "I didn't come down to Lambertfield for the weekend just to go even more north than NYC."

I gave her another hug, then tugged at her bags. "So? Do you have it?"

She scrunched up her little button nose and dropped her bags in the middle of the floor, spreading her arms and legs like a goalie to keep me from getting to any of them. "No 'how's sophomore year, Trixie?' 'Glad you're home for a visit, Trixie?' 'Did any of your work get into any good fashion magazines lately, Trixie?' I'm really feeling the love, Feebs."

I tossed her an amused look before reaching around her

to dig into one bag that had hints of green fabric peeking out of the top. "Oh, it's good to see you, but even better to see the dress."

"Dinner first," Dad called from the kitchen. "You're late, Trixie."

She stopped blocking me for a second to call over her shoulder. "Sorry, there was an accident on the Turnpike that delayed all the buses." Amusement played across Trixie's face as she turned back and swatted my hand away from the bag. "You heard Dad. Dinner."

I reached for the fabric again, endured another swat, and batt my eyelashes at her. "Please can I have the pretty? Please?"

"You're terrible." She swept past me and tugged on my sleeve to pull me away from her things. "And maybe it would do you some good to wait. I spoil you way too much for your own good, baby girl."

"Because you love me."

Trixie shook her head and dragged me back to the dinner table. "Right. Remember, you owe me a sweater after this."

"Hold still." Trixie jammed another pin into the top layer of my dress, just barely skimming my skin.

"Careful! You almost stabbed me."

My older sister just pulled another pin out of the cushion on her wrist. "I told you not to move." The second pin actually scraped my waist and I had to fight not to flinch. "I didn't come down all the way from New York to screw up the fit on this thing."

Between pins, I ran a hand over the incredibly soft green fabric. "This isn't what I bought."

"I used my student discount to pick up some decent stuff in the Garment District. I can't work with crappy fabric," She lifted the skirt of the dress and let the green material run over her hands like a waterfall. "Pure silk." She sniffed a corner of it. "It even still has that real silk smell."

I swatted the material out of her hands. "Stop smelling my dress. That's weird."

She went back to pinning. "You smell books and yarn."

"That's different. There's nothing in the world like brand new book or that sheep-y, wool-y smell."

"Except for silk." Apparently satisfied with sticking enough pins in the dress to make me into a life-sized voodoo doll, she stepped back to check me from a few angles. "Good. Time for the overlay." She reached into her bag and pulled out a bundle of material that was as delicate as cobwebs. "Arms up, bend over."

"Overlay? The description in the book didn't say anything about an overlay on the dress," I complained, but at one look from those dark brown eyes, I complied. Never mess with a girl who owns four different kinds of sewing shears.

She slipped the layers of gossamer fabric over my head, letting it swoosh down my body like a whisper. "Won't need to alter this," she murmured, pulling and prodding the fabric into place. A tiny smile slipped across her lips. "I have to say, I thought this was a weird challenge, but this dress will look amazing in my portfolio. I love that they decided to let you wear costumes to Homecoming." She brushed at imaginary lint on the skirt.

"That's because some parents started protesting that our Halloween Fling was satanic or something and the school had to cancel it. This was our only chance to dress up."

"It's almost too pretty for a costume." We both turned to see Mom leaning against the doorway to our shared bedroom. Since Trixie went away to college, I had taken over most of the room, but we were standing in her still sacred corner of fabric and sewing machines, and sketches that papered the wall so thickly, you couldn't see the violet paint underneath. "It's a shame you're not saving it for your Senior Prom." Mom stepped inside and came over to inspect Trixie's work.

My sister's smile turned into a full-out grin and she shook her head hard enough for the red and orange tinting the ends of her short brown hair to flutter like flames. "No way. Imagine how much better I'll be in a year. Feebs' senior prom dress is going to be epic."

"Why do I feel like I'm just one of your experiments?" I teased, faking a pout.

Trixie added a golden belt to my whole outfit. "Your crazy ideas actually work out. Plus, your body type is a nice challenge." At my glare, she added, "I'm all straight up and down. You might be practically flat chested, but at least your hips give you some curves."

"I don't know whether to be insulted or flattered."

"Flattered. And you can always pad in some fake boobs."

At my Mom's frown, she quickly added, "Could. You don't need to in this dress…" Mom kept frowning at her. "…and, um, because you're only sixteen and not a prostitute?"

Even Mom laughed at that one. "You're beautiful the way you are." She made a twirly motion with her pointer finger. "Turn around, I want to see the entire thing."

As I rotated carefully like a music box ballerina and tried not to stick myself with any of the pins, I said, "I'm using shoes from that Irish dance store and I've got temporary color and extensions to give me 'waves of flowing red hair.'"

I stopped turning at the dismayed look on Mom's face. "Oh, Phoebe. You have beautiful hair. Why would you do anything like that?" Leave it to Mom to say that. While Trixie had gotten dad's straight chestnut hair, I had inherited hers. Our hair was fine, thin, and hovered in this part-curly, part-straight state that was frizzy ninety percent of the time. Mom always kept hers short like Trixie's and probably never noticed. And our color was brown. Not chestnut. Not auburn, not golden brown. It was a nice, boring shade of dirt brown. People never dyed their hair our color.

"Because it's a costume. Maeve is a redhead." I tugged at my puny braid. "The heroines in practically every book always have long, thick hair that flows down their backs. Well, except for that one character in that knight book, but she cut off her braid so she could fight."

Trixie just shook her head at me. "Okay, enough playing. Off with the dress so I can do some alterations."

"Wait." I lifted the skirts and picked my way across the

room towards our full-length mirror. "I haven't seen it yet."

I stood in front of the mirror, taking in the dress with more than a little bit of awe. It really was as if Trixie had just pulled it out of the pages of *Golden*, down to the tiny gold ribbons tying my off-the-shoulder sleeves to the main dress. And instead of looking out of place on me, I looked like I belonged in something this pretty. I looked like Maeve. "The perks of having your own designer," Trixie said, echoing my thoughts. "In a dress like this, you're not allowed to hang out on the side of the dance floor like the nerd you are, you know."

An image popped into my head of Kris showing up at the dance dressed in a green battle tunic just like Aedan's. He'd come up beside me and, as if we were the only ones in the room, would sweep me into a waltz. I wouldn't be invisible dressed like this. A shiver of anticipation rushed through my body and I smiled at the thought.

"Maybe," I said, unable to tear my eyes away from the reflection. "Maybe not."

3

I twirled, watching as the layers of sheer material wafted around me in a green cloud. "Trixie did a good job." Em said, making her way through the school atrium doors. "Now, stop spinning before you hurt yourself."

I stopped midturn and the skirts settled in a sigh around my legs. "It really is perfect. I feel just like Maeve in this." I couldn't help but swing my arms at my side as I walked so the sheer overskirts brushed my hands and rustled as if there was a breeze in the building. My hair shed glitter that dotted everything.

"Too bad nobody will have any clue who you're supposed to be." She tilted her pirate hat at me as we headed into the gym. "Nobody reads books."

"When the movie comes out, all of you will wish you had thought of this."

"Doubt it." She reached over to straighten one of my gold torques. "But you look so pretty tonight. Like something out of a fairytale." Satisfied with the torque, she fixed my hair so a bunch of it spilled over one shoulder.

"Thanks."

"Pretty enough that maybe Jon will ask you to dance,

drag you off to the locker rooms, start making out with you in the showers..." she said with a wink.

I shook my head. "Right. Only in Em-fantasyland." We were early and they were just starting to set up the decorations. I craned my neck, checking to see if Kris was there yet. When I didn't see him, I slumped slightly. "I wish I had half of your flirt-fu."

She smiled back at me over her shoulder. "Since I come from cultures that gave the world Aphrodite *and* Oshun, it's in my blood, you know? But I can totally teach you. Your sister made you a dress that makes you look like you actually have a little bit of cleavage," I made a face at her, but she continued, "so use it. Lesson one, work the nonverbal with the verbal. Watch and learn."

"Can't wait, Yoda." I watched Em make her way over to the DJ stand where Wilhelm, the cute foreign exchange student from Germany, seemed to be struggling with the speakers. She dropped onto his lap like she was already dating him and started pointing at the random cords in his hands.

"That girl is as subtle as a nuclear bomb." I glanced up to find Dev standing right behind me. "You're very...sparkly. What are you supposed to be?" he said, quirking a half smile.

I took in his jeans and white t-shirt with 'Ghost' stamped in faded letters across his chest. So perfectly Dev. One of my torques slid loose and I shoved it back up my arm. "Maeve from *Golden*." He stared at me blankly and I added, "It's a book."

"Oh."

"It's really good. It's been on the New York Times series bestseller list already for thirty weeks. And it's going to be a movie." In my head, I could practically hear Em telling me to stop right there, but I couldn't help it. "It's about a girl who falls in love with a leprechaun."

His eyebrows rose. "A leprechaun? Like, the little Irish people leprechauns?"

Hearing him say it, leprechauns really did sound ridiculous. "Well, kind of. Only they're not little, they're warriors. And hot. And Maeve is supposed to use her powers to save the world but she's almost found out by the evil fae…" My voice drifted off. "Uhm, it's actually a lot cooler than that, I swear."

"I'll take your word for it. It's a nice costume, whatever it is."

"Thanks. Um, so's yours." I watched as he turned back to untangling strings of twinkle lights. "Need help?"

"Yeah. Just hold this for me." He dumped a tangled ball in my hands and started walking with the untangled end to stretch the string of lights along the bleachers.

While he was walking, Em came up alongside me and poked me in the arm. "Arrrrgh, whatcha think you're doin', matey?" she said softly in the worst pirate accent on the planet.

"Helping Dev with the lights."

She shook her head at me. "You're supposed to be sitting your green glittery butt next to Jon, picking out the best lighting gels for tonight. Not playing Tinkerbell to Dev's Peter Pan."

I blinked at her. Sometimes Em made no sense. "What

does Peter Pan have to do with lights?"

"A, you look like a fairy farted on you with all that glitter, b, you're wearing green, and c, blinky lights." She shook her head. "This isn't a book. Guys aren't going to come after you. You have to get your flirt on."

"I know that life isn't a book—"

"And that's why you need to put yourself out there."

I opened my mouth to respond, but was interrupted by a loud yell coming from about a quarter of the way down the gym. "Can the two of you pause for a second in talking about how hot I am and start untangling? This gym isn't going to light itself up."

I stuck my tongue out at Dev and tugged at the cord coming from the ball in my hands, careful to not break any of the bulbs.

"Oh, and your scintillating presence isn't light enough?" I said with a smirk before turning to Em. She looked from him to me with an unreadable expression on her face. "What?"

She shook her head. "'Scintillating?' Who says that?"

"People in AP English. Along with words like 'limpid' and 'epaulets.'"

"Well, Miss AP English, finish that up quick and then get to work with Jon. I'm getting my remedial English butt back to my English as a Second Language project." She waved her hook at me and then sauntered across the gym to the DJ booth.

A sharp tug brought me back to the ball of lights in my hands. "Do I need to crack a whip to get you working?"

"Bossy," I called back with a laugh, but continued unraveling.

The gym did look magical. With the lights dimmed and the twinkle lights in place, you could barely make out the rows of bleachers that lined the two long walls. Floodlights covered in blue gels projected onto the tarps that hung in front of both basketball hoops for a watery effect. And kids in costume, mostly recycled from previous Halloweens or precycled for the coming Halloween, gave the crowd on the dance floor a mostly surreal effect.

I leaned against the bleachers, my fingers itching to pull out my e-reader. As the gym filled, my dress was too hot, too heavy, too different. More than half of the girls dancing were wearing skimpy outfits that barely passed the school dress code and the other half were in the usual witch, vampire, or fairy types of costumes. No one wore anything close to what I was wearing. Plus, Kris never showed up. This had been a really stupid idea.

I took a deep breath. Maeve wouldn't care. *Maeve* would be proud to stand out. I straightened up, tossing my hair back like she always did right before facing the dark fae.

"Was that a twitch or something?" Jon stopped beside me and propped himself on a part of the bleacher that we hadn't been able to push all the way in earlier. He was really tall and lanky and if he hadn't been sitting, I'd have to crane my neck to look at him. He reached out to touch the thick waves of hair that fell to my waist. "Is that real?"

"Clip-in extensions." I tried tossing them again and gave up. "That was supposed to be a really cool shampoo commercial moment," I informed him, trying to sound flirty-ish and not like I just wanted him to go away so I could go back to being a fly on the wall.

He laughed, one of those laughs that showed too much of his teeth. "Cute. You really took the costume thing seriously, didn't you?" I recognized his costume from his project on Socrates in World History. He'd shortened the robe's sleeves, though, and I could tell Em had totally exaggerated about the ROTC pushup thing.

"It's from this book—" I stopped and nodded when I saw his eyes start to glaze over. "Yes. Yes, I did." Unlike Dev, Jon didn't seem to want to hear about it.

"Whatever, it looks good. Em told me to come over here and force you to have fun. Why aren't you dancing?"

Of course Em told him I was here. I hoped my shrug was cool and unconcerned. Maeve-like. "I'd rather watch." After seeing some of the couples on the dance floor, there was no way I was going out there. I think I'd die if someone tried to grind against me. Worse if I got reprimanded by the monitors patrolling the dance.

"Oh." His smile dropped from toothy to close-lipped and he looked from me to Em, who was across the room making dance-y twirly motions at us with her arms. "Maybe when they change up the music?"

I stopped trying to shoot daggers with my eyes at Em and made a noncommittal sound. He apparently wasn't going away any time soon. Silence fell between us and I shifted from foot to foot. Talk. We should talk. I tried to smile up at him.

"So, um, did you see the new mascot uniform concepts for next year?"

He screwed up his face. "How much more can they screw up a muskrat? If we had a decent mascot, it would be one thing, but muskrats?"

"True. They don't really strike fear into the hearts of our rival schools."

"Yeah." Another too-long pause filled the air around us. I heard the bleachers squeak as he shifted his balance, then he hopped off. "You want to go get a cupcake? I heard the snack table is actually decent this time."

Em was still waving at us while slow dancing with the foreign exchange student. Maybe going to the cupcake table with Jon would make her happy.

"Sure." I followed, awkwardly holding onto his sleeve to keep from being separated while we navigated through the crowd.

Just as we reached the three point line, the music changed abruptly. The twang of a sitar filled the air. "Is that—" We stopped and I laughed as Dev slid out on his knees into the center of the floor and started to sing. "What is he doing?"

The whole gym froze and stared as, one by one, other people broke into dance, their voices joining in with his.

"You're effin' kidding me. A flash mob?" Jon laughed and shook his head. "Leave it to the theatre geeks to come up with something like this."

"Even better, a Bollywood flash mob. This is awesome." Some of the girls from the dance team twirled by in matching genie-like outfits. More and more people joined in, mostly theatre, the school choirs, and the dance team. Even some of the chaperones got into the dance until they were a solid formation making patterns across the gym floor. Jon started pulling me towards the cupcakes again, but I swatted at his hand. "I have to see this."

"C'mon. This is the best time to go. Everyone's watching right now."

I ignored him. Some of the teachers had jumped into the dance.

"Look at Mr. Hayashi. I didn't know he could move that fast," I said as I tried to ignore Jon's insistent tugging and kept my focus on the dancing AP History teacher. "I really want to see this."

Then Dev was in front of me, dragging me away from Jon and onto the dance floor while still keeping in his character of a crooning Bollywood hero. He twirled me right into the center so my skirts flared around me in an impressive circle of green chiffon. "Uhm, Dev," I said between my teeth, feeling my face grow supernova-hot, "I can't dance. And I don't know—"

His lips quirked upwards and he winked at me before breaking into the next round of lyrics:

"Your hair like fire, eyes like embers," he lip-synced, finger tilting up my chin and amused eyes meeting mine, "soul like a blaze burning through the room." His arms gestured dramatically at me and the dancers as he sang. He pulled me in, wrapping his and my arms around me, "I am captivated, drawn in, a moth to your flames. Your fire is my doom," and twirled me out again. My embarrassment melted away and I laughed at his exaggerated and cheesy movements.

As the chorus broke out again, he squeezed my hand. "Thanks, Phoebe," he said softly. With another twirl, I fell right into a chair on the edge of the flash mob, as if I had been perfectly choreographed into the dance. Em looked down at me with a grin. "You looked good out there, Pavlova."

"If you put that online, I will kill you."

Em didn't even bother to hide the fact that she was still recording the whole thing. "I won't have to. Someone else will." She tugged teasingly at the ribbon on my sleeve. "If it makes you feel any better, Dev did a good job of making you actually look desirable. You might get an Internet stalker or two out of this one."

I twisted my nose up at her. "That's comforting. Did you know about this?"

"No. He probably planned it the week I had to miss the theatre club meeting. Jerk. I could have gotten a better view of you actually dancing for once if he'd bothered to tell me." She wiggled her phone at me. "Thankfully, with my 'get to the front of a crowd' superpower, at least I got some awesome blackmail material."

I reached up to grab at her phone. "Let me see—"

She held it out of my reach and gestured towards the dance floor. "No way. Besides, look, he's got Ms. Alexander out there now."

When I turned around, he was promenading the little blonde gym teacher through an alleyway made by the other dancers. She was laughing so hard that she could barely stay upright. "Okay. That's proof that Dev is absolutely certifiable."

"Wanna take a guess about who he picks as the brunette?"

"Brunette?"

"Don't you recognize it? It's that song from the movie we watched at your house a few weeks ago. *Viraag*? The one where the guy dances with girls with different hair colors?"

Em was right—this was the point in the song where the movie guy had switched to dancing with the heroine, who was a brunette.

"Funny how he picked a song from this movie." Em said, sounding a little distracted, "He didn't seem to know about it when you were raving about it in band."

"I guess we inspired him to check it out." I giggled as Dev dramatically dropped to his knees and waved Ms. Alexander away like he couldn't look at her anymore.

"Maybe." She paused and narrowed her eyes, looking from me to Dev and back at me again. Then, she shook her head and said, "I guess Dev found English lyrics or something. Too bad it screwed up wherever you and Jon were going, but I think this was worth it."

Jon. Oops. I craned my neck to see him standing on the

opposite side of the gym.

"About Jon. I—"

"Huh? What about Jon?" Em let out a whoop as Ms. Alexander gracefully bowed her way out of the flash mob.

"Nothing." I twisted the dangling end of my rope belt around my fingers like a one handed cat's cradle. "I don't think he cares if I'm over here," I mumbled into my lap.

Em didn't even hear me over the roar of the crowd. "Oh, no. He didn't."

I looked up to see Dev dragging our practically bald Vice Principal dead center of the dance formation and the shock made me immediately forget about Jon and lack of sparks.

"Mr. MacKenzie? No way. He's going to get suspended. And then Ms. Osoba will kill him for screwing up band practice." A ripple of laughter ran through the crowd as Dev reached up to ruffle the little that was left of Mr. MacKenzie's hair while singing about "waves of brown, deep as night." It was just so ridiculous I couldn't help but join in with a giggle that made my side hurt.

To my utter amazement, the vice principal joined in the last part of the dance.

"Holy cupcake, he knew. He had to," Em said over my shoulder. "There's no way—"

Dev slid off on his knees, landing next to us as the song ended. He grinned up at Em, apparently catching the end of her words.

"Never underestimate the power of the musical theatre club," he said with a wink before standing and taking a mock bow. "I'm not stupid enough to screw around with MacKenzie."

"With your grades, you can't afford to," Em joked and he rewarded her with a wide grin. "I'm mad you didn't ask Pine Central's greatest actress to join in, though."

Dev shrugged, poking her in the arm playfully. "I figured you're too much of a diva to want to share the spotlight."

Em put her hand to her chest like she was wounded. "That hurts, even if it's probably true."

As people passed by, clapping him on the back or congratulating him on the 'epicness' of the whole flash mob, a few weirdly even congratulated me. "I didn't—" I protested, but there were just too many of them. Even people who I didn't know were telling me I did an awesome job. As soon as the worst of the crowd dispersed, Dev pat my shoulder. "Sorry for dragging you out like that, but the line needed a redhead. I figured you wouldn't kill me. Or fall in love with my heartfelt but swoonworthy acting."

"That didn't sound egotistical at all," I shot back at him as I stood and straightened out my skirt. "But, it's okay. I think I'll forgive you if you promise to never do that to me again." A smile escaped past my faux-annoyed expression.

"Admit it, you liked it." He tugged at my extensions before peering over at the refreshment table. "I seriously need something to drink. Do either of you want anything?"

I shook my head, but Em grabbed his arm. "I'll come with you." Before I could follow, she pointed at my feet and the gold ribbon trailing off of the ghille on my right foot.

"Your laces are untied."

"Crud." The boning keeping my bodice up didn't let me bend over to reach my feet and I dropped back into the chair to fiddle with the slippery satin. "Trixie warned me about satin ribbon, but I--" I looked up and trailed off, realizing I was talking to empty air. Once my laces were fixed I started towards Em and Dev, but they were already deep in conversation by the refreshment table. I froze mid-step—they looked serious and I totally didn't want to play third wheel. It was like I was eavesdropping, even though they were all the way across the room. Since when were Em and Dev so close?

My eyes searched the room for anything else to watch. Jon stood by the speakers, basking in the flirt-vibes coming off of a curvy sophomore blonde dressed in one of those genie outfits. It relieved me more than it probably should have.

What *would* Maeve do right now?

She sure as heck wouldn't hang around here. She'd be running into the Otherland and back into Aedan's arms. Aedan's strong, magical arms that helped protect her from the dark fae and...I sighed, and the dance fell away. Really, they gave me no other choice. I pulled my book out of its hiding place under a pile of coats, slipped onto one of the opened bleachers beneath a bundle of fairy lights, and dove back into book two of Maeve's world.

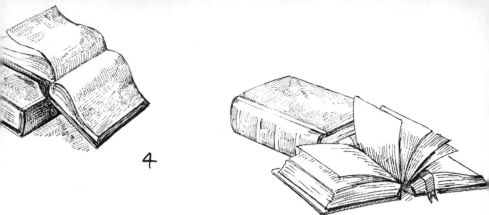

4

Even though she was supposed to focus on self-defense, she was acutely aware of how close Aedan had gotten in his last attack, especially when his laughter had pressed more of his battle-trained hard body against her own. With her back up against the hay bale, she couldn't roll away...and a part of her really didn't want to. The prickly hay snaking in between the laces of her leather bodice and scraping her skin was no competition for the whisper of his breath across her forehead and cheek. Maeve shut her eyes for a second, took a deep breath to regain her focus, and, before he could finish his attack, mimed a cutting motion against his neck with the point of her arrow. "And I win."

Aedan laughed even harder, grasping her arrow hand and pinning it to the ground. Slowly, he moved his mouth towards hers and...

"You're coming with me." Em grabbed my arm none too gently, and dragged me off of the bleachers.

"Hey!" I shut my book with my free hand and tripped after her, trying to keep upright. "What the heck, Em?"

She pulled me into the girl's locker room and pushed me unceremoniously onto one of the benches. "We need to talk." As I watched, she rushed about the room, checking to make sure no one else was in there.

I tried not to laugh at the sight of her crouched on the floor and looking under the bathroom stalls.

"If this is about Jon, he was the one who dropped me for genie girl." I tilted my head and corrected myself. "I think."

Satisfied we were alone, she got up and dropped onto the bench next to me. "Forget about Jon. This is important."

I frowned at her. "Is everything okay?"

She took a deep breath and focused her serious brown eyes on mine. "How do you feel about Dev?"

Out of everything Em could have asked me, I wasn't expecting that. What did Dev have to do with anything? "Dev? I'm not mad at him about the dance thing, if that's what you're asking."

"No, dummy. I mean, do you like him?"

"Dev?" I blinked at her stupidly for a few seconds. The image of him sliding across the dance floor rose up in my mind. "I...I never really thought of him like that. I mean, we're sort of friends, I guess—"

She had that expression on her face that let me know she was getting frustrated. "But do you think he's hot?"

"I—" I had no idea what to say. I cringed under her stare. "I guess? I mean, he's really cute, but he's *Dev*." His grin popped into my head again and I had to shake my head slightly to focus. "What's all this about?"

"He's totally crushing on you."

My brain just couldn't compute this complete and total

course change. It was as if someone had switched books on me and I was having plot whiplash. "No, he isn't."

She grabbed my arm and shook it like she was trying to shake some sense into me. "Yes, he is. I saw him staring at you at the pep rally, then I noticed that every time you're at your locker, or God, even in the middle of orchestra, he keeps looking at you. It's almost stalker-y. And then this whole dance thing—"

I cut her off. "He needed a redhead. I was just the closest one." I ran my fingers through the waterfall of extensions currently brushing my lap.

Em shook me even harder. "Please. Ms. Zhdanova was, like, two people away from you. And her hair is freakin' fire hydrant colored. He totally strayed from the teacher theme on purpose to dance with you."

"Stop being such a conspiracy theorist." I yanked my arm out of her hands.

"I'm not."

I lay back on the bench and stared at the ceiling. "This is ridiculous. I've never seen him watching me." I ran a mental inventory and came up with nothing. "I'd know if someone was watching me."

"You never see anything. You're always buried in your books or one of your knitting projects." Em lay down on the other end of the bench, mirroring me so we took up the entire bench, our feet pressed against each other's. "I think the two of you would be freakishly adorable together."

My neck grew warm again. Of everything I had to

inherit from my father, this insta-blush thing was the worst.

I pressed my neck back until it touched the cool wood of the bench, and replied, "You said the same thing about Jon."

"Jon was an experiment. Unless you like him, which I doubt, because you're not out there trying to keep him from the harem bunny." She kicked the side of my foot. "Just give Dev a chance. This girl," she sat up and pointed at herself with a flourish, "is never wrong when it comes to guys. I'm like the Oracle of Delphi of relationships."

"You're just trying to yenta us together." Maybe that conversation by the cupcakes was Em trying to do the same thing to Dev about me, which made me want to crawl into one of the lockers and hide.

An amused tone came into her voice. "No, I swear, he's been following you like a puppy dog." Em shrugged. "For some reason I can't totally understand, weirdly dressed book nerds must be a major turn-on for him."

I threw one of my arms over my face, partly to be dramatic, partly to hide my blush. "Oh my God. You are so making all this up."

"Am not." She stood and pulled my arm off of my face so I had to look directly at her. "So? What do you say about dating our Bollywood Casanova?" She faked a swoon.

I swatted at her but she jumped away, laughing. "Stop that."

"He's just so dashing and debonair, I can't help but be equally dramatic when I'm talking about him," she said with a flourish, then forced me up to sitting. "Here's the thing. I think you need to give him a chance. "

"I've never not given him a chance. He doesn't think of me like that and I don't think of him that way. Because we're just friends, Em. And not even sitting at the same lunch table kind of friends. We're more like 'snarking about Ms. Osoba making us sit out in forty degree weather for pep band' kind of friends."

"Sitting at the same lunch table regularly will be a good start. I'll get on that Monday."

"Em, don't," I pleaded. Now that Em had me and Dev on her matchmaker radar, I couldn't even imagine how I'd even be around him without turning as red as the lining of his clarinet case.

She shook her pirate sword at me. "We're going out there right now, you're going to look cute and be nice to him, got it?"

"I'd rather stay in here and finish my book." As soon as the words came out of my mouth, though, I cowed to her unblinking stare and stood. "Tell me why I listen to you?" I checked my reflection in one of the long mirrors on the pillar behind me. The sparkly face powder did a pretty good job of hiding the red in my face.

"Because I'm doing what's best for you." She smoothed down a layer of chiffon in the back of my dress and started pushing me out the door. "Now, smile."

5

I pulled the heavy comforter over my head. Snaking my hand out from my cocoon, I felt around on the nightstand for my glasses. A hard corner dug into my back and, as soon as I slipped on the glasses, I reached under myself to free *Glittering*. My fingers ran down the still-straight spine and unbent cover and I breathed a sigh of relief. I had to stop falling asleep on books. Glasses-to-nightstand became automatic after I had broken my last pair by sleeping in them. Waking up to a bent frame pressing against my nose was enough to train me out of that habit. But somehow, I always ended up sprawled over the latest hardcover.

I didn't bother looking for my book light. If I started reading now, I'd never get out of bed. Late night or not, I had to get ready for work teaching the Brunch n' Beginners learn-to-knit class at Oh, Knit! The money was good and I got to be surrounded by tons of yarn and books while sipping bottomless lattes.

I rolled out of bed, grabbing the first pair of jeans and a long-sleeved shirt that crossed my path. Catching a glimpse of myself in my vanity mirror, I cringed. I had fallen asleep with wet hair and now half of it was curly, the other half stick straight and practically standing on end. And still a bright shade of red, despite all the scrubbing I gave it last night after the dance.

I stayed in the bathroom just long enough to decide that I really didn't need to put in contacts today and gave the tub a wide berth on my way out. I didn't want to look. The last I checked, the tub was still dyed an insane shade of pinky orange from my hair dye. My blue towel was still draped over the side, too, now stained with brown blotches.

After trying a few times to tame the mess on my head, I just threw my hair into a claw clip, slipped my 'The book was better' t-shirt over my top, grabbed my knitting bag, and headed out. It didn't matter. Only knitters were going to see me, anyway.

Oh, Knit! was only fifteen minutes from my neighborhood, and usually, I loved the walk this time of year through the piles of leaves in the early morning autumn chill. Today, though, I dragged myself there, barely noticing anything around me until a familiar tug on my messy bun made me jump.

"Sorry, didn't mean to scare you." Dev's voice came over my shoulder.

I stopped midstep and tried not to seem too thrown off as Dev and Alec came up alongside me. "It's okay. Now I won't need coffee since you just gave me a heart attack."

Alec hadn't gone to the dance, so I could understand how he managed to look semihuman that early on a Sunday, but Dev? Even with slicked back wet hair and grungy clothes, he was too awake and too pulled together for someone who had probably been up later than me. Before I could stop myself, I checked my reflection in a passing shop window. Yup. Still looked like a human version of yarn barf. Embarrassment tickled up my neck and I was thankful for the chill that had already colored my cheeks and was keeping my face from getting too hot.

"Nice shirt."

I glared at Alec for calling attention to how utterly ridiculous I looked. He didn't seem to notice.

"Going to work at the bluehair store again?"

Pull yourself together. Maeve would just straighten herself up and keep walking as if she were wearing a designer gown instead of a goofy t-shirt.

As I pulled my back ramrod straight and tilted up my chin, I answered in my best Maeve-y tone, "You realize that a ton of young A-list celebrities knit, right?"

"And grandmoms." Alec kicked a rock off the sidewalk and it clattered into the mostly deserted street. "Besides, it's not like you care about what celebrities do."

"I care about them if they knit." I pulled my circular needles out of my bag and pointed them fencer-like at Alec. The metal needles were gorgeous and a little dangerous in the faint sunlight. "And I have a great way to defend myself when weird guys jump me in the dangerous streets of Lambertfield," I added with a flourish of the needles.

Dev, who had been watching us like a ping-pong game,

broke into the conversation. "Hey, does that mean you can make me a sweater?"

Still on my silly dramatic high, I gave my needles one last twirl and started slipping them into my bag as if I were putting them into one of those sword-holster things. "You have to be knitworthy to get stuff from me, maybe something small, like socks. And you, my friend, aren't knitworthy yet." We shared a grin and I wiggled my needles at him teasingly.

"So, what do I need to do to become 'knitworthy?'"

"I'll…I'll let you know." Suddenly, what Em told me at the dance popped into my head and the air became incredibly heavy—uncomfortable, like a shrunken and felted wool sweater. I was going to strangle her for sticking ideas into my head and making things so awkward around him. I wracked my brain for some change in the subject. "So, where are you two going? The diner?"

Alec had perched himself on one of the cast iron streetlamp bases a few seconds before, but now hopped off. "We're on our way to McCaffery field. Damien's brother is home for the weekend and he said he'd teach us how to play rugby."

I couldn't even look Dev in the eye, so I focused on Alec. "Rugby? Just you two are playing against him?"

Dev answered, instead. "Nah, we're meeting up with some of the other guys there." We reached the store and he waved in the direction of the field. "Stop by when you're finished here, if you want."

My hand froze on Oh, Knit!'s fancy brass doorknob. "I don't think I'll be able to." I let my focus drift to the store's big picture window of yarny goodness. In a few minutes, I'd be inside and I could just sink into the Manos display.

"It's not like you're trying to impress anyone. And I know you don't have anything else today." I was going to kill Alec later.

Dev was making weird faces behind Alec, puffing his cheeks out and bent over like he was using a walker.

I choked back a laugh. "You two are going to make me late for my class. Plus, you're going to offend the *not ancient* customers." I gestured at Dev, and Alec turned around, letting out a loud snort-y laugh.

Alec faced me again, but started backing away from the store. "Yes, Ms. Martins. See you at McCaffery field, then?"

"I'll think about it." I heaved a sigh of relief and slipped inside. It was such a comfort to drop back into my chair at the teaching table and bury my face in a display shawl that Cassandra, my boss, must have left there.

One of the store's regulars reached over and patted my knee sympathetically. "Boyfriend?"

"God, no." I tried not to look out and see if they were gone yet. "Two perpetual pains in the…" I looked up at her, and quickly checked myself, "…well, you know. They're just friends."

She gave me another soft pat and returned to her baby blanket. The rest of the class shuffled in and started chattering softly over the click of needles while waiting for me to pull myself together.

In my dramatic show-offyness, I apparently had disconnected a needle from its cable and now half of my demo shawl was off the needles and threatening to unravel in my bag.

Frak.

6

"Hey."

I jumped at the poke to my shoulder, accidentally closing my locker door on my hand in the process. "Ow."

Dev came into my line of sight, an apologetic look on his face. He reached around me to reopen my locker. "Sorry I scared you."

"It's okay." I examined my poor finger as it started turning an angry shade of purple-y red—of course it had to be in the perfect spot to get hit by the lock. "It's my left hand, anyway. Not like I need it to knit or anything."

"I guess that won't earn me sock points, will it?"

I snorted, forgetting the stinging pain in my knuckle for a second. "You're right. I think I'll have to bump you to the bottom of my knitworthy list thanks to this."

"Which means I wasn't at the bottom before?"

"Nope. Osoba was last for making nonmarchers like me play in the stands in below-freezing weather." I turned back to my locker to pull out the notebook I had been going for before almost losing my finger. A spare knitting needle started to roll off the top shelf, but I shoved it back into place and slowly closed the door.

"How does *you* slamming *your* finger in *your* locker get me lower than Osoba making you a piccolo popsicle?"

I turned back to face him and tilted my shoulder in a half-shrug. "Because you're special that way?"

"I'll just have to work harder to get on your good side, then." He grinned at me, then nodded at someone who called to him from down the hallway. "Anyway, Em said you might be able to help me find a copy of *The Phantom of the Opera*—the book, not the musical. Someone checked out the only copy in our library."

"Em makes me sound like some sort of underground book dealer." I twisted my lips into a wry grin and added, "But this time, she's right. I can lend you my copy."

"That would be awesome." Whoever it was called him again and he waved. "Sorry, I have to go, but you're the best, Phoebe."

"Tomorrow morning, atrium. I'll bring the goods." I cringed at how stupid I sounded.

"Good, I'll be there. Thanks."

"You're welcome," I said to his back as he made his way down the hall to his friend.

Em came up beside me, Wilhelm-the-exchange-student behind her. "What was that all about?"

I blinked up at Em's new German shadow. Apparently, she'd caught his attention for longer than just the dance.

"Um, hi, Wilhelm," I said, then rubbed at my sore knuckle and shrugged. "Nothing. He just wants to borrow a book."

"He asked for a copy of *Phantom*?" she asked, eyebrows

quirked slightly upwards as she switched back and forth between studying me and watching Dev move through the crowd.

Ignoring whatever she was trying to get at with her not-so-subtle looks, I said, "Yeah. I'm lending him mine. I don't need it right now."

A cat-that-caught-the-mouse smile spread across Em's face. "But he can get *Phantom* online."

I did the mental math—she was right, it was in the public domain. "But maybe he wanted an actual copy."

"Mmmmhmmm." That smile grew wider and she leaned against Wilhelm, arms crossed, looking totally self-satisfied.

"Okay, so if you knew, why didn't you tell him to go online instead of telling him to ask me?" I bounced on my heels and resisted the urge to head to class instead of dealing with Em's conspiratorial matchmaking weirdness.

Em poked me in the arm like she was trying to drill her point into me. "Because I wanted to prove how right I am about him liking you."

"It's just a book." The late bell rang and I started moving down the hallway, Em and her shadow trailing behind me.

"Really," she said, "aren't you the one who always says, 'It's never just a book?'" Her last few words were said in a perfect imitation of me.

She was crazy. Absolutely crazy.

"And using that logic, if he asked you first, doesn't it mean he's really crushing on you?" I asked.

She waved her hand dismissively. "We were just talking after drama club on Friday. He mentioned he was looking for a copy and maybe I casually mentioned you. He was the one who decided to ask you. Which, of course, means he wants you for more than your personal library."

"Em-logic makes my head hurt."

"Em-logic," she said, hanging on the door of her Geometry classroom, "is the best kind of logic." She blew Wilhelm a kiss and gave me a little shove towards my class. "I want you to practice safe book lending, you know."

"Eww."

She snorted, imitating my expression, and said, "See you at lunch."

Wilhelm and I shared a look.

"Does half of what she says even make sense to you?" I asked.

He shook his head, but the look on his face was pure amusement. "I find it easier to believe it makes sense to her and just think my English is still bad."

"No, your English is fine. Being around Em is like getting stuck in a whirlwind, It's hard not to feel a little dizzy when you get out." I made my way down the hallway towards class, Wilhelm right beside me.

"Dizzy is a very good word for it." He stopped in front of one of the classroom doors. "But it's a good kind of dizzy, yes?" Wilhelm nodded, like he was answering his own question.

I grinned back at him. "Yes."

"You didn't come to watch," Alec said as he slipped into the seat next to me at lunch.

I finished biting the crust off of my sandwich and shrugged. "Cassandra needed me at the shop."

"Right, because yarn stores must have crazy lines on Sundays." I glared at him but he just grinned and reached across the table to steal a few fries off of Grace's tray. "Your loss. I could have taught you how to tackle."

"You mean you could have demonstrated how to get your ass handed to you by a real rugby player, right, Kohen?" Dev dropped his tray next to my lunch bag and grinned down at us. "Alec spent the most time sitting on the field."

"Who knew Anderson would get so huge after only one year? It was like playing rugby with a Klingon. Damien could have warned us," Alec grumbled. He stole another fry and asked jokingly, "What are you doing coming over here and making me look bad in front of the girls?"

"I asked Dev to sit with us so we can talk about the spring musical prep." Em gave me a significant look, one eyebrow raised, while Dev settled into the space next to me.

His leg bumped mine and I threw Em a dirty glare before smiling awkwardly at Dev and wiggling over slightly to avoid more leg bumping. "Don't you guys usually do this kind of thing after school? Like, in the theatre with your whole crew?"

Dev shrugged. "Em thought it would be a good idea to lay out a battle plan now. We have a pretty epic idea."

"But we're not sure if Mr. Landry will bite," Em finished

with a flourish of her carrot stick. It was show season again, and she was back to her yearly weird preperformance diet. "Besides, I told Dev you'd probably be a huge help since we're thinking of doing a rock version of *Phantom* and that's your favorite musical." Em tried to catch my eyes again.

I poked a hole in the center of the sandwich with my finger. A second hole joined it and now my peanut butter sandwich had eyes. "To watch," I said with a shake of my head. "Or read. I don't do musical theater, Em. Band is where I draw the line when it comes to musical anything." I didn't look at Dev. It was all so awkward.

Grace watched the entire interaction with more interest than I expected out of her, then, looked at me, her slow smile hitting its peak. "This should be good."

"We were thinking of making the Phantom a zombie guitar player..." Dev started when my attention was completely diverted by a silhouette entering my line of sight.

Kris passed, his hair catching the light streaming in from the cafeteria skylights. I forgot about all kinds of zombies and just stared. The world went into slow motion and I couldn't help but watch as he maneuvered himself and his tray around the tables and out the side door. What I wouldn't give to be one of the lucky few allowed at the student council tables, even if it did mean freezing outside. Almost like he lived in one world and I lived in another. Which was kind of true. Except what divided us were lunch tables. There weren't any fae gates keeping me from the Otherland and he wasn't a warrior sworn to defend it. But it was still a great analogy. Or was that a simile?

"Earth to Phoebe." Dev actually waved a hand in front of my face.

"Having an Aedan moment?" Grace asked wickedly.

Dev looked from Grace to me back to Grace. "Who's Aedan?"

I blew air through my lips and contemplated kicking Grace in the shin. Before I could say anything, Alec answered for me.

"It's an in-joke." He took a bite of hoagie and didn't bother to finish chewing before continuing. "The girls are all kinds of screwed up." He swallowed and looked around me at Dev. "Anyway, that zombie Phantom sounds like something I'd watch. Does he try to eat the girl?"

"Gaston Leroux is rolling over in his grave right now over what you're doing to his story," I muttered, even though I was just happy Alec had changed the subject.

Em steepled and twiddled her fingers, evil-style. "Just like a zombie would. Perfect."

As soon as Dev left the table, Em moved back over and nudged me with her elbow. "See, I told you. He likes you." Thank God he probably didn't hear her over the din of the emptying lunchroom.

I looked at her with narrowed eyes. "No. He came to the table because you dragged him here, just like you told him to borrow the book from me. You're so dying for me to get a boyfriend that you think everyone likes me."

"I'm not in love with you," Alec threw over his shoulder before disappearing into the crowd.

"And you're not my type," Grace added to me in amusement as she walked around the table to join us.

I shot her a sour glare. "Shut up."

Grace stuck her perfectly manicured nails into my arm to keep both me and Em from leaving. When I tried to pull free, she fixed me with a death glare that I swear must be handed out to cheerleaders with their pom-poms. "So, what haven't you both been telling me? This whole lunch period was like a bad teen drama."

"Nothing—"

Em cut me off while deftly extracting herself from Grace's clutches. "Dev totally has the hots for Feebs, Feebs refuses to believe it because she's completely oblivious, and Kris is a tool who doesn't even know you exist," —that last part was directed at me— "so you have to give up on him."

"Well, that explains why you looked like someone put cat litter in your sandwich. You're so Snow White innocent, it's actually kinda cute." Grace said with a laugh. "Em's probably right. The social mirroring, the unnecessary touching you…"

"Social what?"

"Mirroring. It's where someone unconsciously copies what you do. But don't change the subject."

"I'm not changing the subject—" I started to protest.

"Why are you complaining?"

I groaned and yanked my arm free. "I'm going to be late to history." Since Grace was in the same class that period, I added, "And I need to stop at my locker." Before they could say anything else, I made myself disappear into the flood of people still trying to get through the lunchroom doors. Tomorrow, I promised myself, I was eating in the band room.

Grace slid into the desk next to mine. "I have practice all week, and a game on Saturday, but you're coming to my house on Sunday and you're getting a makeover. Em enlisted me and my unquestionably awesome skills."

I scrunched my nose at her and flipped open my history book. "Why are you letting Em push you around, too?"

"Because she doesn't know her eyeliner from mascara. I do." She shrugged. "It might be fun, and a little bit of change never hurt anyone. Besides, unlike either of you, I can tell whether a girl is hot enough to date." She winked at me.

I tried not to feel too insulted by that. "Won't Leia get jealous of you making me 'hot'?" I joked. "I hear those Haddontowne Academy girls are really possessive."

"You'll never be that hot. Trust me." She pulled out a pink plaid notebook and matching pen. "So, Sunday? I promise to make it as painless as possible."

"I don't have a choice, do I?"

"Look, I really don't give a crap if you date Dev or Kris or Em, for that matter, but I think you probably *could* use some girly pampering time that doesn't have anything to do with bubble baths and books. Or yarn. Or Em shoving guys at you." She held up her hand to keep me from talking, "It's less about how you look and more about giving you some time away from your everyday stuff. We get to hang out and talk. And if you learn a little bit about how to make the perfect cat's eye in the process, that's just a bonus."

I reached over and hugged Grace quickly before our history teacher started the class. "Thanks. I'll skip the makeover, but I'll take the Grace time."

"If I were you, I'd at least consider a tiny something. Step one would be to get your hair back to one color so it stops looking like you painted red camoflauge spots on your head."

"I hate you."

"Shh, class is about to start." Grace sat up straight, pen poised over her notebook, and stared at the board like a perfect blonde angel.

7

I loved new books. The crisp pages, the smell, and the sense of potential as I carefully broke in the spine made getting them one of the best feelings in the world. Getting one at a book launch with the actual author—an even better feeling. Getting one at a book launch with the actual author when the author is a rock star flying around the country to release the third book in her four book series and has a crowd of fans sitting outside the bookstore and waiting for hours to meet her? Electric.

"The final battle outfit. Awesome," someone said as they passed me. I proudly looked up from my page for a second to smile at the two girls who passed me on their way to the back of the line. They were wearing homemade t-shirts scrawled with all of the best Maeve quotes and clutching fresh copies of *Gilded,* the third book in the *Golden* series.

I tugged at the corset, readjusting the fake leather so it would stop digging into my ribs. The costume might be perfect, but Trixie had built it for looks, not for waiting on line for hours at the mall. At least Maeve wore leggings when she fought. I couldn't imagine sitting on this floor in a skirt. Semi-comfortable again, I dove back in to the book.

If I read fast enough, I might get a third of the way through before the bookstore let us inside.

A pair of beat-up sneakers stopped right next to me, the Sharpie doodles of skulls and crossbones playing in my peripheral vision. "Phoebe? What are you wearing?"

I groaned when I followed those sneakers up to find Dev looking down at me. Of course he'd pick the one day I was in costume to run into me at the mall. I wanted to melt into the concrete wall behind me.

"I'm here for the launch party." I followed his eyes back to the corset and puffy shirt I was wearing. "And there's a costume contest." Warmth crept over my cheeks and I tilted my head forward so my hair hid my face. Dressing up for a costumed dance was one thing, but I hadn't expected anyone from school to be at the mall this early.

"You should have worn that green dress. It was pretty epic."

A little part of me that wasn't dying of mortification warmed at the thought that he remembered my home-coming dress. Why he hadn't yet gone away, though, was totally beyond my understanding. "Wrong scene. I'm in Maeve's battle outfit. You know, like on the cover?" I used my finger as a bookmark and gestured with my new book at the giant version of it on the banner above me.

"Oh. Right." He shuffled his feet impatiently. "And you have a bow because…"

I protectively hugged my recurve with my free hand. "Because Maeve was the reason I became an archer. I want the author to sign it." I dropped my eyes and added, "I know this all sounds incredibly stupid."

"No, that's actually really cool. I didn't know you were an archer." He poked at my bow. "I didn't know anyone did that stuff outside of gym class."

"Hello, it's an international sport, you know. Not just a chance to almost shoot freshmen who run across our field during gym class." I shrugged and added with more than a little bit of pride, "I placed second in States at my level. Coach Rentz thinks I'll make it to Nationals next year. I wouldn't have had that without Maeve. I really want Niamh—" at his look of confusion, I added, "the author—to know that."

"Wow."

"Books are powerful things." I tried raising one of my eyebrows, like Maeve would at a moment like this, but I had to settle for a twitch that probably made me look like I'd escaped from an insane asylum.

"I'll take your word for it." He started backing up and gestured with his thumb towards the escalator. "Uh, I'd love to stay and talk, but I've got to go take care of something."

My heart sunk right into my kneehigh boots, but I just flipped my book back open and tried not to let the disappointment show in my face. I couldn't have expected him to wait on line with me. "Have fun."

He stared at me a moment longer. "How long do you have to wait for this?" He wasn't walking away.

The snarky side of me wanted to point at the poster again, but I didn't. The girl behind me made an exasperated snorting sound and I saw her doing it for me. "It starts at one."

His eyes grew wide. "So you're going to sit here for two hours?"

The girl behind me was practically going into apoplectic fits. Dev and I tried our best to ignore her. "Four hours. I've been on line since the bookstore opened."

"Are you kidding? Who does that?" I gestured towards the people in front of us and then the line snaking along the mall wall behind me. "Okay, stupid question. What *normal* person does that?"

"What normal person breaks into a Bollywood flash mob at a school dance?"

"Point taken." He ran his hand through his hair, leaving it standing in dark spikes. "I gotta go. Maybe I'll swing by later."

"And buy a book? It'll be good for you."

He flashed me a wide grin. "Sure, Dr. Phoebe. I'll pick up two and call you in the morning?" I laughed and watched as he disappeared into the crowd. I could see what other girls saw in him, especially with the messy hair. That smile nearly killed me.

As I turned back to my book, the girl behind me poked me with her copy of *Gilded*. "Boyfriend isn't much of a brain trust, is he?"

I ignored her and turned back to my book. A little bit of Maeve and Aedan would take my mind off of the past few minutes.

8

Maeve doubted any of her teachers or the foreign exchange program organizers would take 'my homework is late because I had to protect Ireland and the whole world from fairytale creatures last night' as an excuse. A small part of her was tempted to take up Aedan's offer to move to the Otherland full time, but—

A milkshake floated in front of my eyes, blocking my view of the page. Condensation dripped off of the plastic cup and I squeaked as a drop hit my page. I scrambled to wipe up the water before looking up at the culprit.

"What the heck—" I stopped short as Dev's greenish eyes came into focus. "Dev?"

He was clutching a bag and bottle of soda in the hand that wasn't holding the milkshake. Dev looked apologetic. "Sorry." He wiggled the milkshake at me again. "Peace offering? It's mint chocolate chip. Your favorite."

I carefully marked my place in the book by closing it around my bowstring and took the milkshake from him.

"Let me guess. Em told you." I took a sip and closed my eyes in pure bliss. There was nothing on the planet as good as that milkshake at that moment.

"Yeah, I texted her. I thought you might be thirsty," he said, then shook the bag before placing it on the floor in front of me, "and hungry by now. Four hours is a long time."

I opened the bag to find those tiny soft pretzel bite things. I had a sandwich in my purse, but nudged it behind me. "This is really, really sweet. Thank you, but you really didn't have to."

He shrugged. "Someday, I'll be in a mall line for something and you can pay me back. Until then," Dev sat down on the floor next to me, folding his tall frame into the small space outlined in yellow tape on the floor, "I've got nowhere to be right now. I'll wait with you for a little bit." The girl behind me started grumbling and he gave me an amused look before turning around to face her. "Relax. I'm not cutting in line. I'm her illiterate, degenerate friend. I'm not into books about—" he squinted at the book in my hands. "What's it about?"

"A girl finds out she can see evil fairytale creatures trying to invade the Seelie Court and our world. She partners with a hot leprechaun and uses her skills to tackle these subversive elements. It's like…CSI meets fairies." I popped a pretzel into my mouth and chased it with the milkshake. Salty, minty goodness.

"I'm definitely not into books about whatever she said, so your precious space in line is safe." He then purposely turned his back on the girl and held out his hand to me with an even wider grin. "Annoying book people make me hungry. Pass me a pretzel."

"Maeve fans are dangerous. We learn how to wield pointy objects," I told him as I handed him the bag. "You shouldn't upset them."

"I'll take the risk. You'll defend me, right?" He picked up my bow and I squeaked as he lost my page in the process. Oblivious to my pawing through the book to find where I had left off, he swung the bow around to check out the sight.

"I don't know," I said, trying to sound cute and not the least bit relieved about finding my page. "If someone shows up with a bigger bow, you're on your own." I gently pried the bow out of his hands

He nearly choked on his soda. "Size-ist," he managed between coughs and suppressed laughter.

Oh. My. God. I didn't need a mirror to know my face had to match the red that still hadn't completely washed out of my hair. "I didn't mean—you couldn't possibly think I meant *that*." I glanced at the other people in line for support, but except for a few audible snickers, everyone's heads were buried in their books.

"Who knows what those books are teaching you?"

"Shut up." I bit my lip. Were you supposed to say shut up to guys who were maybe into you? Unless they were snarky bad boys, but Dev wasn't one of those. Bad boys didn't bring you milkshakes and pretzels and risk whatever standing they had in the high school hierarchy by hanging out with geeky girls in costume. But good guys didn't just pull double entendres on you…did they?

"Hey, you were the one who started talking about bigger bows…"

"*Dev,*" I hissed through my teeth, "there are middle schoolers and parents here."

"I know. You should have known better."

I couldn't help it. I tried to keep my expression serious, but dissolved into a bout of snort-y laughter. "You are so bad."

"And that's why you like me."

That comment stopped me midlaugh and I had to force out a few more giggles to cover it up. What did he mean by 'like'? Was he trying to figure out how I felt? Was he trying to tell me something? I was going to kill Em for making me read things from his comments that probably weren't there and confusing me enough that comments like that made me question what my own 'yes' might mean. My posture stiffened. Maybe combine a yes with some snark?

"Um, yeah. It has to be the bad-boy vibes. It's definitely not your sparkling wit."

His grin quirked up a notch. "I've always wanted to be one of those bad boys. But my parents would kill me. Being bad doesn't get you into 'top universities.'" He air quoted the last two words with one hand while grabbing a handful of pretzels with the other.

I took a long sip from my milkshake and pasted a mock frown on my face. I narrowed my eyes and pretended to study him. "Let me guess…med school?"

His hazel eyes danced. "Engineering, even though I have the mechanical aptitude of a rock. I think they're aiming for a stereotypical Indian kid success story."

I pulled a face. "Try telling your parents you want to review books or own a yarn store. Those went over really well with mine." I took the lid off of my milkshake and ran a pretzel along the side before popping it in my mouth. "I'm sure your mom and dad won't be too devastated when you're, like, starring in impromptu Bollywood flash mobs across the country and becoming an Internet sensation."

That caught him off-guard and he nearly choked on a pretzel. "You know, I never see you outside of school and band. You're fun. In an amped-up book lover kind of way."

I gestured at my outfit. "Comes with the territory."

"I bet." His phone rang and he stared at the screen for a second with a frown. "I really have to go now. Sorry I couldn't stay longer."

I held up my book. "I think I'll be fine. Maeve was about to kick some enemy butt when you interrupted me." I cringed slightly. Why do I say stuff like that?

He didn't seem to notice my cringe. "Have fun with that." Something caught his attention and he paused midway through standing up. He leaned in closer and my breath caught in my throat. "That's incredibly cool," he said, fingering the silver 'chainmaille' hanging off the bottom of my corset.

"I knit it. Out of stainless steel wire," I forced out. As soon as he let go of my costume and finished standing, I breathed again.

"I didn't know you could knit this kind of stuff."

"You'd be surprised what you can do with knitting

needles." As soon as I said that, I regretted it. It was like every other sentence out of my mouth could be made into an innuendo. What was *wrong* with me?

Thankfully, Dev just raised his eyebrows. "Speaking of, when am I getting those socks?"

I lightly whacked his leg and then regretted it. He just laughed. "See you later, Feebs."

Just before he stepped on to the escalator, I called out. "Thanks…for the food and entertainment and stuff."

"I aim to please." He turned on the escalator to face me and bowed with a flourish as it lowered him out of my sight.

"Your boyfriend is insane," the girl behind me said as soon as he was out of hearing range.

"He's not my…" I paused at her look of utter indifference. "Yeah, he's just weird."

"That kiss in the scene Niamh just read? Best kiss in the entire series, am I right?" The girl in front of me said, bouncing impatiently as the line inched closer to the signing table. Without waiting for anyone to actually answer, she added, "I need to find me an Aedan of my own. Too bad real boyfriends aren't as awesome as book boyfriends."

The kiss had been amazing, with just the right amount of perfect prebattle training and swoonworthy dialogue thrown in.

"At least real boys don't get brainwashed by the enemy and try to kill you?" I said, trying to play devil's advocate.

"It wasn't Aedan's fault, though. If Carma—"

"Hey, no spoilers!" The girl behind us said, poking her head over my shoulder with a massive scowl.

"But that's right at the beginning of the book," I said, my brow furrowing. "Which we were all reading while waiting."

"Well, *some* of us might actually want to enjoy our books instead of speed reading straight through."

The girl in front of me rolled her eyes and flipped open her copy to point at the cover flap. "It's on the cover. I don't think it's a spoiler if it's in the book's description."

Spoiler Girl narrowed her eyes. "Whatever. Just stop ruining the book for us *real* fans." She popped in a pair of earbuds and went back to ignoring us and craning her neck to see the front of the line. The girl in front of me shook her head at the ceiling and mouthed "*Nutcase.*"

When we finally made it to the front of the line and Niamh was signing her book, the girl in front of me handed me her phone. "Can you take our picture?" she asked as she rounded the table and squished behind it next to Niamh.

"Sure." I framed them on the little screen, taking two pictures just in case. This close, it amazed me how, even after practically just getting off a plane and reading an entire chapter to a packed, overheated bookstore, Niamh still managed to look like she'd just breezed in from a salon appointment. She held up the book and scrunched next to the girl in a perfect book-signing pose.

When they were done posing for the picture, Niamh handed girl-in-front-of-me her book and grinned at me. "Maeve's battle outfit! I love it! *I* want a picture with *you*, if that's okay."

"Sure?" I said, my voice shaking, and I switched phones with the girl when we traded places, practically floating. Niamh Adams liked my outfit. I couldn't wait to text Trixie about it. I grinned at the camera, trying not to look too squeeful, like a rabid fangirl.

The girl turned the phone around so we could see the screen. "How's that?"

"It's so cute, like I'm taking a picture with a brunette Maeve," Niamh said, then looked over at me for my reaction.

I squinted at the screen. While Niamh looked so put-together with just the right size smile and Grace-worthy perfectly blown-out crimson hair, I had a ridiculous grin on my face, my eyes were too squinty, and a random piece of hair was sticking up in the back. The rest of my hair was practically plastered to my head and neck from the heat of so many bodies in the bookstore.

"Really cute," I forced out as I took back my phone and tried not to sound disappointed. The girl behind me in line was starting to tap her foot and roll her eyes.

Niamh went back to sitting, saying, "Tag me if you post it anywhere," as she picked up her pen. "I'd love to have that picture."

"Okay." When she started writing in my book, all of the cool things I wanted to say flew out of my brain, but words started coming out of my mouth, anyway. "I really, really love your books, Ms. Adams. I've been a fan since forever and Aedan is my favorite book boyfriend and…" I stopped midbabble before I ended up sounding even more like a crazy fangirl, "I'm so glad to finally meet you," I finished lamely.

"Well, I love meeting all of Aedan's girlfriends." She said in an amused tone of voice, then glanced at the sticky note before writing my name. "Phoebe. I love that name, it's so pretty." Niamh finished writing with a flourish and handed my book back to me. "Thanks so much for coming."

Spoiler Girl started making impatient sounds and pushing her book onto the table. Before she could force me to move, I quickly held up my bow.

"Actually, before I go, can you...I mean, I got into archery because of Maeve and you and..." My voice grew shaky and tears just barely threatened at the corner of my eyes. I focused my attention on the teal riser of my bow instead of her face, hoping she wouldn't notice.

"You want me to sign your bow?" Niamh finished for me, her tone gentle.

"Please."

"I thought this was a book signing, not a bow signing," Spoiler Girl snarked.

Niamh carefully signed the inside of one of the limbs, right under the Hoyt logo. "I hope that's okay," she said, hands hovering over the bow as if she was unsure of how to pick it up without breaking it.

"It's perfect. Thank you." I expertly picked up the bow. If I could maneuver it in crowded competitions, I could avoid knocking out my favorite author. "Thank you so much. I—" Before I could say anything else, Spoiler Girl practically hip-checked me and shoved her book at Niamh.

With a lame wave, I walked towards the bookstore exit, trying to look as dignified as I could, flipping open my book to the title page. Niamh's curvy gold signature caught the light from the mall skylights and I hugged both my bow and the book to myself. Meeting her was totally worth every bad photo of me that was bound to pop up online.

9

Frustration bubbled up in me as Em chattered on about one of her elaborate plans before it finally overflowed.

"I am not asking Dev out," I said into my phone while trying to reorganize my way too tall to-be-read pile before it could eat my dresser. "He's the guy. He should do the asking."

"Well, excuse me, Miss Nineteen-Fifties. You realize this *is* the twenty-first century, right? You don't have to wait for a Sadie Hawkins dance or something. Girls do ask guys out."

I dropped onto my bed, switching to video and rolling my eyes at Em with deliberate emphasis. "I'm not stuck in the fifties. I'm just a romantic. Did you know that my granddad actually hired a band and serenaded my grandmom?"

"And I thought my family was dramatic."

I ignored that and pushed on. "I want that. Where would the romantic story be if I just said 'Hey, Dev, Em thinks we'd be great together because we have *so* much in common, like being juniors and being in band. And you know, the whole milkshake thing was actually really cute. Wanna get some pizza?'"

Em stared at me for a second before bursting out

laughing. "You are ridiculous."

"This whole situation is ridiculous. They should have just handed us relationship instruction manuals when we started high school." An idea hit me and I sat up quickly to stare at the incredibly crammed bookshelves around me.

"How to get a guy to confess his undying love in five easy steps?" Em's laugh turned snort-y and it took her a second to catch her breath. "You can't learn everything from books. But you can just suck it up, join the new millennium, and ask him out already."

"I don't know..." I wasn't really paying attention to her anymore. My fingers reached for my copy of *Golden*. I was already always asking myself WWMD—What Would Maeve Do? So why not actually try to apply it? Or act like another one of my favorite heroines? "I...have to go. I'll see you tomorrow?"

"Of course. And then you can tell me all the details about Dev and books and milkshakes."

Golden's dust cover glittered as I absently flipped it around in my hands. "Right."

"'Night."

"'Night." I clicked off the phone and stared at the tower of books shoved on my "favorite" bookshelf. There had to be some way to become more outgoing or interesting. The kind of girl who guys like Dev asked out.

Marissa from the *Hidden House* books was like that. She was sassy and there was that scene with Cyril after she got trapped in the mirror with him...the heat rushed to my cheeks as I shook my head and fanned myself. No way could I do anything like that. My eyes moved to *Meet Me on the Edge of Midnight*. Nope, Saila was linked to Tarak. I didn't think a psychic connection would automatically spring up between me and Dev.

Golden. Maeve. She was brave and smart and witty. And she had to go undercover and not be herself to help Aedan. She'd be perfect. Except for the fact that she was a little bit aloof sometimes…

My focus drifted back to the *Hidden House* series. Okay, so maybe a little bit of Marissa mixed in with the Maeve wouldn't hurt.

I picked up my phone and typed a quick text to Grace. Time to make some changes.

My eyeliner is perfect, making my eyes look dark and mysterious. Ditto my red lipstick. With one last check in my phone, I shut off the camera and yank my hair out of my ponytail. It falls down my back in wild curls. No straightener today.

"You look like a harlot." I turn and smile at Cyril, who is scowling at me from the mirror.

"Maybe in your century. Now, it's just considered hot." I say back to him with a wide grin. I push my peasant top a little bit more off of my shoulders and step back to show him the whole outfit. "Do you think this will get his attention off the house?"

"I think I don't like this idea." But his eyes wander appreciatively from my legs up, up slowly to my face. He shakes his head and his expression grows even sterner.

"Which part don't you like, the mini skirt or the fact that I'm going to be romancing Daniel Shen until he believes there's no point in continuing his investigation here?"

"Both." Eyes that match the silvering of the mirror bore into mine. "I may have been trapped in here for a century, but

Oooh, sounds cute. Maybe Trixie can make me one?

I doubt what you are about to do could be considered right on any moral scale."

"It will be if it keeps him from ghost hunting you into oblivion." I tell him. I grab my messenger bag—backpacks are such a bad idea with minis—and throw my lipstick in the front pocket. "Besides, it might be fun to be the Mata Hari of Brookview High."

"Who?"

Right. He's pre- World War One. I raise one perfectly arched eyebrow at him. "I'll tell you about her later." Getting into character, I blow a little kiss at the mirror and saunter out of the room, putting a little bit of merengue into my hips. He follows me through the mirror on the stairway and the hall mirror, but I ignore his protests and push through the front door.

It's time to save his hot, mirror-trapped self.

10

Makeovers in books and movies looked like so much fun. Not so much in real life.

"Would you please stop manhandling me?" I dug my fingers into the velvety vanity seat cushion as Grace, her own hair flowing down her back in a perfect rose gold sheet, yanked another handful of my now brown-again hair and started threading it into a spiral-y tube roller thingie.

Another tug, this time hard enough to make my eyes water. "You're way too sensitive. Trust me, this is nothing. Wait until I tackle those eyebrows."

My hand reflexively went up to my eyebrows. "You're not touching me with any sharp objects. I take care of them."

"I didn't say that you don't. But I can make them better. Geometry actually comes into play if you do it right." One last pull at my hair and she stepped away, letting me see myself in the mirror. Between the pore strip across my nose and the spirals of curlers sticking off of my head, I looked like something out of *Star Wars*. "Besides, you're the one who changed her mind about the makeover. I could totally get a few blackmail photos of you right now," she said with a laugh.

"Don't even joke about that." I took a deep breath. "So,

what's next, oh guru of Fifth Avenue?"

She reached forward to yank the pore strip off of my nose and I cringed at the sharp skin-tearing feeling. "Clothes. I'm going to reevaluate your wardrobe later, but a makeover isn't a makeover without that moment where you walk into school and everyone stares at you. We need the full effect tomorrow." She grabbed my hand and pulled me over to her massive walk-in closet. "I think I might have something that will work for you."

Right. Grace was built like a dancer. I...wasn't. But I let her pull me along, anyway. As she rifled through hangers filled with designer clothes, I shifted from one foot to the other nervously. "What do you think about what Em's been saying about me and Dev?" My words were a little more halting than I had hoped.

Grace looked up with a frown, her dark eyes studying me for a minute before saying in a measured tone, "A bit of advice? Never let anyone tell you what you should or should not do or who you should date. Em and I are like this..." she held up two crossed fingers, "but sometimes she gets so carried away with things that she forgets it's your life, not hers." She held a plaid skirt up against me. "Well-meaning people are going to always try to butt into your life and make you fit their idea of what's best. Believe me, I know. But if you try to make everyone else happy, you're going to end up miserable."

I tried not to frown as she paired a white, cabled sweater with the skirt. I would look like a preppy cheerleader wannabe, and the commercial cabling was just plain uninspired. I could cable a better pattern in my sleep.

"I know. But I also get that I'm socially inept and don't always catch things, like that social mirroring stuff you were talking about."

Grace pursed her lips, shook her head, tossed aside the sweater, and reached for a black top instead.

"Yes, you are socially inept. You also have this incredibly big heart, which is so much more important than being socially savvy. It's all part of what makes you Phoebe and why we love you." She dropped the outfit on a chair with a pair of dark tights and made her way towards the bathroom door. "Okay, put that on while I get all my hair stuff ready. You're curvier than me, but they should fit."

"Thanks," I said dryly. I changed into the clothes, yanking up the skirt when it caught on my hips and alternating between pulling up the deep v of the shirt and tugging it down to reach the skirt's waistband. With more than a little bit of trepidation, I slowly made my way in front of the full length cheval mirror and stared at myself in shock. What was schoolgirl prep on Grace was punkier, shorter, and tighter on me. I looked kind of badass. And I'd never shown this much leg outside of gym class. "Are you sure I won't get in trouble with the dress code police?" I called in the direction of the bathroom.

"As long as it's fingertip length, you're okay."

I straightened my arms at my side. The tips of my fingers just passed the bottom of the skirt. "I have freakishly long monkey arms, remember?"

"So, scrunch your shoulders a little and you'll be okay. This isn't a Catholic school. Nuns aren't roaming the halls with tape measures."

"I don't know." I wandered into the bathroom, turning a full three-sixty in the doorway.

Grace looked at me from head to toe. "You're hot in that. I'd do you." As I blinked at her, unsure of what to say, she grinned. "Actually, I wouldn't, but you have to admit it sounded a lot less egotistical than 'I am the most awesome stylist ever.'" Grace pointed at the vanity seat with her hairbrush.

I grimaced as I sat, squirming a little in my seat. "You know that weirds me out. It would be just as freakish if Alec suddenly said something like that."

"I know. It's fun to see you freak out sometimes." She started sliding out the curlers until my head was a mess of Shirley Temple-like ringlets. "But I'll try to be better, oh delicate one."

As she messed with my hair, fluffing and spraying at the curls, I tapped my fingers on the top of her spindly white and gold vanity. "I ran into Dev at the mall yesterday. Well, actually, he ran into me while I looked like an idiot in my costume."

"I'm sure you were very adorably Phoebe," she said gently. "And what happened?"

"I don't know. He was actually really sweet." My tapping turned into a staccato rhythm. "I've known him for, what, five years? And I never really realized how his eyes kind of sparkle when he says something funny." My heart did something strange when I thought about that grin.

"Okay, stop or I might die from all the saccharine." Grace turned me away from the mirror, saying something under her breath about my not needing foundation. Instead, she came at me with an eyeliner pencil. "I know you're not big on makeup every day, so I'm not bothering with anything fancy." I tried not to flinch as she practically touched my eyeball with that thing. "Now, it sounds to me like someone's developing a crush." Just when I thought she was finished, she grabbed another pencil and attacked my eyes again. As she drew around my eyes, her mouth made a little O of concentration.

It was hard to talk while fearing an imminent blinding poke in the eye. "Is it really bad if I say I don't know?"

Grace shrugged. She took a step back and studied me for a second before pulling out a tube of mascara. "It's not like you have to know right now. It's a lot more important for you to take your time figuring out how you feel than to just jump into something because you think everyone expects it." She wiggled the mascara into my eyelashes. "But, you know, it might be good to figure it out eventually. Until then," she turned me back around, "you can rock a look like this."

The black and copper eyeliners made my grey eyes actually bright and not stone-like. My hair fell around my face in pretty spiral-y curls and waves. I looked like I'd stepped out of the nineteen-forties, in a good way. "Woah. It doesn't even look like me." I could be a different person, not just bookish knitting Phoebe. There was so much *potential*.

Grace grinned. "It's definitely you, only more dramatic. I can't wait to see what people think. Things are going to get really interesting tomorrow."

11

Marissa had Operation Save Cyril. This was day one of Operation Figure Out Dev.

Standing in the doorway of my A.P. English class with about sixteen pairs of eyes staring at me was pretty much on par with those nightmares of realizing you're naked in a crowd. Makeover reveal scenes always had the character growing bolder and happily glowing with the attention. Marissa even sashayed her way into her classroom. I wanted to hide behind my color-coordinated binder. Instead, I took a deep breath and, imitating Maeve's badass walk into the Fae court, pulled back my shoulders and headed for my desk.

Like Marissa in *Hidden*, I casually slung my messenger bag over my shoulder as I stepped into the classroom, but, unlike Marissa, messenger bags and miniskirts didn't mix on me. Five steps in, I had to stop and tug on my skirt to keep it from riding up into suspension territory. Ten steps in and I resorted to holding the hem of my skirt down with one hand while walking.

"Cute outfit, Phoebe," "Since when did *you* start channeling slutty?" and "Nice boots" followed me to my seat. But I didn't pay attention to any of that. My lungs were already compressed into a golf-ball-sized lump somewhere in my throat.

I passed Dev's desk and tried to make my hair bounce so it would fill the air with the scent of the cherry blossom shampoo I'd borrowed from Trixie. But instead of leaving behind a cloud of flowery prettiness, strands of my hair got stuck in the lipgloss Em had pushed on me the second I walked into the lobby. Ducking my head, I swiped at my face and hoped I didn't pull pink streaks of gloss all over my cheeks.

I barely made it to the front of the classroom between fussing and tugging and feeling tempted to turn around and dart to the nurse's office. It was just Dev, the same Dev as always. So, why were my palms all sweaty?

Maybe he'd see me differently, now that I looked different. Maybe he'd see me dressed like this and ask if I wanted to grab a water ice at Marranos after school or something?

Never in a million years.

I focused on the new binder Grace had given me as an 'accessory,' my finger tracing the cute little teal skulls. Leave it to her to think of details like this that fit me perfectly. One skull even sported a pair of oversized glasses and a giant bow.

I didn't hear him at first. The skull and crossbone Converse entered my line of vision and I looked up. Dev dropped his bookbag onto the floor and slipped into the seat in front of me—which was going to annoy Sarah, who had had that seat since September—and turned around to wave a book at me.

I took it out of his hands and studied the cover. "Sentinel Eighteen?" It was the latest YA dystopian novel, number two on the New York Times bestseller list for weeks. I passed the book back to him, but not before catching that he was a dog-earer. It hurt my heart to see page abuse like that, but I'd deal.

"You told me to pick up a book or two and call you in the morning. I didn't have your number, so I figured this is second best." He flashed *that* grin again, the one that had gotten under my skin on Saturday and now made me speechless. What was wrong with me? Maybe it was the way he held the book, with his thumb absently running over the raised swirls on the cover. It was kind-of hot. Sarah appeared over his shoulder and glowered over both of us before making a grumbly sound and moving up to an empty seat no one ever took because they said a kid died in it. She was too much of a kiss-up to take a seat in the back of the room. "I also picked up *Ghost Warrior.*" Dev added, like he was prompting me for a response.

Ohmigod, Phoebe. Talk. I forced my jaw to move. "Nice picks. I've heard awesome things about both of them."

"It's really good so far." He slipped the book back into his backpack and leaned closer in the process, his eyes scrunching a bit as his smile grew wider. "So, how did the signing go? Did the crazy girl behind you tackle anyone for cutting in line?"

His comment caught me off guard and I let out an embarrassingly loud non-Marissa-like snort. "No, but she almost shoved me out of line to get to Niamh." He raised his eyebrows, as if prompting me to keep speaking, and so I added, "And the signing was really good."

"You got your bow signed?"

I nodded. "I did, and she said she loved my costume."

"Definitely sounds like it was good."

"It was." My manners kicked in and I quickly said, "Thanks for hanging out with me in line."

"It was fun. When I'm done these, we'll have to hang out again so you can give me some more book suggestions."

Ohmigosh. Was he asking me out or did he mean just a lunch table/band/the next time he bumped into me at the mall kind of "hanging out?" I hunted for something to say. Something Marissa-like. Flirty or witty or just anything. Like tugging on his shirt and saying it made him look as hot as the model on the Sentinel cover. Or pretending to fake-steal his book so he'd have to reach into my bookbag to get it back. But then my mouth defaulted to book-geekery info dump. "Maybe. Sounds like you're into sci-fi/dystopian."

"Um, okay…"

I smiled as the late bell rang and Ms. Zhdanova stood up. Marissa always glanced up winsomely through her eyelashes. I tried, nearly crossed my eyes, and had to blink a few times to see straight again. "I'm paranormal and fantasy, myself. Well, mostly. But I'll think about it and let you know."

Dev turned to face the board, but threw his answer over his shoulder in a stage whisper. "Aren't those books about girls who make out with vampires or ghosts?"

He caught me off guard with that one and I gave off a snort-y laugh that made Ms. Zhdanova pause midsentence and look right at me. I covered my mouth and waited until she went back to talking about *Brave New World*.

I never talked in class, but I couldn't help one last answer. I leaned forward and whispered as seriously as I could. "Leprechauns, actually."

Dev's shoulders shook with silent laughter.

12

"Wait. Say that again?" Em pretended to study her sheet music while Ms. Osoba ran the clarinets through their section for the fifth time.

"He said he didn't have my number so he wanted to show me the book he bought." I told her, trying to keep the annoyance out of my voice. Why she insisted on dissecting every tiny conversation was beyond me.

Em frowned at me. "So, did you give him your number?"

My brows knit together. "He didn't ask for it."

The clarinets stopped and Em looked over at Osoba. Happy that the band teacher was absorbed in chewing out every clarinetist one by one, including Dev, she leaned closer and hissed,

"Yes, he did. When a guy says something like that, you're supposed to then say, 'Oh, here's my number for next time.'"

"Are you sure? He really didn't ask."

"Hello, I'm fluent in flirt, remember? Next time, you just reach over, grab his phone—"

"What if his phone is in his pocket?"

"That will definitely get his attention."

"Eww, Em."

She grinned. "You asked. Anyway, you grab his phone and—"

Just then, a shadow fell over us and Em let out a little curse under her breath. Ms. Osoba stuck her head between ours and we both sat up ramrod straight. "Phoebe and Ephemie. If the two of you used your tongues to practice hitting those staccato notes as if they were actually staccato instead of flapping them around all of the time, you might someday sound like decent musicians."

I looked down and played with the practice cork plugs in my keys. One popped out and went bouncing under Em's seat, but I didn't dare move. Em, though, blinked innocently up at Osoba. "I was just asking Phoebe about the counts for our duet. I need to know where I can breathe before we have to hit that high G."

Osoba scrutinized me and I tried to look as guiltless as Em. I did not need another hour long after school detention cleaning out the instrument room. "I told her I breathe right, um, before the phrase starts. But I have big lungs." Another practice plug went sliding down the inside of my flute, probably straight into Em's purse. My toes were crossed inside my boots.

She stared at us another second more and then, with an unconvinced frown, went up to her podium. "Okay, again from the top." She pointed glanced at us. "Your section had better be perfect, or the two of you will be cleaning the loaner tubas this afternoon."

"Crap," Em whispered. But before hitting the first note,

she murmured over the top of her mouthpiece. "And don't look now, but he's been checking you out this whole time."

I couldn't help it. I tilted my head at an unnatural angle so I could see the clarinet section. Hazel eyes met mine. My throat clenched and my fingers slipped on the keys. I quickly turned back to my stand and just tried to focus on the music. I didn't like him. And watching him watch me was not worth wiping up rotten tuba spit. Still, it took every bit of willpower to keep from checking if those eyes were still looking my way.

13

"I broke up with Wilhelm." Em declared, dropping Alec's box of Copic markers on the table like it was the exclamation point on her words.

"You might want to go back and try telling him that a little more slowly, because I don't think he knows," Alec said, failing at hiding his smile.

"See, that's the whole reason we had to break up. Miscommunication."

"You do talk really fast sometimes," I pointed out.

She shot me a LOOK. "It was really nice while it lasted, but it's for the best. He's going back to Germany at the end of the year and I'd be left behind, brokenhearted…"

"Overdramatically brokenhearted," Alec added, his smile morphing into a grin.

"Very overdramatically." I mirrored Alec's grin and went back to flipping through the sketches he'd handed to me. It was the second time Em had "broken up" with Wilhelm this week. She'd be back with him in about an hour. "These are awesome, Alec. It kind of reminds me of *Lord of the Rings*. Really Tolkien-ish." I moved my finger from box to box, following the story he'd outlined in neat pencil sketches.

Alec dropped onto the couch next to me. "You think? It's not too derivative, though, is it?"

"No, you're good. I like the steampunk thing and I really like the story between Liliel and Aladir. It's epic in a nondepressing way."

"Fine, you two, ignore me in my hour of need."

Alec grabbed her arm and pulled her down onto the couch next to him. "You'll be fine."

"You two are completely useless when it comes to interpersonal stuff." She slumped into the sofa like she was annoyed with us, but her lips twitched up ever so slightly. "It's like you're permanently stunted when it comes to romantic relationships."

I shared an amused look with Alec. "You're totally right. So," I reached over Alec and handed her his storyboard, "what do you think of these?"

"Heartless." Em took the notebook and lodged her tongue in the side of her cheek as she flipped through it. "That's a lot of detail. Do you think you'll be able to animate all this?"

"I can try. Think of how cool all those gears will look on screen."

"Like whenever Liliel extends her parasol-gun?" I bounced excitedly next to him. "This is going to be the best game ever."

"Oooh, I like the idea of hiding the steam-powered rocket thrusters in her bustle. I bet you can even have the support hoops and her corset stays light up whenever she powers up." She handed the notebook back to him and shook her head. "As awesome as it looks, you're going to be stuck behind a screen for the rest of your life working on this."

"Making a cane cannon come to life will definitely be worth it."

She arched her brows. "As your unofficial big sister—"

"By a month," Alec said under his breath.

"I think you need to balance your gaming stuff with, you know, real life? And I don't mean just hanging with the guys or us."

Alec snorted and his eyes met mine. I rolled my eyes in sympathy.

Em didn't even notice. "Look at how good things are going with Phoebe. I can totally do the same for you..."

I frowned over at Em. "Things are going good?" I tugged at my turtleneck for the millionth time, trying to breathe and wishing I'd stopped at home to change instead of coming straight to Alec's house. I'd knit it out of incredibly soft bronze-y merino from the store's remnant bin, but it always suffocated me. Grace had dug it out of my knits drawer and declared it a perfect fit and color, but apparently, perfect meant a size too small.

"Yes, like that adorable flirt-fest between the two of you the other day in English? Alec, you know Dev. He's totally into Feebs, isn't he?"

"Whoa." He put his hand up in the "stop" position. "I'm Switzerland. I'm not getting involved. You already dragged Grace into whatever insane plan you have going on—don't pull me into it, too." They stared each other down and he added, "And no, I don't want you to set me up with anyone, either."

"Fine." She crossed her arms and fake-pouted. "Keep cultivating your reclusive nerd aura in your goal to become the next Howard Hughes."

Alec suppressed a smile as he deliberately grabbed a tissue and, in imitation of the famous recluse, used it as a barrier between his hand and her arm as he gave her a shove. "Working on it. The only thing I need now is a couple million dollars."

I let out a snort, which set off Em's stifled laughter. She looked from him to me and shook her head. "I don't know what I'm going to do with the two of you."

"Why do you have to do anything with us?" I asked.

She leaned into Alec and reached over him to squeeze my arm. "Because you're both so stinkingly talented and awesome and fun and I want the rest of the world to see that."

Alec narrowed his eyes at her. "I'm not sure how getting set up by you does that."

"It's a good first step." She looked from me to Alec. "Trust me."

Alec stuffed the tissue between her arm and his in one last Howard Hughes imitation. "Pass."

She twisted her lips and shoved Alec so we were in a big heap on my side of the couch. "Good thing I love you both enough to ignore your wishes and do what's best for you, anyway. You're lucky I'm so selfless."

Alec and I shared a glance over Em and he rolled his eyes while I held back another laugh.

I practically danced off the bus. My handknit Maeve-inspired shawl wrapped me in cozy, sparkly, merino silk goodness. One of the few seniors who still rode the bus had dropped into the seat opposite me and fawned over it the entire ride. And it was a perfect shawl day—foggy, autumn-y, and breezy. Just like the day Maeve first entered the Otherland.

Today was one of those days when everything seemed to come together, like I had woken up in a Disney movie. It wasn't going to last, but I basked in it while I could. And I had to fight to keep from skipping down the hall to my locker with my shawl swirling around me, or running while singing out to the hill behind the football field like Belle in *Beauty and the Beast*.

Grace stood at her locker and I whacked her with the edge of my shawl as I passed. She looked up and watched me with an unreadable expression as I twirled the combo and opened my locker.

"Please don't tell me you're planning to wear that today."

Okay. Not that unreadable. "Yes, I am." I gripped the locker door until the metal cut into my palm. Buh-bye Disney movie mood. "I wore skinny jeans today. I haven't worn anything comfortable for almost a week. I took an hour this morning to curl my hair. I'm wearing eyeliner, for frak's sake. Let me have my wool." My patience had suddenly worn as thin as lace weight mohair.

Grace blinked, taking a step back. "Moody much? God, if it means that much to you, keep the damn thing. I quit as your stylist."

Someone stepped between us and I backed up a bit to see Grace. "Oh, come on. I read *Teen Vogue*. Knitwear is all over the runways."

"Quit. As. Stylist." Grace said, but then closed her locker and walked over to tug at my shawl. "Fine. One day a week, you get a pass to dress like my grandmom. But Monday, I'm bringing an eyelash curler." Before I could protest, she waved and headed for her homeroom. "Later."

I stuck my tongue out at her, but quickly hid behind my locker door when Kris turned down into the hallway. My face grew warm and I resisted the urge to press it against the cool metal. "Crud, crud, crud," I said under my breath.

"Hey Phoebe," Kris called out as he passed, but I didn't turn around, hoping he hadn't seen the tongue thing. Of course. The *one* morning he actually noticed me was the morning I acted like a two year old.

As soon as I thought I was safe, I peeked around my locker door to watch him. His hair was getting longish, curling in dark waves above the collar of his jacket just like Aedan's would. I caught his profile as he turned to walk into his homeroom and caught the hint of a smile as one of his friends said, "Man, I don't know what happened, but she got hotter." Right before they disappeared through the door.

I was not one of those girls who cared about appearances, but maybe Grace was right about the skinny jeans. I clutched my shawl and floated down the hallway to my homeroom.

14

Late fall home football games meant huddling in ridiculously cold weather in clumps of woodwinds and brass on the metal bleachers, trying to keep at least slightly warm between fight songs. I was wrapped in enough woolen goodness to make a sheep jealous, from my hand-knit tam to the matching scarf and fingerless gloves, all in Pine Central's signature red and orange, but my nail beds were still a purplish-blue color. I rubbed at my fingers and went back to knitting.

Before starting my next row, I glanced up and frowned at the figures on the field. I still knew nothing about football, but if the players were closer to the goal post and one person wasn't getting jumped on, chances were good we'd have to play.

"Touchdown!" One of the few of us who actually understood the game yelled, and we all scrambled for our instruments.

"Crud." I dropped my knitting in my lap and grabbed my piccolo, bringing it up to my lips and hitting the opening, ear-piercing notes of the Victory March. After a frenzied minute of music, it was back to status quo and I picked up all of the dropped stitches in my shawl. Maneuvering a piccolo and knitting took skill. I had to be more careful next time.

My fingers fumbled on the needles. "It's so cold I can barely purl," I complained.

"So, stop knitting." Dev turned around and nudged my boot with the end of his clarinet. "Or is it physically impossible for you not to?"

I made a face and kicked so he had to move fast to save his clarinet.

"Physically impossible," Em said. Her fingers were wrapped around little pocket heat packs, her flute perched precariously on her knees. "You have to admit, at least it's better than reading. Osoba docked her a bunch of participation points after last week's game because she missed all the cues."

"Wait, you actually lost points? I didn't think it was possible to lose points in band."

I ignored him and squinted my eyes in a sideways look at Em. "The person who once made us *all* miss our cue has no right to make fun of me for missing a touchdown thingy once in three years of this." I waved at the field full of guys in tight pants and helmets basically smashing into each other.

"Like Susan B. Anthony said, 'Cautious, careful people always casting about to preserve their reputation or social standards can never bring about reform.' I was *trying* to bring about reform to this whole stupid making nonmarchers a part of the pep band. You were just reading."

"I don't think Susan B. Anthony meant trying to get out of playing at football games by standing up and pretending to stab yourself with your flute while quoting Shakespeare."

A wide smile spread across Em's face. "I'll have you know that was my best *Macbeth* soliloquy. It was worth all the tuba cleaning and the B that marking period."

"It was pretty awesome," Dev said over his shoulder. He glanced at the field and, apparently satisfied that nothing was going to happen any time soon, turned to face us again. "Speaking of theatre, we need to start figuring out costumes for zombie Phantom."

"You know, Phoebe's sister is this amazing costume designer. Maybe she could do it." Em tugged my sleeve and nodded, like she was agreeing with her own idea. "You should talk Trixie into helping us out."

"Right. She'll definitely drive down from New York and take time from her class projects to make costumes for a high school musical. Don't you guys have, I don't know, a whole theatre club full of people to do that? Isn't that the wardrobe master's job?"

Em waved her hand dismissively. "He's useless. What we need are really amazing costumes to go with our really amazing idea, especially when I get cast as Christine. You know that role *needs* something that stands out on stage."

"Oh, so it's 'when' you get Christine?" Dev asked in an amused tone. "We haven't even auditioned yet."

"C'mon, we all know I'll be her and you'll be Phantom.

Lexie is dying to get Christine but she can't sing or act her way out of a B in Theatre so she'll probably just stick to stage manager to boss everyone around again. And there aren't any guys half as good as you."

"And you're not a diva, no," I shot at her, stretching the 'no' out for emphasis.

"If I'm a diva, then I need a majorly diva-worthy costume."

I shrugged. "I'll try, but I really doubt Trixie will be interested in this project."

"For once it would be nice if you stopped hoarding your sister." Em blew into her cupped hands, then rubbed and flexed her fingers. She tossed a dark look at Osoba before turning back to us with a grimace. "I think my fingers are going to fall off."

She was right—my metal needles were practically freezing to my fingertips. I gave up on knitting and flipped the convertible mitten tops over my fingers so my fingerless gloves were now full mittens. "I think I have an extra pair of gloves in there," I said with a nod at my knitting bag.

"Perfect." She dragged my bag onto her lap and dug past my yarn in a way that made me cringe before pulling out a pair of grey alpaca fingerless gloves. Instead of dropping my bag by my feet right away, though, her brows knit together and she dug a little deeper. "Phoebe Martins, did you lie to Ms. Osoba? I thought you said you didn't bring a book. She'll probably fail you if she finds out."

"I didn't." I could have sworn I'd taken my 'in case of an emergency' book out of my bag.

"Oh, wait, it's just a notebook," Em pulled my teal glitter notebook out of the bag and her expression grew even more confused. "Why do you have a notebook in your knitting bag?"

My whole body froze as if a giant snowball had fallen on top of me. *Please don't open it, please don't...* "It's my, um, knitting project notebook. You know, lots of boring pattern instructions..."

Em ignored my silent pleas and grinned as she slowly opened the cover. "You don't want me to look at this because it probably has plans for our Chris-Yule-akkah presents in it, huh?"

"She knits presents for you? Now I'm really feeling left out," Dev said with a mock hurt look, fake pout and all.

I couldn't focus on him or even fake a laugh. "Not knit-worthy yet," I said absently. Wishing I were telepathic like Evie in the *Daydreamer* books, I stared at Em and added with a frown, "Can you put that away before Osoba sees it?"

Em's expression as she flipped through the notebook jumped from confusion to understanding, a little smile spreading across her lips before she snapped the notebook shut. She handed it to me, eyebrows arched and one side of her lips turned up a little higher than the other, like she was stopping herself from grinning. "You're right. Just a whole bunch of Ks and Ps and YOs. It's like you knitters have your own language or something."

For someone who refused to learn to knit, she must have paid more attention to my patterns in the past than I'd ever realized. "It's Y.O. for yarnover," I corrected her, trying to sound light but also shooting her a "please don't tell anyone" look as I stuffed my reference notebook back into my bag. When she gave a barely visible nod, I let out my breath in a puff of white cloud and squished my bag between my feet where Dev or Em couldn't go for it.

"I thought stage directions were weird, but I should have known your hobbies would be weirder. Dev, you need to help me get this girl into this century."

I opened my mouth to say something, but was interrupted by someone yelling out, "Third down. *Louie-Louie!*" In a Pavlovian reaction from almost three full seasons of football, we all quickly grabbed our instruments, I flipped back my mitten tops, and we started rattling out the familiar notes.

An elbow jabbed me in the side midsong and I looked over at Em, who tilted her chin at Dev and winked without skipping a note.

I "accidentally" poked her in the arm with the end of my piccolo.

The moment we got into the band room to prep for the halftime performance, Em grabbed my arm and pulled me into one of the soundproof practice rooms. "Is that notebook what I think it is?"

On the other side of the glass door, the marchers were scrambling into their uniforms while the nonmarchers thawed under the heating vents. I stared longingly at the closest vent for a minute before turning back to Em.

"Thanks for not saying anything."

"What could I possibly say beyond telling Dev you're absolutely insane?" Em invaded my personal space and reached into my bag before I could stop her. She pulled out the notebook and flipped to one of my carefully laid-out pages where I'd taped a scene I'd copied from *Golden*. My handwriting was all over the page in little notes and annotations that analyzed every single word in the scene where Maeve first met Aedan.

At that moment, I had to become Maeve. Brave, bold, and with my eyes trained on Em so she wouldn't see how I wanted to snatch back my notebook and curl up behind the snare drums. "Don't criticize my way of figuring out how to deal with guys and I won't criticize yours."

"You're so…bookish." Em pursed her lips and flipped through to another section. "You know people have been hooking up for millennia without the help of books, right?" She turned the page and her eyebrows shot up again, "Whoa, but I totally approve of this one. You should totally just march up to Dev right now and pretend he's this Aedan guy because this," she poked at the page enthusiastically, "is make-out gold."

I snatched the composition book out of her hands and hugged it to my chest. "Don't you have lines to memorize or something?"

"Later. Right now I'm too busy memorizing the look on your face so I can use it the next time I have to act really embarrassed." Another look at my face and she reached out to give my arm a comforting squeeze before opening the door onto the overwhelming, clashing noise of marchers warming up. "Sorry. But you're kinda asking for it."

I made my way towards the double doors that opened closest to the football field, where a lot of the marchers and nonmarchers were already clumping in groups. "No, I'm not."

"You don't use this, uh…method…for everything, do you?"

"No."

"It *would* explain a lot about you."

This time, I poked her in the arm. "You walk around in character all the time."

"That's for roles. I'm an actress. It's completely different." Another look over her shoulder at me and she shut her eyes with a "saints preserve me" expression. "Fine. Do your book-thing, bookworm. I'll be here to help when you decide to embrace reality again."

I hugged my notebook tighter. "Fiction is the best kind of reality."

"No, reality is the best kind of reality."

"Can one of you help me out?" The voice came from behind us and I turned around to see Dev pulling on his marching hat, its orange feather drooping over the edge of the red column of silliness. "I can't get this stupid braid untwisted without taking off the jacket."

Em took my notebook out of my arms and shoved me at Dev. "Go, put your research to use."

Because we were standing right in front of Dev, I held back my urge to run and, instead, tried becoming Marissa when she flirt-fixed Dan's tie at the dance.

"Let me get that for you," I quoted straight from that scene, and stepped half a step closer than necessary. But, as much as I tried to go even remotely flirty while straightening out the gold braid hanging off his epaulets, I couldn't stop giggling. Our school's over-the-top red uniform with its rows of brass buttons made Dev look like a reject from the Steadfast Tin Soldier fairy tale, down to the elastic squishing Dev's ears to his head. "There," I said, still echoing Marissa's words, if not her tone. "Better." I stepped back and pretended to check if the braids were even and, in perfect imitation of Marissa, bit my lip and tilted my head while studying him.

Biting my lip *hurt*, and I had to fight not to cringe.

Dev looked up from checking his braid and frowned the moment he saw my face. "Are you okay? Are you bleeding?"

I covered my embarrassment up with another giggle, trying to hide my mouth by holding my hand in front of it in a cutesy way, like Min in *Cityedge* whenever she laughed. "No, I'm fine."

Dev opened his mouth to answer, but before he could, Osoba yelled out over the noise in the room. "Line up!" All the marchers snapped to attention, hurrying into freakishly straight lines while us nonmarchers watched in amusement.

"Gotta go." He grinned and waved his clarinet at me as he hurried in the direction of the other clarinets. "Thanks,

Phoebe."

"So," Em said, handing me back my book and zipping up her coat, "was giggling uncontrollably like a middle schooler at a boy band meet-and-greet a part of whatever book you were trying to copy?"

"Yes," I said, wiping at my lip and trying to pull together my dignity. I crammed my red-and-orange beret on my head and tilted my chin up in the air as I headed out the side door back to the stadium with all the other nonmarchers. "All part of the plan."

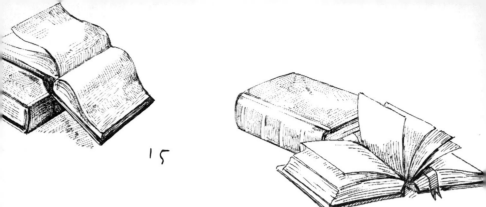

15

"I can't believe you dragged me away from my one day off to come here." I half-spoke, half yawned. I had been up until four am finishing *This Side of Darkness* and it was way too early to tolerate the mall.

Em pulled me through the mall doors and headed for the escalator. "Grace and Leia said they'll meet us at the bookstore," she dangled that last word over her shoulder with a grin. "You need some time away from that note-book and I need coffee, so we figured this would be a good compromise."

I had a to-be-read pile about as tall as me back home, but I'd never say no to a bookstore. "I like your compromise."

"And then I was thinking we could catch the matinee for that movie based off *Fallen Leaves, Fallen Hearts*." Em said, winning me over in one mention of our favorite K-drama. "I can't wait to see Han Min-Su being his hot, cute self in English."

"Let me guess, you're going with me instead of Wil because you're afraid he'll get jealous of your celebrity crush?" I asked jokingly.

Em waved her hand dismissively as she stepped off the

escalator. "Nah, I just want to spend some quality girl time with my best friend." She scrunched her nose at me and added, "Well, my best friend and Han Min-Su."

I froze. I had friends and better friends, but no one in sixteen years had ever called me a best friend. It was weird and awesome at the same time. My cheeks stretched almost painfully into one of the biggest grins of my life. I paused awkwardly, unsure of what to say without sounding incredibly uncool, then, to cover up the pause, grabbed her arm and practically started dragging her towards the bookstore. Time to change the subject. "Speaking of hot guys, Kris said hi to me the other day."

"Alert the media," Em said, twirling her finger in the air. "Dev. You need to focus on Dev. How many times do I have to tell you that Kris is a tool?" She pursed her lips like she'd just bitten into a lemon. "You know what he said in homeroom the other day? He said band and theatre suck up resources we could use for 'better' things. That guy is such an ass and I can't believe you think he poops gold."

I ignored her rant—Em was only biased against Kris because he wasn't Jon or Dev or any of the other guys she'd picked out for me. "I bet you heard that out of context. Kris is definitely into supporting the arts. His best friend's in the theatre club," I reminded her.

"I bet you're wrong and need to admit I'm right. You should listen to my wise advice and give up on him."

"Whatever."

As we walked into the bookstore, Em grabbed a book off

the new release display with a picture of a hot guy. "Who's your favorite book guy?"

"That's a weird question," I said, making a beeline for the new YA releases bookshelf. "Um, it's hard to choose."

"Pick one."

Ooooh, the new Marcus Easton paranormal romance was out on the shelves. A few days early. I grabbed a precious copy.

"Okay, Cyril from the *Hidden House* books. Marissa loves him, but if she touches him, he'll possess her. He's just so swoonworthy."

Em shoved the book she had been holding into a random shelf, making me cringe, and stared at me for a second. "You realize how messed up that sounds, right?"

"He won't risk touching her. It's so romantic, and the tension between them?" I fanned myself with the book.

"I'm not going to psychoanalyze you, but no wonder you have a thing for a guy who doesn't know you exist."

I couldn't take it anymore. I pulled the incorrectly shelved book out and dropped it onto a reshelving cart. "He does know I exist. He said hi."

"Who said hi?" A familiar voice came from behind me and I turned around to see Dev making his way towards us.

I quickly mouthed, "What's he doing here?" to Em before forcing a smile at Dev. "No one." Suddenly, my 'In love with fictional dead boys' t-shirt felt incredibly silly. I should have listened to Grace's advice when she wanted to toss all my t-shirts.

Em tapped me on the arm with a hardcover she must have pulled from the new releases. "I'm going to go see if Grace and Leia are at the café yet." She ignored my pleading look and practically skipped away.

I looked up at Dev. Okay, time to be cute, like Marissa. "Funny seeing you here. I thought you were an illiterate degenerate or something like that." I inwardly cringed at my miserable attempt at flirty teasing and hoped he didn't take it the wrong way. I made a mental note to tear out all the cute insult passages in my notebook.

He didn't seem to notice, or at least ignored it if he did. He held up the book he was carrying. *Sentinel Twenty*.

"You've converted me. Just finished the first *Sentinel* and I had to get the next one." His lips curved into the nicest smile, like he was sharing a secret with me.

Realizing that I was staring, I quickly tried to take in his whole face and found myself talking to his left cheekbone. "That series gets such good reviews." I flipped the book in my hands so the utterly embarrassing cover of a girl wrapped in a guy's arms wasn't facing out.

"Good? I was up half the night because I couldn't put the first one down."

I think my heart skipped a beat. I shifted from foot to foot, trying to find something that didn't sound stupid. "I'll have to move that to the top of my reading pile, then." My gaze unconsciously drifted back down to his lips, a line from *Golden* popping into my head. *Aedan's lips left hers and started trailing their way down her neck. She gasped and arched back, melting into a puddle of sensation as his hot breath tickled her collarbone. His hands burned, tickling the line of exposed skin between her shirt and jeans. It looked like he didn't mind modern clothes now...*

As my face grew warmer, I forced my eyes to focus on a bookshelf over his shoulder. What if he noticed me staring at his mouth? I resisted the urge to dive behind the shelves.

"Phoebe, are you okay?" Dev asked, concern in his voice.

"Um, yeah. I'm just..." Distraction. I darted my hand out and grabbed the first familiar book off that shelf. "amazed they put this out in paperback."

"That's really—"

Grace's face appeared over Dev's shoulder. I've never been so happy to see that bouncy blonde ponytail in my life. "We're here to steal Phoebe. She's supposed to be hanging with us."

Leia, pixie-tiny, showed up at my side and grabbed my arm. "Sorry for breaking in on your cute little flirt-fest." Her short black and purple hair swung into her eyes and she pushed it back with a swipe of her hand.

I gave her a death glare and shrugged free of her hold. Just because she was with Grace didn't mean she could tease me. "I gotta go, I guess. Have fun with *Sentinel.*"

He tilted his head and smiled confusedly. "Thanks. See you Monday."

"Don't stay up too late with that one," I called out, and then wanted to kick myself.

Luckily, Grace's nails digging into my arm was enough

to keep me moving.

"We came to rescue you. That looked painful," she said softly as she dragged me towards the café.

Leia gave me that preschool-teacher-in-training smile of hers. "Someone has a crush," she said in a singsong voice. "You were so red, I thought you were going to combust." She and Grace had been dating since Grace's sweet sixteen that summer and Leia seemed to assume all of us instantly became her friends, too. From the minute Leia first met me and said in her sing-song voice that my "little knitting hobby" was just so "archaically adorable," her voice always grated on me. Being around her was like knitting with bargain bin acrylic yarn.

I wanted to punch her. Maeve probably would. "Flirt-fest, Leia? Really?"

"It's so *adorable* how you wouldn't even look at him." I never really knew if Leia took me seriously. She always made it sound like everything I did was little-kid-like, as if I was the baby of the group. It was annoying, like she thought of herself as so sophisticated compared to me. "You're just so cute sometimes."

We reached Em and the table. I widened my eyes in a pleading look at Em and reluctantly took the latte she held out. "*Help*," I mouthed silently at her.

"So, did you ask him out?" Leia slipped into the seat next to mine.

"No! I can't do that." I didn't need Leia jumping into my personal life, too. Em and Grace were bad enough.

Leia pat me on the arm and said, "You should—"

Em poked Leia in the arm with a still-wrapped straw. "I'm tired of talking about Phoebe and Dev. She's hopeless," she said, emphasizing "hopeless" and rolling her eyes in an over-the-top way. "Let's talk about something else, okay? I need your opinions on what I'm thinking of getting Wilhelm for Christmas."

My eyes met Em's and a tiny smile flitted across her lips. It was nice having a best friend.

16

My arrow skimmed the top of the target and slammed into the fabric backdrop we'd hung up on the far wall of the gym before practice. I grimaced and nocked another arrow. I couldn't even get a group of arrows to cluster all practice long, much less get anything to land anywhere remotely near the ten point circle.

Coach Rentz came up behind me and I could feel her gaze move over me, taking in my positioning.

"You need to relax your grip. That's why your arrows are all over the place." When I looked over at her, she was focused on my bow hand. "You've been practicing with that other bow again, haven't you?"

I almost said yes, but then decided not to since she'd probably confiscate my wonderfully Maeve-y carved bow until after my next competition. "No...I just can't focus today." At least that was the truth. Another disastrous lunch period, where I'd ended up stumbling in the heels I'd worn in an attempt to be more Marissa-like and barely missed dumping my lunch on Dev by inches kept haunting me, popping up when I needed to focus.

Coach Rentz raised one eyebrow and shook her head,

letting me know she didn't buy my excuse, then tapped my hand before moving over to fix another archer's stance. "Relax that grip," she said to me over her shoulder.

I shook out my bow hand, then took a deep breath and aimed, my arms shaking the tiniest bit as I tried to get my sight perfectly dead center. My bowl of southwestern quinoa salad landing right next to Dev's feet popped into my head again and I lost focus as I released the arrow. It wasn't a huge surprise that it almost missed the target altogether. I needed a break to clear my head. I stepped off the line and tried to look like I was checking my bow.

"Phoebe, do you have a minute?"

I paused midway through adjusting my sight and smiled up at Coach Rentz. "Sorry, I promise I'll do better at tomorrow's practice. I'm just a little distracted today."

Coach shook her head, but smiled as she did it. "A lot distracted, and that other bow of yours isn't helping. But," she waved a paper at me, "that's not why I wanted to talk to you."

She hadn't mentioned any new competitions in her team announcements, but the paper looked suspiciously like an application.

"Okay?" I said, warily, squinting at the paper to try to make out the writing on it.

"They want to run an archery range at sixth grade camp this year and Mr. Cooper asked me if any of my archers would be able to help out. Since you're certified to teach, I thought this might be a good experience for you."

I regretted letting Coach talk me into getting my level one certification last summer. The thought of teaching a bunch of eleven year olds about aiming at targets and not at each other made my stomach turn. Instead of looking back up at her, I twirled one of my arrows between my fingers, watching the teal and black vanes blur together.

"I don't know. I'm not really good at this kind of thing." A camp book series I'd read over the summer popped into my head, tempting me with the idea of s'mores and cute campers singing around campfires and hot counselors, but I pushed those thoughts away as quickly as they had come. "I don't think I'm good at teaching."

"You really don't give yourself enough credit. I've seen you helping out new archers and think you do a great job." She handed me the application and pat me on the arm. "Think about it." As she walked away, she turned around and walked backwards to look at me while adding, "And if I catch you with that other bow, I'm confiscating it. Understand?"

"Um, okay," I said with crossed fingers. As soon as she turned around again, I shoved the application into the black hole at the bottom of my bow bag, down under a few folded up old targets. Camp, just like shooting a perfect session a few minutes earlier, wasn't going to happen.

Propping my bow in its stand, I checked the gym bleachers behind me. Dad always came for the last half of practice, waiting on the bleachers with the two or three other parents who came to watch. Most of the other kids hated when their parents watched practice, but I kind of loved that archery was something he and I shared, even though he refused to even *hold* a bow.

I dropped down next to his feet and looked up at him, slipping my blue shooting glasses onto the top of my head. "You know, most people who come to watch practice actually watch." I pointed with one of my arrows at the thick mystery bestseller he was balancing on his knees.

"They do," he said calmly, slipping a bookmark into the book and gently shutting it. "But usually the shooting is much better."

"That's harsh."

He let out a laugh and shook his head. "That's me, your really harsh Dad. So, are you done?"

"I think it's best for everyone involved if I stop before I hurt anyone." Maeve *never* had bad archery days. But, then again, her destiny kind-of made it impossible for her to mess up. I thought of the paper now squished in my bow bag. "And after seeing me shoot like this, can you believe Coach Rentz wants me to volunteer to teach archery at the sixth grade camp?"

He looked up again over the rim of his glasses and suppressed a laugh. "Sixth grade camp? Did anyone tell her about the cryogenically frozen Jesus fiasco?"

I didn't need to be reminded of my last, disastrous attempt to volunteer with kids. "It's not my fault people let six year olds watch the Science Channel. You would think Father Sam would be the first to forgive and forget."

Dad choked back a laugh. "You and kids just aren't a good mix. It might be a good idea if you volunteer with inanimate objects, instead."

"Yeah. I'll stick to knitting chemo caps and preemie hats. Less chance of getting calls from angry parents. Still," I side-eyed him with a fake annoyed look, "thanks for the vote of confidence."

"Always, kiddo." He pointed me back towards my bow and opened his book again. "Now, pack up and let me finish this chapter. I was just getting to the next clue in this mystery."

17

"Sunglasses, Ms. Martins," Mr. MacKenzie said as he passed in his usual morning "just a reminder I actually get out of my office" stroll through the hallways before the first bell.

I straightened up by pressing my back against the wall next to Em's locker and reached up to pull off my sunglasses. The hallway was way too bright for that hour in the morning. "Okay."

Em poured me another handful of chocolate-covered espresso beans. "You do this to yourself, you know."

"I couldn't stop. *Timeswitch* was too good." I slouched again and dropped my sunglasses back into place. "I think it was maybe five-thirty when I finished and got to sleep." I yawned.

"You're the only person I know who has book hangovers."

The first handful of espresso beans were finally starting to kick in—the world was getting a little less fuzzy. "It was worth it. I had to know if Lara and Fabien got together and saved the world."

"Spoiler alert: they always do." Em slammed her locker shut and I jumped at the sound. "You could have just skipped ahead and read the end." She shouldered her bookbag and added, "That's how I figure out if something's even worth reading."

"No, that ruins everything." I yawned. "Part of a really good book is *how* they get to the end. And holy love triangles, it was good."

Em opened her mouth to say something, but then she shut it and wrinkled her nose like she'd just tried some sour milk. "Ego alert."

"Breaking the dress code rules, Phoebe?" Kris came into my line of sight, stopping and looking straight at me. He pushed back his hair in a smooth movement, even though it was already perfect, just like the rest of him. I prayed he hadn't heard the love triangle comment.

It took a minute to remember to breathe. "Huh?" He pointed at my sunglasses and I quickly reached up to push them down and look over them like Maeve did when she first met Aedan on the hill of Tara. "Oh, I'm just rebelling against the social restrictions at this school that you try so hard to protect." I hoped my dark circles weren't too huge and that my sweater looked Maeve-y and wasn't bunched weirdly at my waistband or anything.

Em poked the hand that I was using to prop up my sunglasses. "Stop doing that. You look like my Great-Aunt Simone trying to read the newspaper," she hissed at me under her breath.

Frak. I tried to look cool as I quickly pulled the glasses off my face but I scratched my cheek in the process.

"Can I tell you a secret?" Kris said with a wry grin. He

leaned closer, making my heart stop, and said, in a loud whisper, "I'd join in your rebellion if I wasn't class president. Sunglasses are cool."

Before I could come up with any witty banter, one of the seniors mock-punched Kris in the arm as he passed us and said, "Hey, cuz, you gonna be at the club later?"

Kris did some sort of midair guy-high-five/handshake hybrid with the senior. "Yeah, Aunt Rose needs me to help with the gala. It'll be epic."

"Always is." The guy kept walking and called over his shoulder. "See you at four, then."

Em's expression was a combination of boredom and annoyance. "Do people even say stuff like 'epic' anymore?"

He ignored her comment, but gave me a little wave. "I gotta go talk to Matt before homeroom, but don't worry, I won't report you to the dress code police. Your rebelling is safe with me, Phoebe."

"Thanks." I tried to make my smile cool and mysterious, like Maeve's, but it moved at light speed straight into what had to be an embarrassingly goofy grin.

"See you in homeroom, Katsaros." Kris disappeared down the hallway and I leaned back against the wall to watch him.

"Not like I have a choice," Em muttered.

Her dark cloud of disapproval popped the bubble of happy in the air around me. "Do you always have to be so rude to him?"

"Rude? That 'club' he was talking about is the country club

off Lake Crest. You know, the fancy one that only lets people with personal gold mines and sticks up their butts join?"

I waited patiently for her point, and when one didn't come, I said, "So? I think he just flirted with me. What's wrong with that?"

"What's wrong with that? Everything." She started pushing me towards homeroom. "You're way too nice for uppity jerks like him."

I ignored her comment and pointed at the ceiling as the bell started going off. "You're going to be late."

"I'll be fine. Now, you, don't be late for lunch. I have a plan." Em gave me one last push into my homeroom and hurried off before I could say anything else.

"Oh, joy." I said to myself as I took my seat and lay my head down on my arms.

"She's so freakin' desperate," Em muttered before taking a fierce bite out of her sandwich.

I hadn't been paying attention. Looking up from where I was making notes on a Maeve/Aedan scene in my notebook, I asked, "Who are you talking about?"

She pointed the corner of her sandwich in the direction of the lunch line. "Lexie Rossel. She's the stage manager for *Phantom* and, ever since we started rehearsals, she's been using the whole stage manager thing as an excuse to hang all over Dev."

I looked down the line until a familiar head of messy black hair jumped out at me. I couldn't help but grin at the book spine sticking out of his backpack. Even from all the way over here, I recognized the cover art for the *Sentinel* series. Next to Dev, Lexie laughed at something he must have said. She reached out to untwist his backpack strap, her fingers lingering on his shoulder for a few seconds too long, and something unfamiliar rose up in me. It was like the scene in *Golden* where Maeve saw Deirdre flirting with Aedan. My fingers twitched and I promptly shoved my hands under my thighs to keep them from doing anything I'd regret.

"Does Dev like her?" I asked, softly. The senior always reminded me of Dax from *Star Trek: Deep Space Nine.* Long, shiny brown hair that, unlike mine, was naturally straight, a model's body, and she was so confident. There wasn't one ungainly thing about her.

"Don't be an idiot." Em pursed her lips when Dev let out a loud laugh, loud enough that we heard it across the lunchroom. "But it looks like he really likes the attention," she added. She reached over the table and grabbed my arm, making me turn around to look at her. "You have to start coming to rehearsals."

I shook free of her hand. "Like I don't have a life outside of being stalker-y?"

"Since you refuse to be on the crew, bring a book or knit something. You can get a ride home with me afterwards. He won't even think about Lexie if you're there."

"You do realize that sounds creepy, right?"

"You realize that I saw your claw hands come out, right?" My eyes widened and I curled my fingers under the bench.

"Last time you did that, it was for the last copy of that book, when the mom almost got it."

"I did not do claw hands."

My skin felt the warmth behind me, like a force field, before a tray slid next to my lunch bag.

"What are 'claw hands'?" Dev asked, stepping over the bench to sit next to me. Lexie followed, like the other slice of bread in a Dev sandwich.

"Notebook," Alec said, covering the word up with a cough, and before it could even fully register in my brain, Grace quickly reached over to shove my notebook under her lunch tray.

Em's lips turned up in the type of smile she usually reserved for her particularly evil little plots. "Oh, that's when Feebs wants something really badly and is willing to kill for it. Her fingers get all claw-y." She demonstrated in an exaggerated, monster-movie way.

Dev glanced curiously down to where my hands were glued to the bench and under my knees, before looking back up at the two of us. "So, what did you want?"

I threw an acidic look at Em. "Not like the whole claw-hand thing actually exists, but since I wasn't doing them, obviously nothing."

"Mmm-hmm," Em sing-song hummed before taking a sip of her soda.

My nails dug into the bottom of the bench—*not claw hands*—when I saw Lexie touch Dev's arm to draw his attention. "So, like I was saying, I think we need to get the shop class to help us find a chain long enough for the chandelier scene."

Maeve knew exactly what to say in a situation like this. My notebook's blue, sparkly corner taunted me from where it peeked out from under Grace's tray.

Dev nodded. "Em, what do you think of Lexie's idea? She thinks we can pull off the chandelier part of the musical in the auditorium."

Em blinked, her fingers tapping in a rolling motion up and down her soda can. "I don't know, *Lexie*. Don't you think the stage crew might be better to answer this better than me or Dev?"

Lexie looked surprised. "Whatever. It's my job and I just want us to have a great show. Dev *did* come up with the zombie theme. I thought we could brainstorm about this, too." At *we*, she stared pointedly at Dev.

Dev nodded. "It won't hurt." He nudged me in the side. "What do you think, Phoebe?"

I couldn't even shrug since my hands were firmly and safely trapped under my butt. Logical. Maeve was calm and logical whenever she dealt with Deidre. "Would the school even allow it? If someone in the audience gets hit with anything, they'll probably sue us all."

Lexie stopped mid-drink, looking as if she had just downed sour milk. "You know, Em's right. Maybe this should stay inside the theatre club. Pedestrians won't understand."

Deidre put her hand on Aedan's arm. "I don't think you should be discussing matters of the court in front of," she threw

Maeve a distasteful look, "outsiders with the potential to turn on us."

"Phoebe's probably right. I've seen the bookends some of those guys in shop tried to make." Alec said, looking up from his textbook and making a tilting gesture with his hand. Before Lexie could retort, he went back to ignoring her and saying things in mangled French to Grace.

Maeve dug her nails so deep into her skirt, she was positive the silk would never recover. Still, she wasn't going to stoop to Deidre's level—not now, and not ever. "Since you've hinted about my goblin blood at least three times just now," she said calmly with a smile, "I think you need to remember that it's the reason the court still exists." Then, she stood and walked over to give Aedan a kiss, a small part of her taking satisfaction in how Deidre was seething mad. "But, anyway, I have class, so this is whole conversation is totally moot. I'll see you later."

"I think—" I started to say, but Lexie cut me off at the "I" and my voice faded away on "think."

"Oh, please, it's a rope with a pulley setup. I doubt they could screw that up."

A hard kick landed on my shin and I looked up to find Em grinning at me. "Well, as much fun as this was, I'm getting out of this debate right now because I have a doctor's appointment. But I totally support using Phoebe as much as you want."

I kicked her back even harder. Too bad my ballet flats weren't as hard as her boots. "I'll walk you out. We need to talk."

Another whack to my shin. I was going to be black and blue. Em's smile looked a little bit forced. "Dev needs your help."

Dev watched us like a bad ping-pong game. "I don't—"

I narrowed my eyes at her. She moved her legs so my last kick didn't make contact.

"I need to go to my locker anyway. I forgot my history notebook." There was no way I would last two seconds against Lexie. She was witty and I would be the invisible third wheel, totally not like Maeve, who was able to effortlessly flip Aedan's attention away from Deidre with only a few words. And Grace and Alec were too busy practicing for their French quiz to bail me out.

"*Mauviette*," Grace broke away mid conversation with Alec to kick me, too. I stuck my tongue out at her when Dev wasn't looking. I wanted to know which French teacher thought it was smart to teach her the word for wimp.

Em threw me a pointed look, and then softened when she saw my face. "C'mon codependent."

I grabbed my bags and notebook and followed her away from the table with an apologetic little wave at a very confused Dev.

"I couldn't stay there. It's bad enough trying to be a part of the conversation when you're there to help me. Lexie would eat me for lunch."

Em shook her head at me. "You're using me as an excuse because you didn't know what to say? That kinda sucks." She elbowed me. "You did fine in English class."

"But that was different." We passed the sixth grade camp counselor volunteer sign-up table and I stopped short, Coach Rentz's words about volunteering running through my head.

"We really need to work on your witty banter." Em had walked a few feet ahead before realizing I wasn't next to her. Turning around, she made a face when she saw what I was looking at. "You really want to be a counselor for sixth grade camp?"

"It's only a week."

"In the woods. With no real showers. And ten year olds." Em waved her pass at the door monitor as we made our way out of the cafeteria. The monitor didn't even blink at me, one of the perks of being a notorious rule follower. "You're not seriously thinking about it, are you?"

"You should be supporting me when I try to branch out to new experiences." We reached the front entrance and I poked her in the side. "But, if it makes you feel any better, I'm not."

"Good, because if you can't even stand up to Lexie, I can't imagine you standing up to a cabin full of kids." She poked me back, then added, "Call me tonight. We need to talk about growing you a spine." She waved her phone at me, and the sound of her pushing open the doors echoed in the empty hallway. "Later."

I watched her back as she made her way out of the double doors before heading to my locker. Being spineless felt like a good option at the moment.

The arrow hit the target dead on. The second shot was even better than the first. Third, fourth, fifth—all of the arrows were crowded at the heart of the swinging target.

Aedan turned to look at Maeve, the shock on his face mirroring hers. He quickly schooled his features back to neutral. "And you didn't lie about not having training?"

"It has to be part of being the Harper." Those weird, creepy powers were taking her over like some sort of superhero-y disease. Her body didn't feel like her own anymore. She dropped the bow even though her fingers ached to shoot some more, just like her entire being was dying to touch the harp again.

"It could be that I'm an incredible instructor."

Maeve snorted. Did *Aedan* just make a joke? "Or, I'm just amazing. Maeve, the Goblin Slayer." She mimed a slashing motion.

Aedan stiffened up, all humor draining out of his features. "Harper or not, you've never been in battle. We are only working on this so you can defend yourself if the goblins break our lines." His hand gently brushed her arm. "You're not a warrior."

The whole 'you're a weak human' thing was starting to get on her nerves. She drew herself up, looking him straight in the eye. "I *am* part goblin, you know." She bared her teeth in what had to be an awful grimace. "My ancestors probably had yours for dinner."

Be challenging and awesome. No damsel in distress stuff

Aedan stared at me for a moment before breaking into a laugh. "I think you might win the battle on witty commentary alone."

"Then, you agree. I can be on the front lines," she said lightly, rolling an arrow between her fingers.

Aedan grew dead serious. "Only if you want to be killed. I can't defend the gates if I need to protect you."

"Oh, you're worried about protecting me because I'm weak?" Somehow, her body just knew what to do. Without a second thought, she yanked the brooch off his cloak and threw it in the air, whipping her bow into position and letting an arrow fly. The arrow hit the wooden pillar with a thunk, the circular brooch swirling around its shaft. "I disagree."

18

"What are the chances, between 'No way in hell' and maniacal laughter, that this might actually work?"

"In my time, we'd say we have the same chance as a cat in hell without claws."

"Thanks for the confidence."—Marissa and Cyril—*The Hidden House series book 3, Found*

I nocked my arrow and pulled back, anchoring at my chin as I took aim before letting it fly. Completely off the mark. "So, how are things with you and Wilhelm?"

Em handed me another arrow from her perch on the grass beside me and heaved a theatrical sigh. "Status quo. He wasn't able to get another foreign exchange year. Something about visas or whatever."

"That sucks." I took aim again and this time hit slightly off-center. With a sigh, I dropped to the ground next to Em. "Do you want to try?" I asked, gesturing my bow towards Em. "Turning targets into Swiss cheese always makes me feel better."

Em laughed, poking at my bow with her finger as if it were a snake. "I never hit the target."

I gestured around us at the empty football field and

baseball diamond. With school out for the teacher's convention, we had the athletic fields to ourselves. Coach Rentz never locked our practice shed and didn't care if we dragged out the targets as long as we put them back again afterwards.

"No one's here to see if you miss." I wiggled my bow at her temptingly.

"I'll probably stab myself, become one of Rentz's horror stories, or shoot you. No, thanks."

"You don't know what you're missing." I rubbed my thumb gently along the smooth wood grain of my Maeve bow. It was hand carved and beautiful, no sight, no stabilizer, definitely not for competition, and Coach would have a fit if she saw me sneaking in a practice with it. Maeve would definitely love a weapon like this one.

Em's burst of laughter made me look up. "Do you want me to leave you two alone? You look pretty cozy."

I tossed a handful of leaves at her, most of which didn't even make it half the distance. "You need to get a hobby. Preferably something that keeps you too busy to talk."

"Oh, I have that. His name is Wilhelm."

"Making out in the movie theater isn't a hobby."

"I disagree. Plus, the people who called it French kissing apparently never made out with a German."

Em's retort was so fast, it took a minute for her sentence to fully register. I resisted the urge to facepalm. "I really didn't need to know that."

"You're the one who mentioned making out."

"Believe me, I'll never make that mistake again." I

rubbed at a spot of dirt on my bow that had lodged in one of the carvings. "You'll need something to keep yourself busy this summer when Wilhelm's not around," I said, trying to really lightly gloss over the "not around" part. "Are you going to do community theater again?"

"Actually," she said, while pulling apart a clover, leaf-by-leaf, "I was thinking of auditioning to be one of those historical interpreters in Philly. How cool would it be to get paid to dress up, talk about the revolution, maybe sing a colonial song every now and then, and do improv all day long?"

It actually sounded like Em heaven. "Cool? In the city in the summer? Only if they let you wear ice packs under all those skirts."

"I'll just make sure I'm so dazzling in the audition, they'll have to give me an indoor job." She put her hand to her chest and put on a starry-eyed ingénue expression. "I could be the daughter of a wealthy merchant from the islands. Maybe you can teach me how to fake that I'm knitting something, like a sock. Or maybe embroidery—I can stick a needle in the fabric every now and then and make it look like I'm making a tapestry or something."

"Or you can just learn how to really knit."

She waved her hand dismissively. For someone who loved history, she wasn't big on actually *learning* historically accurate handicrafts. "Who has time to do that? I have a life, you know."

"I know," I said dryly.

"So, what do you think?" She looked up at me, and a

little bit of insecure Em shone through her confident grin.

"It sounds awesome and you're awesome, so how can they not pick you?" When the worry melted away from her features, I knew I'd said the right thing. "Can I sneak in when you're on shift and play with the spinning wheel if they have one?"

"Maybe. Can you make it look like I was the one who used it so I can get extra awesome reenactor points?"

"Deal."

"Great." She leaned back on her elbows, letting the sunlight wash over her. After a minute of basking in the sun, she reached up to look over her sunglasses and said, lazily, "Looks like we weren't the only ones who thought this might be a nice place to hang out." I looked up to see Dev and a group of his friends dribbling around what appeared to be a soccer ball, then turned back to Em with a frown. She tried to shrug but only succeeded in wiggling her shoulders. "Don't look at me. I didn't tell them you were here."

Dev seemed to say something to his friends before jogging over to us. "I'm surprised to see you here."

I floundered for a good response. Witty. Maeve was always smart and witty. I changed around her prebattle comeback from *Glittering* to make it fit.

Rolling back my shoulders and tilting up my chin like she would in a situation like this, I said, "Do you think I just sit inside all day and read?" I did a mental inventory of my outfit. Sporty and loose, but nothing awful today. Grace would be pleased.

"Actually, yeah. And knit." Dev said, and Em choked on a laugh.

"Well, then." I tried to let my lips slowly grow into a smile like Maeve's always did, and stood. Confident. This had to be awesome. "If I sat around eating bonbons all day, would I be able to do this?" I bent over to grab an arrow from the pile and ignored my racing heart. This was my turf. I could do this. Giving him one last glance, I took a deep breath and pulled back on my bowstring, counting my heartbeats. This wasn't States, just practice. With a guy watching me.

A guy who, for some crazy reason, I was trying to impress.

I let out my breath and, with fingers that shook a little bit more than I would have liked, released the arrow. I grimaced as it skimmed the top of the target and landed somewhere in the grass behind it.

"Maybe you could." Em said with a little note of snark in her voice. She looked over at the group of guys and sat up. "Is that Wilhelm?"

My sneaker suddenly planted itself right on the back of her sweater, jerking her back down. "No extracurricular activities, Em. We were supposed to hang out today."

She extracted her sweater and rubbed at the dirt I had gotten on it. "God, just land a bullseye and impress Dev so I can go work on my German." Both Dev and I stared at her. She rolled her eyes. "What?"

Dev shook his head and turned to me. He bent over to pick up an arrow and held it out. "Try again?"

All of my Maeve-esque bravado had melted into a slouch, a furious blush, and an overwhelming wish to roll back time. "I'm usually not that bad," I said softly as I took the arrow. A little voice inside of me corrected that statement. *Never that bad.* At least not at this distance on this target.

"Prove it." The sunlight brought out the green coloring in his eyes, and there was a little note of challenge in his voice. Very Aedan-like in that moment. I tugged on the arrow until he released it.

"Okay," I breathed. My fingers gripped the carved wood of my bow, taking comfort in its warmth. I was Maeve guarding the gates. I had killed the first goblin to rush me and only had to prove my skill. And I would prove it. She wouldn't let a cute guy throw her off-aim. She'd also be insanely dramatic.

I nocked my arrow and, before I could change my mind, whipped around, raised my bow, pulled back, and released in a split-second shot. And like something straight off the pages of *Golden*, it hit the bullseye. Slightly off-center, but still awesome.

"Damn, that was cool," Dev said for me, his eyes focused on the target. "Like something out of a movie."

"Yeah, she does that all the time, Little Miss Robin Hood, etcetera," Em said in a bored tone. "Now, can I go steal Wilhelm away?"

It took a second to make my own voice work. I tore my eyes away from the target to look down at her. I was good, but that had been a one-in-a-million trick shot, at least for me. "You have such a one track mind."

While Dev's back was still to us, Em mouthed, "*Oh my God.*"

And I mimed back, "*I know.*"

Dev turned back to us and we quickly resumed our carefully cultivated looks—Em's of boredom, mine of confidence.

"Uh, yeah, Wilhelm. Actually, we're meeting some of the other guys for a game, so I've gotta go. I only came over to say hi." He stared at the target. "Maybe I'll stop by afterwards if you're still here."

I waved my bow at him. "Maybe."

"Great." He jogged off, waving. "And remind me not to tease you about your hobbies."

I tried that slow smile again and scrapped it for a normal grin. "Mission accomplished."

As soon as he was out of earshot, Em grabbed at my arm. "Holy crap, where the hell did you pull that from?"

I looked back at the target, wishing someone had caught that on camera. "I wish I knew. 'Little Miss Robin Hood?'"

"It was either that, or jump up and down in shock. You officially impressed me."

"I—" but before I could finish, a yell came from Dev's direction.

"Am I knitworthy yet?"

I burst into laughter and ignored the confused look Em threw my way.

19

By the time I got to English class on Wednesday morning, Dev was already in the seat in front of mine. He and Sarah had been in a mini desk war for the past few weeks and it looked like he had beaten her today. I never realized my desk was in prime sitting territory.

Dev turned around without even saying hi and said, "Are you doing anything for Thanksgiving?"

I made a face. "Driving up to Massachusetts. My aunt's hosting this year. You?"

"Quiet. Mom's talking about making tofurkey and inviting my sister's boyfriend over for dinner. Dad's been sharpening his sword collection."

I let out a laugh. "Sounds better than watching Gran look for her false teeth and Aunt Sophia's soap turkey." His brows knit together and, laughing some more, I explained. "It actually tastes like soap. I swear, it's like she scrubs it down every year with bar soap and never rinses or something."

"That's...wow." Dev leaned closer, propping an elbow on my desk. "I guess I can't complain about tofurkey anymore."

"Nope. Sounds delicious. Your mom can adopt me if she wants." I tried not to get flustered by his closeness and instead forced myself to lean closer. "We're leaving tonight. Wanna trade?"

"As tempting as soap turkey sounds, no. But it's too bad. I'd been hoping you would show me how to use a bow this weekend. I guess I'll have to go looking for something else to entertain me." He really did seem disappointed.

Dev's cellphone sat on top of his desk. Before I could talk myself out of it, I pulled a Marissa-like move and reached around him to grab it, quickly programming my number into it.

"In case watching your dad threaten to kill someone isn't entertainment enough, text me if you need any book recommendations," I whispered as I handed it back to him. His fingers brushed mine and I couldn't tell if the little shock I felt was from static, the phone, or him.

"Ms. Martins, Mr. Jacobs. Will I have to separate you two?" Ms. Zhdanova asked as she stood up from her desk, earning a few giggles from somewhere in the back of the classroom.

I quickly sat up straight, trying not to look guilty. But Dev tossed a small grin over his shoulder before turning to face her, looking incredibly cool and composed as he pulled out his copy of *1984*. A minute later, my bag vibrated. I snuck my cell out and checked it under my desk. Zhdanova turned back from what she was writing on the board at my stifled laugh.

Do you think Zhdanova would die of shock if I used dystopian in a sentence?

I froze, and when she started writing again, texted as fast as I could. *I dare you.* As soon as I hit send, I regretted it. Counter witty sentence with a fifth-grade dare. Yeah, really intelligent. I held my breath as he looked down at his phone.

His shoulders shook in silent laughter and I breathed a sigh of relief, until he looked back over his shoulder. "Watch me," he said so softly I practically had to read his lips. "Ms. Zhdanova, would this be classified as a dystopian?"

Our English teacher froze before nodding with a surprised expression. "It looks like Ms. Martins is rubbing off on you. But, yes, it would be." She broke into a discussion of the future worldview in the book and I started taking furious notes.

My phone vibrated, this time rattling against the underside of my desk. I glanced down and felt that electric shock run through me one more time. *I agree. You are definitely a bad influence on me.* I started to try and write a not-stupid reply when Zhdanova's voice cut through the air:

"Phones!" The woman had eyes in the back of her head, I swear.

Fifth-grade me whacked Dev in the back with my copy of *1984.*

20

As a concession for surviving Thanksgiving dinner and Great-Aunt Amelia's two-hour breakdown of every health problem she had had in the past year, including a TMI blow-by-blow of her UTI, Trixie and I were given a pass from the rest of the family visits in Massachusetts on Friday. Dad dropped Trixie off in the part of Boston packed full of fabric shops and I was left in front of The Midnight Read. The indie bookstore was probably my favorite part of family visits.

I snapped a picture of the bookstore's logo of a book on horseback with a tri-corner hat and sent it to Alec before stepping inside. With all the weird video game characters he'd come up with, he'd get a kick out of that. The smell of old and new books mixed with coffee hit me the second I opened the door and I broke into a grin. *Home.* Lambertfield didn't have anything this awesome. I ordered a gingerbread latte and settled into one of the big couches in the antique book section. Just being in the same space as them was amazing. The store even had the peacock-feather-cover version of *Pride and Prejudice* and a first-edition *Anne of Green Gables* behind carved wood and glass doors. I angled my seat so I faced them. My eyes traced the pattern of the covers as I sipped at my latte. Maybe if I took quadruple shifts at Oh, Knit!, I could afford them. In a year or two or three.

My phone buzzed and I nearly dropped my latte. Balancing it on the arm of my chair, I pulled up the text. After Wednesday, I hadn't gotten any texts from Dev, so I was surprised to see his name on my screen.

What are you up to?

I stared at the books in front of me and felt bolder than I ever was in person.

Soaking up literary greatness. Let him think I was weird.

???

Before I could really think or stop myself, I placed my latte on the floor, stood, and took a picture of myself grinning and pointing at the rare bookcase. That would totally be something Marissa would do. At least I was wearing eyeliner and what was left of this morning's lipgloss application. I texted the pic, and sat back down to finish the latte and wait for his response.

I didn't have to wait long.

Don't most people go to Boston to see the Old North Church or something?

Don't hate on the book geekishness, I typed back and then quickly followed with, *How was Thanksgiving? Any dead boyfriends?* It was so easy to be flirty via text.

My latte finished, I got up and started making my way to the YA section. With some of the pocket money slipped to me by both sets of grandparents and Aunt Sophia, I had enough money for a few new releases and another ginger-bread latte, but I needed to space the two coffees out.

Dev's next text made me laugh.

Mom and I hid Dad's swords. Could have been bad. How was the soap turkey?

I paused mid-book-fondle to answer. *Extra soapy. No near-homicides here.*

Ha! GTG, last minute rugby lesson. When are you back?

Sunday afternoon.

Silence. The raised title on the new Emma Sanderson book had probably permanently imprinted itself on my palm at this point. When he finally answered, my heart nearly stopped.

We'll have to hang out then and compare notes. Text me later?

My fingers moved jumpily over the keys, misspelling so many words that I could never blame them all on autocorrect. I slowed down and retyped everything.

Sounds good. Have fun. Don't break anything. Cute and not desperate.

I'll try. Later.

After that last text, I slid down to the ground. Surrounded by the best instruction manuals on the planet, I reread our entire text conversation at least three times, cringing over some of the stuff I had written. Not awful, but I couldn't wait for round two. I had ideas.

21

Ideas like texting a picture of myself in front of Old North Church, even though I'd been there a million times. And a picture of me with Bryan Forster, the author of the *Sentinel* series, who just so happened to work at the same high school as Aunt Teresa, with a copy of Sentinel Twenty he'd signed for me. It was like I was a different girl—a girl with a quirky sense of humor and witty responses. Like someone had mashed Marissa and Maeve together and shoved them into my phone. Problem was, I didn't think I could be that person in real life.

When we pulled into our driveway on Sunday afternoon, I shoved my reference notebook into my bag, wiping away the telltale blue sparkles on my jeans. I'd studied every cute interaction scene I'd copied into that notebook, just in case. At that point, I could almost quote every flirty line Marissa ever used on Dan or Cyril. Grace was sitting on our front steps, and I practically jumped out of the car and into Grace's arms.

"Thanks for coming. Make me pretty."

Grace laughed and held me at arm's length as my parents watched with confused looks on their faces.

"You really don't need my help for that." She held up one of those reusable shopping bags filled to the brim with stuff. "But I grabbed what I could when I got your text and I'll see what I can do."

I pulled my knitting bag and duffel from the car and dragged Grace up to my room, flinging open my closet to stare at its contents. "Dev texted to see if I wanted to meet him at the diner in half an hour. I look like crud. And I don't think I fit in anything after this weekend."

Grace pulled a makeup and hair tackle box-like thing out of her bag and started laying some of her more alien-looking items on my desk. "You're wearing your skinny jeans and those boots I made you buy last week. And that cute grey sweater you knit that actually makes your eyes almost blue." Before I could protest that none of those would fit—except maybe the boots, she shoved me none-too-gently to the closet. "I doubt you expanded that much."

"You're like a fairy godmother with an evil streak."

"And you're the one who asked me for help on the last day of a four-day weekend. Get changed."

As soon as I changed into the outfit that surprisingly still fit, she sat me down and started attacking my hair with her straightener.

"So, he texted you?" she asked.

"Yeah. All weekend." I watched in fascination as she used the straightener to make perfect spirals, like she was curling ribbon.

"Huh, maybe he's not as big a chicken as I thought."

She put the straightener down and gathered my hair into a ponytail.

"Dev, chicken? No, that's me." I grimaced as I saw all that hard work get smushed in a hair elastic. "A ponytail?"

"You're supposed to look like you came back from a five-hour road trip and this is just natural for you."

"You've done this before," I said while she held my face in place to line my eyes and apply some shimmery liquid stuff to my cheeks and eyelids.

"I run with the A-crowd, hon. Looking naturally stunning is a part of the job description." Grace stepped back to check out her work. "So, why the sudden 'go get him' attitude? The Phoebe I know would have begged off and said she'd catch up on Monday."

She turned me around to face the mirror and I spoke to her reflection.

"Remember how last time I said I didn't know if I had a crush on Dev or not?" She nodded at me to go on. "I think I'm definitely crushing on him now. Not as much as Kris," I added quickly, "but Dev's actually really funny and now that I'm paying attention to him *that* way, kind-of hot."

Grace fluffed my ponytail. "And he doesn't look like what's-his-face from your book? Be still my heart."

"No more soul bearing for you if you keep up the sarcasm." I checked my reflection. Whatever she had done to me was amazing. I still looked like me, just a me that had spent a weekend relaxing on a beach somewhere instead of bouncing from house to house and staying up late knitting in suburban Massachusetts. "Even if you have the magical ability to make me date-worthy."

She rolled her eyes and started repacking her stuff. "You're dateworthy with or without makeup. Now," she added, "want me to walk with you to the diner?"

"Please?" I grabbed a scarf and handwarmers out of my basket o' warmth and followed her out of my bedroom and through the front door. A hoodie would have been better for this freakishly-warm-for-late-fall-but-still-finger-numbingly-cool weather, but Grace probably would have nixed it. Unless it was like the Pine Central one she herself was wearing. I had to get myself some fashion-appropriate school spirit.

"What happened when I was gone? How was Thanksgiving at Leia's house?"

"Uncomfortable. Her uncle started quoting religious stuff at us, her mom broke down in tears, there was a bunch of political debate, and then half the people who'd been debating fell asleep on the couch watching football. The usual." Grace smiled over at me. "Plus, you missed the Thanksgiving game drama at school," she said as we slogged through a pile of leaves that had taken over our cut-through.

Even though there were more leaves on the ground than on the trees, it was still autumnally pretty and, like a two year old, I couldn't help but shuffle my feet so the leaves flew up around us as we walked. I tilted my head to in confusion.

"Drama? No one told me there was drama."

"Jon was under the bleachers making out with Cassie.

You know, from the squad?" It took me a second to register that she meant cheerleading squad. "Her ex-boyfriend, Mike Lyons, was on the bench, saw them, and, I didn't see the whole thing because I was cheering, but I heard that Mike dangled Jon by his ankles from the top of the bleachers and Mr. Winters had to go all Marine on the two of them. And then Cassie got all googly-eyed and got back together with Mike because she thought it was 'romantic.'" She pulled her hands out of her sleeves to air-quote "romantic."

I blinked, trying to picture the entire thing. "I'm sorry I missed that. Mike is usually so nice." I tried to choke back a laugh. "Poor Jon, though. First me and my awkwardness, now Cassie's ex-boyfriend."

"Yeah. I'd pity-date him if it weren't for Leia and the fact that he's a guy." We stopped in front of Carlo's Diner, which looked more like a Victorian tea house from the outside, thanks to the town's architectural "vision."

Grace gestured up the steps. "Go be awesome and make me proud."

I impulsively hugged her again and made my way up the steps. Time to try and be a Marissa-Maeve amalgam in person.

It turned out I only had to be a Maeve, keeping my expression completely devoid of what was really going on in my mind while still looking cute and interesting. Yes, Dev was at the diner. With a bunch of his theatre friends, including Lexie. And, yes, he did drag a chair over and make room next to him at the table for me, but this wasn't what I expected.

I did what I always did in crowds of people I really didn't know. I turned into a silent lump of fake smiles and nods at conversations full of people and things I didn't even know about. Em was still at her grandfather's shore house, or she'd at least be someone to talk to. Part of me was tempted to text Grace and beg her to come back and save me.

Lexie reached over from her spot across the table and took the sleeve of my sweater between her fingers, rubbing the material. I hated people who didn't ask permission before manhandling my knits.

"Did you make this?" she asked. I nodded, and she sat back, studying the sweater. "You'll have to make me one of those. It's pretty."

Years of comments like that made my answer automatic. "I can teach you how to knit and then you can make your own." Even though I didn't like her, I could already picture the bright blue Madelinetosh from the store that would make her skintone glow. As well as the pattern that would make the yarn and her body look great. Because I was, like, the yarn whisperer or something.

"I don't have enough free time to do any knitting," she said with a dismissive wave, "but I can pay you to make it for me."

Another automatic answer, this one something that would definitely make Maeve proud. "You can't afford me." Like my free time was any less valuable than hers.

Dev broke away from a rugby conversation with Damien and bumped me with his side. "Good one."

Lexie looked like she had just bitten into a lemon.

Not wanting to sound like a jerk, I sputtered. "But, really. I charge twenty dollars an hour plus material costs. And you don't want to know how many hours it takes to knit a sweater." She still looked like she wanted to stab me with her fork. *Plus, I only knit for the knitworthy and you, hanging over the table trying to get Dev to look down your top, are definitely not knitworthy.* But I didn't say the last part. Lack of sleep definitely made me a little bit snappy.

Lexie blinked. "Huh. I can buy something like that at Target for fifteen bucks." She took a sip of her soda and sat back with a self-satisfied smile.

To keep myself from saying something I'd regret later, I stuffed a piece of cannoli in my mouth and pretended to turn my attention to the rugby conversation. I had no idea what they were talking about and I don't think they did, either. It was like a battle of the phones, where each of them would surreptitiously look something up and try to sound impressive with some sporty term or another to one-up everyone else. Well, except for Damien, who could probably make stuff up and get away with it because he'd been to his brother's games. Even Lexie found ways to chime into their argument.

I didn't get it. Dev's texts had made it sound like it would be just us at the diner, or at least I, like an idiot, had read them that way. And now, it seemed ridiculous that I got all excited and asked for Grace's help. I could have shown up here in sweats with no makeup for all the attention he gave me. I started picking the chocolate chips out of the mascarpone filling of the rest of my cannoli, making a little pile on the side of my plate that I could eat in one chocolate-laden shot.

Dev nudged me with his elbow and I looked up from my chocolate Everest to see a concerned frown on his face. "Are you okay? You've been quiet."

I forced a smile. "I'm just tired. Boston's a long drive."

"Oh, sorry. Did you want a coffee or something?" His eyes searched my face and I tried to smile wider.

I held up my half-filled mug. "Beat you to it."

He looked down at my mug and… was that a little bit of color in his cheeks? "Right. I forgot about that. I didn't even ask how your trip—" Lexie cut him off and started asking him something about the theatre club meeting.

I ate my mini mound of chocolate and debated my next move.

Marissa would sit on his lap, like the cafeteria scene in *Hidden* when she tried to distract Dan. I voted that out automatically.

Maeve would blend in and then impress him with her brains and selflessness. I could be like her in chapter twenty of *Golden*, maneuvering through the Otherland court like she'd been born fae. Or I could imitate her graceful but dramatic exit from the pub in *Gilded*, catching Aedan's—I meant, Dev's—eye and leaving him wanting more.

The exit sounded wonderful at the moment. I didn't need to keep being that girl who was so socially inept that she had to pass her time reading the backs of sugar packets and trying to lip-read the conversation of the couple in the booth opposite me. Downing the last of my coffee, I pulled a ten out of my purse and dropped it on the table.

I stood, slipping on my handwarmers and artfully draping my scarf around my neck. "I have to go, I still haven't unpacked." I tugged at my ponytail tie so my hair could fall in graceful waves down my back, just like Maeve pulling out her hairstick as she left the pub, but it wouldn't budge. So no one would notice my hair fail, I tried to make it look like I was pulling the ponytail out from under my scarf.

Lexie blinked up at me, delicately waving her spanakopita. "Already? Oh, well."

I wasn't sure if I saw disappointment in Dev's eyes or if it was just wishful thinking. "That sucks. Are you sure you can't stay?"

Faking my best perky-smile, I said, "Positive. Thanks for inviting me. Happy Thanksgiving and see you tomorrow." I tried turning on my almost-three inch heel and stumbled, grabbing at a chair to steady myself.

"Was there more in that coffee than just coffee?" Damien called out from across the table.

I gave Damien the evil eye. A line from *Hidden* popped into my head and this seemed like the perfect moment to use it. "I don't know. Is there more in your head than just air?" It sounded so much cooler on the page, but the guys didn't seem to notice.

"Oooh, burn. Good one, Martins." A senior whose

name I didn't know reached across the table for a fist bump. He winked at me before turning to Dev. "Where have you juniors been hiding this one?" I broke into a genuine grin. Marissa saved the day. Again.

"The library," Lexie said in a tone that made the library sound *bad*. As if.

"Anyway, I really have to go." I wracked my brain for something smart and funny. "This time without almost falling on my butt." Success. They were definitely laughing with me and not at me. "Bye." Random 'goodbyes' followed me but I didn't turn around to look at anyone, especially Dev. Maeve wouldn't do that. I put spice into my step, which wasn't hard in these heels, and loved the feel of my ponytail bouncing as I walked towards the front door. I couldn't tell if I looked hot or stupid, but Em had once said that I had a butt built for walking away in heels. I hoped this was what she meant.

As soon as I reached the Oh, Knit! storefront, I started breathing again.

On Monday, Dev won the coveted seat in English again. He threw a grin over his shoulder, then pulled his phone out of his pocket and started texting something. Zhdanova was going to kill him.

My phone buzzed and I snuck a peek at it.

Sorry I didn't ask you about your trip yesterday. Talk at lunch?

No sitting at our table to talk about the spring musical

stuff—he just wanted to hang out with me. A giddy little feeling rose up into my head like I was filled with helium and I boldly tapped his shoulder. When he turned to face me, I nodded. My grin matched his, like we were sharing our own little secret.

December was going to be amazing.

"So, if you hadn't found me and I hadn't touched the harp, someone else would have become the Harper?"

"Yes, if they had the potential." Aedan finished pulling on his embossed leather breastplate and turned around so she could fasten his straps. "It's lucky for us it was you, with the advantage your goblin blood will give us." He added over his shoulder.

She'd been so focused on tightening the leather buckles without letting her fingers linger too long on the muscles of his back that his last sentence registered only after she was done. Maeve pulled back and covered her mouth and nose with her hand, unable to hold back a snort-y laugh.

"What's so funny?" He strapped on a pair of gauntlets and side-eyed her when she let out another snort.

"The luck of the Irish?" She peeked through her fingers and scrunched her nose at him. The air in the weapons cavern had been so heavy with battle, it felt good to laugh. "Or maybe Leprechaun luck? Next, you're going to tell me I need to defend your pot of gold, too."

"Stereotypes, the whole lot of them." He shook his head. "Americans. We should have banned travel to and from the New World centuries ago."

"Mmm-hmm. You're just *lucky* to have me. Maybe I should kiss the blarney stone or jump a bonfire before the battle or something to make me even luckier." *sarcasm win*

"Those superstitions aren't about luck," Aedan turned to the pegs on the wall holding the leather armor the weaponsmith had fashioned especially for her. "And even if they were, luck isn't going to—" he started, switching back to serious warrior mode.

She took a deep breath, steadying herself. It was now or never. "Before you say anything else, I want to give you something for the battle." She reached into her pocket and tried to keep her voice light. "I have my lucky coin, but you need something, too." The small, clear resin oval started cooling the minute it hit the air. "I had one of the girls in the dorms make this for you."

Aedan reached out to take the stone from her upturned hand, his fingers brushing her palm with the barest of touches that shot fire up her arm and nearly stopped her heart. Silent and serious, he held it up to the light, the trapped four leaf clover glowing green at the heart of the clear stone.

Bracing herself for another rejection, she barreled on. "I found this clover on the hill at Tara the day I met you. My grandmom always told me the best good luck charms come from someone who loves you." Her eyes met his golden ones and suddenly, all her doubts about his true feelings dissolved. "I didn't think it was lucky back then, but—"

With his free hand, he pulled her as close as his armor would allow, dropping his forehead to touch hers. "It's better than lucky, because it brought me you." *cutest idea on the planet. I wonder if I can come up with something like that???*

22

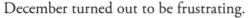

December turned out to be frustrating.

"Again, from the top," Osoba ignored our groans and lifted her baton. "I'm not letting any of you go until you get this phrase right."

I glanced at the clock, trying not to look too obvious. At the rate we were going, we would miss the late bus, which meant bumming rides off of the seniors or playing parent pickup roulette. Even though Osoba had the power to call after-school orchestra practices for our winter concert, I wondered if she was actually allowed to make us stay this late.

We started again from the top, and, as we got to the flute section she always picked on, Osoba yelled out, "Stac-cat-to!" I staccato-ed the heck out of those notes and could hear the other flutes do the same. When the entire orchestra hit the last note, we froze, silently waiting for her verdict. As soon as Osoba put down her baton and said, "Fine. We'll fix the rest tomorrow," we dove for our cases.

"Totally obsessive," Em muttered as she speed-cleaned the spit out of her flute.

I shoved my piccolo case into the pocket on the side of my flute case. "I know. It's just a holiday concert. No one's going to care if we're not 'stac-cat-to' enough for Carnegie Hall or something."

"And half of the people in the audience will be asleep, anyway," Dev said as he passed us, then stopped and looped around to stop right next to Em. "If it makes you feel any better, it sounded staccato enough to me."

I zipped my flute case shut and pulled my coat out from under the chair, totally aware of how Em was hovering around us, pretending she wasn't listening. "You are kind. Deaf, but kind."

His smile stretched across his face. "We could debate that, but I gotta go. I've got a youth religious thing in Philly. I'll see you both tomorrow."

I tried to give him a quirky-but-cute grin. "Not like we have any other choice, right?"

"Right." He started walking away, then turned to look at me with a teasing expression on his face. "You're making those socks for me, aren't you?"

"Ugh, you're still not knitworthy," I said, but my face actually hurt from how wide I smiled.

"You two are so cheesy, it's disgusting. Get together already," Em said to me, tugging on her coat. She headed for the door and I had to rush to keep up with her.

"Like it's that easy," I said. One sleeve of my winter coat trailed on the floor as I tried to wiggle into it while hurrying through the hall behind her. "Do you think they'll hold the bus for us?"

Em ran through the front doors of the school and cursed

at the empty parking lot. "I swear, this lack of transportation thing has to be illegal." She dug in her bookbag for her phone and searched though her contacts. "Dad can't leave early on Wednesdays and Mom's teaching tonight. Your parents are still at work, right?"

"Mmmhmm," I mumbled around the one glove I tried to hold in place with my teeth while buttoning it with my free hand. It was an awesome design, but a pain to put on.

Em looked at me and shook her head. She went back to her phone. "Wanna wait here and see if we can bum a ride?"

I'd managed to get both gloves on and wiggled my fingers happily before shoving them into a pair of mittens. Double cozy warmth. "There's always Alec and his Cinderella license if we can't find anyone else. You know he's always dying for excuses to drive."

"Right." She shoved her phone and hands in her pockets and sat down at the base of the pillar she had been leaning against. "God, I hate waiting." After a barely a second's pause, she looked around the parking lot and added, "These people are taking forever. Don't they know that some of us need to bum rides off of them? It's starting to get Arctic out here."

I laughed. "It's only been a few minutes. Isn't there a saying about beggars and choosers?"

"Impatience is a virtue and I'm cold." She pushed to standing. "Y'know what? Let's walk to Marrano's, split a water ice, and bum a ride from there. At least we're not just sitting around." Her eyes swept the parking lot again. "And if no one else shows up, which I totally doubt, we can bribe

Alec with a cheesesteak."

"Or hang out until Mom gets out of work." Marrano's was never crowded on Wednesdays, so no one was bound to complain.

"Or that." Em said over her shoulder. "We can plan what you're going to do about Dev. Maybe there's actually something in your notebook we can use."

I dragged my messenger bag back onto my shoulder and followed Em as she cut across the school lawn, the tail of the goldenrod yellow scarf I'd knit for her blowing behind her in the wind like a ribbon. I froze, a flash of inspiration hitting me, and Em nearly tripped because of my sudden stop. "I have an idea. I'm making Dev socks."

"What, like 'I like you, here's my declaration of love' socks? Don't you have, like, a gajillion charity hats still to finish?"

I ignored her. "It'll be just like when Maeve gave Aedan the clover." That was one of my favorite swoonworthy book scenes. "Or when Sara gave Mikhail that brownie pizza in *Zero to Forty*."

"Oh God, let's get you somewhere warm. Maybe you'll get some sense when your brain isn't frozen."

I already knew the exact yarn and pattern. "No, this is going to be super cute. He knows I don't just knit for anyone."

She tugged on my arm. "Walk." Em dragged us out the front gates. "Sometimes you really scare me."

"Says the girl who just starts randomly making out with

foreign exchange students."

"No crazier than the girl who's planning to knit a weird-ass sock thing for a guy or who crushes on people who aren't real." She hooked her arm in mine. "Why are we friends, again?"

"'Cause Osoba sat us next to each other freshman year?"

"True. Forgot that."

We walked on the side of the street towards Marrano's Deli in silence for a minute before I said, softly, "I'm glad she did."

Em squeezed my arm and nodded.

23

Night one in Winter Concert hell.

Em and I propped ourselves onto the windowsill of the art room where they had herded us orchestra people to wait for our turn on stage. The millionth choral song piped into the room on the loudspeaker and half of us cringed as a soprano hit a sour note. "One night of this crap is bad enough. But I swear, if they're still singing 'Carol of the Bells' tomorrow, I'm running in and stabbing them with…" Em reached for one of the woodcarving gouge-y things on the file cabinet next to her, "whatever this is."

I resisted the urge to tug at the barrel curls Grace had worked into my hair. She was out in the audience and would definitely notice if I had messed up her work. Instead, I tried to keep my mind off of the concert and how I'd soon be on a stage where people would be looking at me. My nerves also weren't helped by the knit gift sitting in my flute case.

"Dev wasn't in class today," I said, trying to sound casual. My fingers fumbled as I put together my flute and piccolo.

Em turned her head so that one heavily lined eye peeked out at me. "I heard he has to leave before break starts and was taking his midterms in the guidance office. Wil saw him in there during fourth period." She rotated slightly so she faced me completely but still managed to look like a tortured soul.

"That makes sense." I slipped the knit into my palm and held it under Em's nose. "What do you think?"

Em sat up quickly, grabbing the two mini socks out of my hand. "OMG, these are so fucking cute!" I had knit them out of our school colors and she danced the little flame-colored socks on the drafting table. She squinted at the note I had pinned to one of them. "'As requested'?"

"Cute, right? I'm thinking of sneaking these onto Dev's music stand before the concert." The thought made my nerves tick up another notch.

"Not how I'd flirt, but I guess it works." Em flipped one of the socks inside out and I had to fight to keep from grabbing them back.

Instead, I blew air through my lips. "I've tried hints. I've texted. I've worn cute clothes around him. I have a notebook full of the best flirty ideas from a ton of books. Seriously, Em, I couldn't think of anything else."

"Um, you could just ask him out."

I frowned at her. "Hello? Shy, bookish knitter here. I don't ask people out. The thought of doing that gives me hives."

She made the little socks twirl before handing them back to me. "You're a lost cause."

I slipped the socks into the sleeve of my dress. "I just need to figure out how to get this out there without Osoba killing me for getting out of line." I hummed the Mission Impossible theme song. "At least I'm wearing black."

"Y'know, I heard that Kris is supposed to be in the audience today."

I deflated ever so slightly and stopped my silly little spy dance. "Really?" The mini socks burnt my arm, reminding me that I was betraying my feelings for Kris.

"Just kidding. You know he doesn't do anything that won't help his student council standing or GPA. The jerk even said they'd have to pay him to listen to the hand bells." She fiddled with her flute and grinned wickedly at me. "I just wanted to see your reaction."

"That was mean."

"Why? Because you don't want to admit that Dev has risen to higher crush status than Kris? A situation of which I fully approve, by the way."

I wasn't going to dignify that comment with a response. Em never understood my undying crush from a distance on Kris. Instead, I looked around the crowded room, squinting my eyes at the clarinet section. "I just want to get this whole night over with."

Em waved her hand in front of my face. "You're so boring when you go into freak-out mode."

"I'm not freaking out," I said, biting my lip and twisting the mouthpiece on my flute again.

A pair of black-and-white Converse caught my attention, followed by a familiar voice.

"Who's freaking out?"

I followed those Converse up to a pair of black suit pants and Dev, looking cuter than I'd ever seen him in a black dress shirt and tie. All of the other guys in band were wearing white dress shirts and black ties, making him stand out even more. He twirled his clarinet nonchalantly.

"Feebs. She's always like this before a concert." Em jumped off of the windowsill and grabbed her purse, the spangles on her sparkly black flapper dress playing music of their own. "I'm going to go check my makeup before we start. You calm her down." She skipped off before either of us could answer.

I looked back down at my flute before he could think I was staring. When he slid into Em's former spot, I had to work to ignore how his shirt just barely brushed my arm. Marissa would smile up at him and slide closer, telling him how good he looked, but I could barely talk.

"I like the black shirt idea. Really different." I stopped twisting my mouthpiece for a second and looked up at him, quickly adding, "In a good way, I mean." Darn, he smelled good. Like a mix of soap and spice. I dropped my eyes back down to the linoleum floor.

He started swaying very slightly in time to the choir's medley of some medieval carols and I was acutely aware of every miniscule touch of his clothing to mine.

"Thanks. Mom nearly had a heart attack when she saw me, but Osoba said black and white. She didn't say how to wear the black and white."

I felt his eyes on me and I looked up in time to see him

take in my black heels and dress in the same slow, sweeping motion I had used. Heat ran up my body following the path of his gaze and suddenly the room felt too warm. "You look really nice, too." His grin revealed a dimple I hadn't noticed before. I was screwed.

I wiped my sweaty palms on the skirt of my dress, praying that I wasn't also wiping streaks of pastel chalk onto the velvet. "Thanks."

I loved this dress. It was sleek and figure-skater-y with a deep u-neck and a short, full skirt that threatened to twirl on its own. I was torn between the urge to jump up and demonstrate the swirly-ness, and shrinking and hiding in my flute case. I racked my brain for something to say next, too wound up to even remember anything Maeve would say. *Don't babble on about the dress.*

I swung my legs, my heels making a metallic sound against the old radiator. "Em told me you're leaving early for winter break."

"Yeah, my cousin's getting married in Mumbai, so the school's letting me take my midterms early." He said Mumbai in the same offhand way I would have said Massachusetts.

I blinked, forgetting how close we were sitting. "Whoa. Mumbai, as in India?"

A grin flitted across Dev's face. "That Mumbai. We're leaving Monday and I'll be back on the thirtieth."

"That's, um, a long flight, isn't it?"

"Eighteen hours straight from Newark."

The choir stopped singing and the chime of hand bells

playing their own version of "Silver Bells" piped into the room. Ten more minutes before it was our turn to go on. My heart jumped into my throat to choke me, and it had nothing to do with Dev. "Wow." I managed to say. My fingers nervously tapped out the notes on the flute's keys.

Dev's gaze drifted down to my fingers. Amusement danced across his features. "Nervous?"

I forced my fingers to still, closed my eyes, and took a deep breath. The spicy-soapy scent just made my heart beat even faster, like I had pressed the accelerator on an already speeding car.

"No." I tasted the lie and tried to come up with something to say that wasn't about me. "You're going to spend Christmas over there? It must be really different."

Dev blinked at me. "Uhm, I guess, sort-of. I'm not Christian, so no birth of a savior or Silent Night or anything like that for me." *Oh, crud.* "But I guess you could say I celebrate Santa Claus day." He winked. "And I'm sure my uncle will be putting up a tree like he usually does."

I opened my mouth, closed it, and opened it again. "Ohmigosh, I didn't mean to assume anything." But I had. And automatically wished I could melt into the vents like a wet wicked witch from Oz.

It didn't seem to bother him, though. The dimple in his cheek grew larger. "My mom's Hindu and my dad is Christian, so I was raised Hindu. I don't celebrate Christmas, really, but Diwali and Holi make up for it."

Holi. Right, the festival of colors. That had been in a

Bollywood film Em and I had watched last summer.

"Holi must be awesome, with all the color and stuff." The handbell/madrigal choir started some old song. Five minutes left. Over Dev's shoulder, I saw Em mouthing "ask him out" and pointing to an invisible wristwatch. I pulled straight from one of Maeve's lines in *Golden*. "That means we won't have time to hang out before you leave, will we?"

"Actually, I was thinking—"

But before he could finish, Osoba hurried into the room and clapped her hands. "Get organized into your lines, now," she shouted over the general din. Everyone started talking again. "Now. Without a peep."

Dev jerked his chin towards the other clarinets and whispered, "I'd better get over there before she threatens to throw me into the orchestra pit." He reached over and squeezed the hand still clutching my flute. "Relax."

Em reached me while I was still watching Dev push through to the clarinet section and poked me in the arm.

"Okay, if you're going to do this ridiculous thing," Em whispered, "which I still think is crazy as hell, go right after we tune. I'll bring your flute and sheet music. Osoba usually doesn't check our lines." Her whisper was hidden by a blare of tuning oboes.

I brought the flute up to lip-level. Osoba would be over soon to tune us. "You're right, this is stupid."

She waited until the clarinets hit their C in unison. "Yeah, it is."

I took a deep breath. "But I can do it." I still felt the

ghost of his fingers on mine, and where his pants had brushed my tights. My skin tingled, like it was stretched a little too tight in those places. It was impossible to even imagine concentrating on anything but those feelings. "I'm Maeve. I'm not afraid of anything."

"You are completely and totally insane."

After we tuned, I hurried backstage, pushing past stagehands as they finished setting up our seats and stands. Maeve would be so much more stealthy than this. Marissa would probably charm a stagehand into doing it for her, but I was Phoebe. Clumsy, not stealthy, and too short on time to play superspy.

Dev was the third chair from the end on the front row, almost exactly opposite Em. I hurried around the edge of the stage, trying to keep to all the shadowy areas. The curtain was touching the first seat of the front row, so I slipped into the second row to keep from bumping into it.

Keeping to the shadows, Maeve crept through the castle hall, her every movement a whisper. As she got closer to her target, she quietly nocked an arrow and held her bow at the ready. She only had one chance to get Carman's scroll and couldn't mess it up.

When I was positive no one was around, I slipped around the second-row music stands and leaned over the back of the Dev's chair, stretching as far as I could to reach the stand. I almost lost my balance in my stupid heels, but, like Maeve on Carman's windowsill, I caught myself last minute and touched the lip of the stand without knocking it over. Exhaling, I slipped the socks onto his stand and ran out, almost crashing into Em as the flutes started filing on stage.

"Good timing," she mouthed at me, handing me my things. After I had settled, I looked up to watch as the clarinets filled in their spots. Dev started putting down his sheet music and paused, staring at his music stand.

I held my breath as he picked up the socks and studied them, reading the tag with a quizzical look on his face. Then, he started laughing and his eyes raised up to meet mine. I tried to appear cool and composed as my heart went completely arrhythmic and my neck felt like it was bursting into flames, but a wide smile snuck through, anyway. The socks weren't a clover, but it looked like they were good enough.

As we were making our way out afterwards, I felt a tug on one of my curls. "These are awesome. I think you made the wrong size, but I'll deal." Dev jogged up next to me, a mini sock on each pointer finger and his clarinet and sheet music under his arm.

I forced an indignant expression on my face as I slicked my hair back into place, but knew I failed miserably. Probably even verging on goofy-grin territory. "You never said they had to fit."

"Thank you, anyway."

I mocked a little midstep curtsy. "You're welcome." Emboldened, I poked at the heel of one of the socks. "Now that you have those, no more teasing me about socks, right?"

In the dim lights backstage, his eyes reflected back a

brighter shade of green than usual. "Nope. I think you need to make me a sweater next."

Maeve would keep up the witty repartee, and I tried to make my response lightning-fast. "Get in line, sock-boy." At his laugh, I knew that worked.

Dev walked a little slower down the hallway, bumping his arm against mine every now and then, just enough that my arm was constantly tingling. I could have avoided him by walking closer to Em, but I didn't. And he kept veering close. "I have to take my history and physics midterms tomorrow morning, so I have to go study, but are you coming with us to Marrano's after the concert tomorrow?"

"I don't know. Maybe."

Dev grabbed at my hands and turned to face me. "C'mon, I need someone to keep me company with all of these band geeks." I was frozen in shock and I guess he took it as indecision because he gave me a pleading look. "I'll cover your milkshake? It's my last chance to hang out before I fly halfway across the world."

I finally shook awake and forced a wan smile. "Sure. I'll try."

"Good." He dropped my hands and started walking backwards. "Gotta go study."

"Kick some midterm butt," I called after him, then covered my mouth and turned to Em. "That was a little loud, wasn't it?"

"That was unbelievably awesome. And lame at the same time." Em pulled me aside. "When a guy you obviously like asks you to hang out, you don't say 'maybe.' Sometimes, I swear, you're like Sandra Dee on steroids."

"Ooohh, a *Grease* reference. Now I'm really worried."

Em shook her head in an 'I love you but I can barely tolerate you' way. "Let's work on dropping some of those super holy virgin habits of yours before tomorrow night, okay?"

"Em! Oh my God."I looked around, hoping no one heard that.

"Calling it like it is. You need a lot of work."

24

"Someone's happy."

Mom's voice broke my reverie and I stopped my off-key humming. I pulled my headphones out of my ears and looked up to find her standing in the doorway to my room with an amused expression. "How embarrassed should I be right now?"

"I think I saw that last bit where you waltzed with your yarn." Mom walked in and dropped into my desk chair, laying her book on my giant to be read pile. "At least, it looked like waltzing."

I sat on my bed, grabbing a set of needles and starting to cast-on. "Life is really good," I said, not even caring if I sounded incredibly goofy. "Like, burst-into-song, movie musical good."

"That's…" Mom broke into a smile that made her look so much younger and a lot like Trixie. "… good." She nudged the basket of knit gifts with her foot. "Even with your Sisyphusian knit task?"

"Yup." I wasn't one of those girls who told their moms everything. But today the words just tumbled out of my mouth as I knit. "There's this guy in band…"

Mom leaned forward so fast, her knee smacked against the basket. She reached out to steady it before it could fall over. "Band?"

I was so glad I had my knitting to look at. I didn't think Mom would appreciate the eye roll that almost snuck out. "Marching and concert. Rock band guys are more Trixie's type."

"Oh, good. Go on."

"He's just really nice, is all." And cute, and funny. But I didn't bother adding those.

Mom hesitated, flipping through the new dystopian on my desk before saying in a measured tone, "You've made a lot of commitments, including passing your midterms and your job. I don't want to make it sound like I don't want you to date, which I don't, by the way, but do you even have time for this boy?"

I closed my eyes. My needles still clicked away. I'd made so many of these hats, I could knit them in my sleep. "Even if we were dating, which we're not, he's going halfway across the world until New Year's. I don't think I need to worry about distractions, Mom."

"I think I like this boy already."

"And then you wonder why I never tell you anything." I looked up at her and frowned.

"I'm too young to have grey hairs and your sister has already given me a few. Please don't add to them. You're supposed to be the easy daughter," she said.

Of course I was the easy daughter, the one born without

social skills. "I'll try harder to be boring."

"That's all I ask." She stood and reached out to gently smooth my hair. "But I'm happy you're happy."

"Thanks."

"And I'm happy that you like a boy who isn't going to be in our time zone. Any chance he'll stay there?"

"I'm really, really never telling you anything again." I tossed a ball of yarn at her as she snatched up her book and ducked out of the door.

Alone again, I fell back onto my bed and stared at the ceiling, my heart dancing in my chest as I thought about Dev and the concert. I couldn't turn into a useless block when I saw him again. And, even though common sense screamed at me for dreaming about something that might not happen, I couldn't help but imagine the possibilities. Maybe he'd pull me out into Marrano's summer patio and kiss me under the twinkle lights, just like Daymeon and Taylor in *Starbound*.

Fireflies—a December miracle would make that happen, of course—would fill the air around us. A light breeze would pick up, swirling my dress around me. Our eyes would meet, and neither of us would be able to look away. He'd look a little nervous, like he was trying so hard to make the moment perfect. I'd drop my eyes and start to walk away, saying something about going home, and he'd grab my arm, tugging me to part of the patio furthest from the streetlight.

"Wait," he'd whisper, "Don't go."

He'd step closer and his free hand would come up to push

back the strand of hair that had come loose from my updo. *Note to self, do hair in an updo and tug a piece of hair free right after the concert.* Daymeon—um, Dev—would then cup my cheek with his hand, his thumb almost skimming the edge of my lips. *"You were amazing tonight. A real shining star,"* he'd whisper to me. He'd slide his thumb down to touch my bottom lip again and I'd visibly catch my breath,

I would look up at him, my eyes reflecting the twinkle lights. Maybe not as prettily as Taylor's golden brown ones, but at least I'd do Grace's bronze eyeliner trick tonight. *"I couldn't do it without you,"* I'd say, reaching up to wrap my arms around his neck.. *"I—"* But, before I could say anything else, he'd close the space between us, sweeping me into an epic kiss as the wind picks up and fireflies and leaves swirl around us. He'd pull me closer, close enough that I could practically hear his heartbeat, and then...

I giggled, burying my face in my knitting. The cool silk fabric made my cheeks feel even hotter.

"Oh holy hotness," I said. That probably wouldn't happen, I reminded myself, but it was nice to imagine.

I put aside my knitting and pulled my copy of *Starbound* out of the pile of books next to my bed, as well as my notebook. Nothing like any of Taylor and Daymeon's epic makeout scenes would happen, but a little bit of advance research definitely wouldn't hurt.

25

The last notes of *English Folk Song Suite* died away and I dropped my flute to my lap, waiting for Osoba to take her bows and for the curtain to close before getting up.

"Move." I nudged Em, who purposely took her sweet time gathering up her sheet music.

She gave me an impish look and stood. "What? In a rush?" She nodded at something over my shoulder and I turned to find Dev standing right beside me.

"Meet me in the lobby?" he asked in a backstage whisper as he passed my music stand.

"Sure," I said, trying to look like I was interested in the order of my sheet music when what I really wanted to do was latch on to him like a rabid fangirl at a book signing. I bumped Em impatiently with my hip. "C'mon. You're so slow tonight."

"Dev's not going anywhere." She finally started walking off-stage. "And the goal here is to get to the lobby a little bit after he does so you don't have to do that whole awkward standing-around-checking-your-cell-phone-or-looking-at-the-awards-on-the-wall thing. Some people can pull that off and look good, but you really kind of suck at that."

So, I moved slowly, carefully packing up my flute. I tugged some strands of my hair free and Em forced some of her lip gloss on me. And, with one final check, she shoved me out into the lobby and headed off to find her ride home.

I searched the crowded lobby for Dev. As soon as I caught sight of him by the offices and started making my way towards him, a bright blue streak zipped across my line of sight, focusing into a girl in a way-too-short blue dress who threw her arms around him. For a minute longer than anyone would consider a friendly hug, the dark-haired girl hung on his neck while Dev bowed his head low to talk to her, all smiles. Maybe it was a sister or a cousin...

They turned slightly to let someone pass and I saw Lexie's unmistakable profile. I froze midstep and a wave of dread washed over me. I was an idiot of epic proportions.

Of course Dev didn't want to *date* me. I was a geeky book nerd who dressed up like her favorite characters and read too much into everything. I bit back my embarrassment and irrational urge to cry. Not in public. If I could just duck down one of the hallways, I could call my parents for a ride, or maybe see if Em hadn't yet left. I started backing up towards the language hallway when those too-familiar hazel eyes caught mine. *Crud.*

Dev walked across the lobby and I stared up at the flags hanging from the ceiling to look like I wasn't—and hadn't been—watching. And like my heart wasn't somewhere by my ankles. "Hey, Phoebe, ready to go? Matt said we could catch a ride with him."

I could have gone with them. Like Maeve in the beginning of *Glittering*, I could have reached out and taken his
arm, smiling smugly at Deirdre—uhm, Lexie. Of course,
that was book two and Maeve and Aedan were together by
that point, but it really didn't matter if Dev was interested
in me. If I was Maeve, I wouldn't let any doubts keep me
from doing anything, not even hanging out at Marrano's. I
took a deep breath, ready to turn myself into her.

But one glance over at Lexie, who was checking her cellphone with a self-satisfied look on her face, and my resolve
crumbled. "Actually, I realized I can't hang out tonight. I—I
need to go." I shifted my weight from foot to foot and added,
"Home." The stupid little strand of hair that had 'artfully'
fallen out of my updo got in my eyes and I tried to blow it
out of the way.

Was it my imagination or did his face fall a little bit?
"Are you sure?"

"It just came up." I tried to come across as apologetic
but detached, not like I had just had a bucket of cold water
dumped on my head. *Chin up.* "Really, don't worry about
me. Lexie, and—and people are waiting. I won't keep you.
Have fun. I'll see you when you get back."

"O-kay. I guess I'll see you in the New Year?"

"Not like we have a choice, right?" I gestured around
the school.

"Right." Dev reached over tentatively and squeezed my
hand. *Like a friend would,* I reminded myself. *Alec would do
the same.* "Have a Merry Christmas, Phoebe," he said softly.

It was as if someone had made me swallow a porcupine, but I forced my smile to grow wider. "And I hope you have a safe trip and a great Santa Claus day."

A click of impossibly high platform heels announced Lexie's arrival. She was perfect, from her thick, long blown-out hair to the tiny rhinestones on her nails. "Dev, c'mon. Matt's waiting." She said, tugging on his arm.

Dev nodded at her, then gave my hand one last squeeze. "I'm sorry you can't make it."

I shrugged. My face hurt from this fake smile and I just wanted them to go away already. "Happens." I backed up a step. "Sorry."

Without letting go of his arm, Lexie managed a one-handed check of her cellphone. "We're going to lose our ride." She then gave me a smile that made my insides twist a little bit more. "That little flute solo thing you did was really cute. Too bad you can't come." When I didn't say anything, she slipped her phone back in her purse and wrapped her other hand around Dev's arm. "Oh well, I'll see you on Monday. Bye." With that, she pulled Dev towards the front doors and he turned slightly to give me a little wave before disappearing into the night.

I bolted for the Language Arts hallway and slid down the wall, burying my face in my skirt. It was such a relief not to have to pretend anymore. I tried to take deep breaths to loosen up the tight feeling in my lungs. This wasn't a fairy tale and it wasn't a book. Dev wasn't going to run after me with a glass slipper or dive in front of me to protect me from evil fae. Why had I been so stupid and naïve to think otherwise?

Another deep breath. I needed to find a ride. Focus now, fall apart later. I pulled out my phone and sent a mass text to everyone I knew was going to be in the audience tonight. Someone was bound to still be here.

As I waited for my phone to buzz, a pair of glittery heels that looked a little bit like Dorothy's shoes from the *Wizard of Oz* stopped in front of me.

"I thought I saw you duck back here." I looked up to see Grace waving her phone. "We got your text."

Leia kneeled next to me, not even caring about the dirt that got on her long skirt. "What happened? Grace said you were supposed to be going to Marrano's tonight." Her voice was soft with no trace of her usual, condescending kindergarten-teacher-like tone.

I blinked at both of them, their expressions mirror images of concern. I wasn't going to say anything… and then it all came spilling out.

I never really liked Leia before, but the gentle way she rubbed my back and just listened without any of her usual "oh, aren't you the most adorably naïve five year old" commentary made me think of her differently. I finished my story and she and Grace shared a long look, like they were communicating telepathically. Leia nodded. "What you need right now is a good cup of freakishly expensive coffee."

Grace tugged me to standing and swung my flute case onto her shoulder. "And I know the perfect place."

26

"I don't know why bookstores need to be open until eleven o'clock at night, but as long as they have coffee and free Wi-Fi, I'm not complaining." Leia announced as she placed a tray on our tiny café table. She slid a ceramic mug of something topped with a giant mound of whipped cream at me. "One full-fat gingerbread latte with extra gingerbread and extra whipped cream for you. I talked them into throwing in a cookie."

I picked up the little gingerbread man on the side of my coffee cup and balanced him, head-down, in the whipped cream. "Thanks."

Grace swirled a chocolate spoon in her nonfat soy latte. "The concert was nice. Your solo was really high-pitched and squeaky."

When I twisted the gingerbread man free, his head had absorbed some of the whipped cream, becoming soggy and decapitating him. That plus her comment made me crack a smile. "You make it sound like I was playing a mouse, but thanks."

"Dev's an idiot if he picked that girl over you. And a jerk for leading you on." Leia said bluntly, bypassing all the pleasantaries. "I don't really know them, but, at least from an outsider's opinion, you're better than both of them."

"Thanks, but Dev didn't really lead me on. Not really." Leia made a dismissive sound and the need to defend him surged up in me. "Em's matchmaking radar was probably off. You know how she's always harping on me to date. Dev would never go for someone like me."

"Excuse me?" Leia put down her mug with a clang and leaned forward. Grace, meanwhile, sat back and watched us like we were a tennis game, or like she was an anthropologist in the wild. "Someone like you?"

"Come on. I'm a geek. I'm on first-name basis with every librarian in the county, but I don't even know who sings the song that's playing right now." I pointed to the speaker above my head, blasting some pop-rock-whatever song. "Dev is so much hotter than me—"

Grace almost choked on her coffee. "If you say so." She muttered something about shoes and hair and marching band that I didn't catch before shaking her head and waving. "Go on."

I took a sip of my latte before continuing. It was hard to be miserable while drinking something that could potentially give me a whipped cream moustache or nose. "And Lexie is gorgeous, put-together, smart, nothing like me. Of course he'd like her."

"I think you're wrong. And blind." Leia said, sitting back again. "There's nothing wrong with being who you are, which is pretty kick-ass, too. But, you probably aren't going to listen to either of us because I'm sure it's easier to feel dramatically depressed right now."

I didn't bother arguing with her. "You know what sucks the most about all of this?" I waved my headless gingerbread man in the air to make a point. "I could have left things alone and been okay, but no, instead I texted him and tried to flirt with him and wore makeup and dressed like Marissa and I made him *socks*. Who *does* that? No wonder he'd rather date Lexie." My voice wobbled on the last sentence and I took a deep breath, blinking back tears that were threatening to come out. "It sucks. It majorly sucks. And I made such an idiot of myself trying to impress him."

Leia pat my back lightly. "You kind of did look stupid the last time I saw the two of you flirting over there." She gestured with her chin towards the new releases. "But he looked stupid too, if I'm remembering right."

I let off a shaky laugh. "Is that supposed to make me feel better?"

"It should. Being mutually stupid cuts any feeling that you made an idiot of yourself in half. Besides, when you graduate in about a year and a half, you'll probably never see him again, anyway, so why should you care what he thinks?" Leia said, handing me a tissue. Her voice had somehow morphed to gentle and comforting instead of grating. "Perspective. Don't ever regret trying."

My fingers went to work twisting and picking at the edge of the tissue rather than wiping my nose and eyes with it. "The scariest part about trying is what I could lose from it all."

"Your pride?" Grace asked.

I hadn't thought of that. "Okay, my pride, too." Instead of looking at them, I focused on the tissue. "Before all of this, my life was perfect. I had my book boyfriends and it was enough for me to read and dream about these guys because they weren't real. I'm so scared I can't go back to that. I'm afraid that maybe reality ruined me for fiction. And that means I really did lose everything." My chest constricted, forcing me to choke out the last sentence. The thought of losing Aedan or Cyril or any of my other book crushes physically *hurt*.

Leia scooted her chair next to mine and gave me a one-armed hug. "No, you didn't. I doubt you'll get over books that fast. Besides, I know you won't believe me now, but the real world can be awesome, too. Until then, you know you have us, right?" She gave my arm another squeeze and stood. "I'm going to get more napkins."

When Leia was far enough from the table, I turned to Grace, who still watched me with that psychologist expression. And then I said something I never thought I'd say about Leia. "Your girlfriend is pretty awesome."

She went from serious to grinning in a nanosecond. "I know."

I used my headless gingerbread man like a spoon, flattening some of the whipped cream in my mug. "Is it weird to say I'm jealous?"

Grace let off a little laugh and looked over her shoulder

at the brunette. "It's only weird if you're threatening to steal her."

I grinned back at her, in spite of myself. "Yeah, no. Still like boys."

Leia got back to our table, dropping a pile of napkins in the center. "Feeling better?"

"You two make being melodramatic like a Regency heroine kind-of impossible."

"Well, this isn't one of your books. I'm not a fan of the whole 'spend the next few months crying into a pillow while listening to depressing music' thing. Please don't tell me you're planning on doing that, because if you are, I'll have to change lunch tables."

Nudging her with a teasing expression, Leia said, "We're supposed to be supportive, Grace."

"You don't go to our school. You don't get a vote." But Grace's voice was light and she winked at me. "Fair enough, you get a pass on a few days of moping. But if you start acting like Alec did when Katie broke up with him, I'll personally escort you to the outcast table."

That made me smile again. "If I start writing really bad poetry and reciting it every time Dev's in earshot, you have my permission to send me to Coventry." At their shared look of confusion, I added, "You know, exile me? Regency?" Leia had an excuse because it was impossible to know what they taught in her snobby private school, but Grace really should have gotten the reference. "We learned that in English class last year during the Jane Austen module? You two seriously need to read more."

Leia dropped her chin in her hand and winked at Grace. "Sounds to me like she's feeling better already."

Grace studied me for a second and nodded. "Totally agree. She's saying English nerd stuff already."

"I think I liked her when she was a little bit depressed and not so much of a know-it-all," Leia said in a bored tone.

I feigned offense. "Hey! Thanks to that comment, I'm taking back what I said about you being awesome."

"Aww, you actually liked me?" Leia twiddled her fingers in an evil-professor fashion. "My world domination plan is slowly taking effect."

I laughed, then sobered up, leaning back to get them both in my line of sight. "Thank you for making me forget the whole miserable feeling of rejection thing for a little while."

Grace reached over and squished me in a one-armed hug. "I'm glad we could help. Plus, I put a lot of hard work into making you look presentable and I don't want you to use this as a reason to slip back into your old ways." She tilted her head and grinned at me. "You're coming to my New Year's party, right?"

"Of course. Why?"

"So's Dev. We're going to make you so gorgeous, he'll see you at the party and regret not picking you. And then you can ring in the New Year looking like you stepped out of *Vogue*."

"I don't know if that's a good idea…"

"Trust me, it'll be fun. Being a little bit evil always is."

Sunday.

All I wanted to do all day was go through my notebook and figure out what could have gone wrong. Or fall into a pile of books and only come up for air when I'd forgotten the last few weeks. But every book I picked up was as substantial as onion skin, without that magical spark that usually dragged me into a story until I forgot everything. And reading about feeling like my heart was put through the blender definitely paled in comparison to the real thing.

I slipped the record out of its sleeve and carefully positioned side two on the vintage record player Trixie had bought in Philly during her senior year. Bouncy 70's guitar filled the room and I dropped onto my bed. Mom had stolen this *Partridge Family* album from Grandmom's house and I had stolen it from the rec room record player.

David Cassidy started into a cheesy voiceover monologue about wanting to be wanted and being lonely and a wave of nausea rolled over me. If I was honest with myself, my pride hurt as much as, or more than, my heart. None of this would have happened if Em hadn't told me about Dev. I could happily still have kept dreaming about Kris. From afar.

It was embarrassing enough I'd let myself get carried away like I did. Dev was probably laughing over the whole thing right now while cuddling with Lexie before his flight. A suffocated, overwhelming feeling rushed over me at the thought, but I forced in a deep breath and pulled myself together. I could be cold and heartless, like Marissa after Cyril disappeared. Or at least, I could work on not feeling anything.

I swiped the back of my sleeve across my face and coughed from my clenched throat. I needed to *do* something. Something that would channel these feelings out so I could keep going on. I stood and changed into one of the tight-fitting workout shirts and a slim fleece Trixie had bought for me to use in the winter when I'd complained about how it was hard to practice outside in a jacket.

Shooting things always made me feel better.

My sweater slips off my shoulder and I don't bother to push it up. In fact, I'm glad I'm wearing it today. It's bright red and bold and as non-Victorian as I can get. I pull myself up and stare at the back of the bathroom door, gathering the courage to go out there and confront Cyril.

He doesn't want to fight for us, and if he really does still love Virginia—even though she's been dead for over a hundred years—then I have to stop caring about him, too. I need to be strong and draw this line in the sand between us.

Especially since it's like someone asks me to tear my own heart out of my chest every time I see him.

"Screw this," I say to my bath towel and combs before opening my bathroom door.

Just as I cross into my room, though, the dried tussie-mussie catches my eye. I turn on my heel to grab the little Victorian-style bouquet, head back into the bathroom, slide up my window and screen, and throw it as hard as I can into the night. A little bowl of potpourri that mom had put in my bathroom follows, and then the dried rose I saved from the dance.

Throwing things feels amazing.

Life stinks

27

I nocked another arrow and took a shot, not even pausing before my quickly numbing fingers reached into the bucket of the school's loaner arrows to grab and nock another one. It was wonderfully mechanical. Whoosh, thunk, shoot again. The already calloused tips of my fingers were turning red from the continuous motion and my arms were burning. There was definitely something therapeutic about this. Maeve was right.

Maeve's shoulder ached, but that distracted her from the ice that was slowly taking over her heart. The memory of Aedan's blank stare snuck back into her brain and she let out a frustrated scream as she let fly another arrow.

"What the hell are you doing out here? It's freakin' cold, you know." Em jogged up next to me, looking from my bow and me to the overloaded target. "Holy crap, Feebs. Don't you think that's a little overkill?"

I let another arrow fly. It just skimmed an arrow in the red of the target. "No."

Images flashed through Maeve's mind and she punched them away. Memory upon memory. Aedan, leaning a little bit too close when he blocked her during their last training session.

Pushing his hair out of his eyes as he joked with her. Holding her in his arms and comforting her after watching their friends die in the last battle. They came fast and relentless and she hit harder until her knuckles left dots of blood on the dummy.

Alec came up on my other side, wheezing a bit from the run. "Damn. Remind me never to piss you off. I forget that you like turning things into pincushions."

"Very funny." Two arrows left. I shot them off in succession, then lay down my bow and marched over to the target to start pulling them out.

"Grace told us all about last night. I know I said I was staying out of things, but I think you might have read too much into what you saw," Em said, close on my heels.

Instead of wiggling the nearest arrow out, I yanked hard until it popped free. Coach would be having a heart attack right now. "Em, you don't have to defend Dev. And I really don't need to talk about this."

Em joined me in pulling out the arrows, except she was much gentler on the target than me.

"Alec, tell Phoebe she's being an idiot."

Alec came into my line of sight, carrying my bow and plucking at the bowstring. I was too worked up about Dev and trying to sound like I didn't care about the whole situation to ream Alec out for touching it. He shook his head.

"I don't know why you're dragging me into the middle of this, but Dev's not dating Lexie. At least, not the way he made it sound when we hung out this morning. She's just the hugging type, I guess." He flipped the bow over in his hands. "These carvings are awesome. Why don't we get to shoot with bows like this?"

"Because 'bows like this' cost hundreds of dollars." I said, reaching over to extract my baby from his hands. I finished yanking all of the arrows free and marched back with my bucket to a line about five feet past where I had been shooting. Barely waiting for them to move out of my way, I started shooting again.

"Okay, now you're just being freakishly dramatic. Normal people eat a pint of Chunky Monkey and move on. And didn't you hear what Alec just said?"

I shrugged, then adjusted my aim to make up for the extra distance. "Guys don't really talk about the girls they like with other guys."

This time, Alec snorted. "Right, like you're the expert on guys. You know, he asked me if I knew if he did anything to piss you off last night."

I froze mid-draw. "He did?"

"Yeah. I told him that it was probably your introvert nature kicking in."

"Thanks," I said dryly.

"Look, he's leaving for India," Em checked the clock on her cellphone, "about now, and I doubt your phone lets you do international texts, but you're going to have to step things up when he comes back. Like at Grace's New Year's party. He'll be there."

"What about Lexie?" I turned to Alec for help, but he was too busy checking out the arrows and eyeing my bow.

With a sigh, I handed the bow over to him. "Go for it. But if you break my bow, I break your gaming stuff."

Em shoved her phone in her coat pocket and kept her hands in there. "What about her? I'm telling you, yesterday was a fluke."

I bit my lip and picked at the fletching on one of the damaged arrows. Distantly, I noticed that my nail beds were turning purplish-blue from the cold.

"I just don't want to keep making an idiot out of myself and putting everything out there, only to find out this was some kind of joke or a bet, like in those old 80's movies."

Em looked at me like I just said I hated her favorite puppy. "Do you think I'd ever do that to you?"

"No," I said, shuffling my feet in the grass. Some frost-coated blades made a snapping sound as I moved. "But who knows what goes through guys' heads."

"I thought you just said you did," Alec said as he let an arrow fly miserably off-target.

"Very funny." I reached for the bow, but he held it over my head. "Give me that so I can go back to practicing."

He managed to stretch it even higher above him. "No way. We're going somewhere warm before you start looking like the white witch."

"*Narnia* reference, I'm impressed." I dropped my hands to my hips and tried to put on my toughest face. "So don't make me go all Susan on you and beat you up with my arrows."

"Kinky. But you might want to try that with Dev, instead."

"Gross," I shot back, but when he wouldn't give me my bow, I gave up with a huff. "At least Grace and Leia were comforting. You both are just being bossy. I'm so sick of people giving me advice and telling me what to do." My neck grew hot as my frustration bubbled over. I bet my nails weren't purple anymore. "Look at where all of your *help* has gotten me. This is my life and these are my choices to make. For once, I'd love to just be left alone to decide what I want to do and how I feel."

Alec looked sheepish and lowered my bow enough so I could swipe it out of his hands. Em took on a hurt air before turning away from me and looking at Alec.

"Let's go. She's obviously not interested in our help."

"Obviously." I faced the target again and reached for an arrow. The overwhelming urge to turn around and apologize bubbled up in my stomach, but I kept steady, nocking the arrow. They seemed to hesitate, but then I heard their footsteps as they left a few seconds later. I let out the breath I held and relaxed my posture.

I was a cold huntress, the target my only focus. Feelings were irrelevant distractions. Resisting the urge to scream out my frustrations, I pulled back my arrow and let it fly.

28

"Distance is good sometimes. It keeps me from strangling people."
—Marissa, Hidden

The following week of school was awkward. Something in me still mad about Sunday wouldn't let me accept Em's and Alec's apologies, even with Grace playing peacemaker. After two torturous lunch periods, I ended up eating my lunch in one of the band practice rooms the rest of the week and, at home, locking myself in my room every afternoon. Even though I missed them, I couldn't let my so-called friends push me around anymore. It was time to start growing a spine, like they were always telling me to.

I Think I Love You blasted from my record player and I rolled onto my back, belting out the chorus at the top of my lungs. My phone rang halfway through the instrumental break and I answered without bothering to get up and lower the volume.

"Is—Is that seventies music playing in the background?" Em sounded distracted, like she hadn't meant to ask the question but couldn't help it.

I padded over to the record player and gently lifted the needle so the music was replaced with the hum of the speakers.

Holding back the urge to say hi, I responded with a clipped, "Yes it is. Don't judge." I looked over at my alarm clock, checking the time. I'd give her one minute before hanging up.

"Right." There was a deep breath on the other side of the line before Em continued in the most depressed voice I'd ever heard, "I've fallen into the deepest pits of despair."

I froze halfway to the bed, my plan to grow a spine crumbling with that one sentence. Em needed me and I couldn't ignore her. "What happened?"

"I did it. I broke up with Wil again, this time for good. I'm going cold turkey."

At that, I unfroze and tried to project comfort and understanding through the phone, failing with the first words to come out of my mouth.

"You said that last week." A part of me was positive the actress in her loved the drama of her on-again-off-again relationship.

Em made a huffing sound. "I don't need commentary about this, peanut gallery. What I *do* need right now is some commiseration from my best friend."

The hurt in her voice, exaggerated or not, cut straight through me. Grabbing Em's finished Yule/Festivus present, I tossed it into my bag and made my way downstairs. "Okay. I'll get there as soon as I can."

Downstairs, Trixie's red and orange-bobbed head went up like a shot as I rushed into the kitchen. While Em continued to spill her sorrows through the phone in a way that would make Shakespeare proud, I mouthed,

"I need a ride."

"Your big sister is pretty awesome," Em said to me as she ate another spoonful of the frozen custard Trixie had thought to pick up on the way over. Em was perched on top of her bed's dove-grey comforter, the only neutral color in the whirlwind of old movie posters and furniture straight out of wonderland that made up her room. Her parents had even managed to find glittery paint for her bright yellow walls.

"Trix has her moments. She's probably just happy I'm getting out of our room so she can work on her winter break projects." I sat down cross-legged on her bedroom floor. "Now, tell me all the awful details."

"Don't mock me in my time of misery." She was washed out, her dark hair a stark contrast to her ashen skin. But, in typical Em fashion, she had still managed to throw on some lip gloss. "Wilhelm said 'I love you' when we were making out in the park last night after our date. Or at least, I think he did." She paused, then added, "It was kind of in German. And I might have freaked out a little bit." She flopped onto her back, almost dropping her custard in the process.

"So you broke up with him. Again."

"Do you have to keep saying 'again' like that?" She twirled the spoon in the air and didn't wait for me to answer. "I keep thinking it's better than letting myself become the long-distance girlfriend when he goes back home. It's like guaranteed heartbreak. But every time I break up with him, it's awful, like someone's steamrolling over my heart." After a moment of mutual silence, she turned her head to look at me and cracked a smile. "Maybe you're right. Maybe I'm just blowing all of this out of proportion."

"I didn't say that, but it sounds good." I picked at a dried dot of nail polish on the carpet. "You realize I'm the worst person in the world when it comes to relationship advice, right?"

"True. Damn, it's hard to feel upset and be on a sugar high at the same time." She ate another spoonful of custard and pointed the spoon at me afterwards. "You've gotten better about not telling me how some book character solved the same problem, though."

"Because you never listen, anyway." To distract her, I reached over to the desk chair and pulled a little package out of my book bag. "I thought you could use some cheering up, so happy random winter holiday."

"Breaking tradition, huh?" We usually all traded gifts on Christmas Eve at the diner over spanakopita and matzo ball soup, except for Alec's gifts, which we usually gave to him in an eight nights of Hanukkah-style randomness. Hiding presents over eight days was probably more fun for us than for him, but it was *tradition*.

"This is a special situation. I still expect something from you at the diner," I said as I handed her the gift. As she unwrapped the black and pink knit corset and held it up to see it better, I explained, "I adapted an antique pattern of Trixie's for shaping. You can wear it on a make-up date with Wilhelm. I think it might look nice over a henley—"

Em's smile grew the tiniest bit. "It's perfect." She set the corset down on her lap and played with the ribbon lacing. "I'm sorry about being so pushy lately about Dev. You know I just get that way sometimes."

"Sometimes?"

"Shh. I guess a part of me wanted to keep my mind off all of this. When I can't control things in my own life, I sort of try to fix other people's lives. Mom says it's just an extension of my control freak nature." She looked up, her eyes still a little watery and her voice a tiny bit shaky as she added, "Thanks for coming, Feebs. You don't know how nice it is to know I can count on you."

Em was always the strong one. It was weird and hard seeing her so vulnerable. I forced a smile that I hoped was reassuring. "Always."

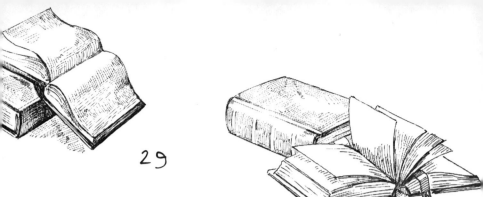

29

"That is awesome," Em said as she watched Trixie stitch the last bit of gold trim in place and start fluffing up the white blousy thing that peeked over my laced-up top. "All my sister does is steal my things."

"The privileges of being the baby of the family," I told her primly. "People just love to spoil me."

I felt a pinch in my side and glared down at Trixie, who innocently hid her needle in her palm. "Just spoiling you, baby sis." She tied off her thread and stood. "Which reminds me. You still owe me a skirt."

I nodded towards a mound of crimson-firefly colored merino silk on my nightstand. "On the needles," I said distractedly.

"Don't forget our deal—one dress for one skirt." Trixie straightened my necklace, then stepped back to check the outfit as a whole, adding, "No shiny new project syndrome allowed, okay? When things get tough or boring, you have a habit of just stopping and moving on to something new."

"Thanks for the diagnosis, Dr. Beatrix." I turned to take in my reflection. It was like Trixie had ripped the dress right out of the pages of the harp scene in *Golden*, from the golden white velvet bodice that skimmed my body snugly to the sleeves that ended in a point and hooked to my middle fingers. The short skirt tickled the back of my knees.

The girl looking back at her from the mirror was almost a stranger, an ethereally beautiful fey girl all in varying shades of gold and white.

"I'm not Phoebe, not a confused human dragged into a world where I don't belong. I'm a changeling version of myself," I whispered at the mirror, just like Maeve did when she put on this dress. A vision of me twirling in the snow with my cobwebby gold lace shawl popped into my head and I held back the goofy grin that would have messed up my picture-perfect Maeve-y reflection.

Em got up off of my bed and stood next to me, her sequined gold dress bright next to my gold and white outfit. "We look good, girlie."

I smiled at her reflection and started yanking out the curlers. "Stunning enough to make Dev sorry he went with Lexie?"

My sister's head went up sharply and her eyebrows drew together in her best Disapproving Big Sister look.

"Trying to make a guy jealous by looking awesome is a waste of a good party and a good dress," Trixie said in a disinterested tone while walking over to her vanity. She leaned closer to the mirror to swipe on some bright red lipstick. "Just be awesome and have a great time."

I scrunched up my nose. "Thus spoke the big sister."

"And the voice of infinite wisdom, kid-lin." Trixie tugged the sweater I made for her in place and rummaged through my scarf basket until she pulled up a bulky, bright red infinity scarf. "I have to go. I'm supposed to meet up with Petur at the River Rink in an hour."

"Don't break your neck."

She reached out to ruffle the mess of tight curls on my head. "I'm the coordinated one, remember? I can skate and watch fireworks at the same time." She grabbed my red mittens from where I had left them on the vanity and waved them at me as she headed out the door. "Have fun and don't waste your time with stupid boys. Happy New Year."

Em blinked at our reflection and reached over to pull at one of my curls so it bounced back like a spring. "We still look awesome. And you're not Phoebe tonight, you're— what's that book character you're probably going to try to imitate tonight?"

I laughed. "I don't do that."

"Right. You've never done anything like that." She nodded at my nightstand and the giveaway sparkle of my notebook.

I smoothed down my skirt. "But this is Maeve's dress from that book I told you about. The one set in Ireland. She's pretty kick-ass."

"So if I see you spouting stuff off in Gaelic?"

I blew a raspberry, like I was five again. "You'll be too busy making out in German to even notice if I start speaking Elvish."

"You know me so well." She grabbed a sparkly hair tie and pulled her straightened hair into a low side-ponytail. "C'mon. Grace wants us there by eight-thirty."

"Don't feel obligated to be with me," the ghost of his voice whispered through her memory and she shook my head to push it away. The part of her still stinging from their "discussion" that morning wanted to run back to the dorms and mope, but the rest of her kept moving forward on autopilot. Aedan *needed* her to help protect his people.

Even though she was just a means to an end.

Maeve's attention returned to the harp. It was beautiful, but no more so than any other artifact in these Archives. Still, something about it kept drawing her to it like a sailor to a siren. She crossed the room, reaching out towards its smooth wood surface.

"You're beautiful," Aedan's voice came softly from behind her, making her fingers freeze millimeters from the harp's surface. She didn't turn to look at him. "White makes you glow. Like you're all light." He sounded serious, so unlike his usual self.

"Don't," She whispered, straightening her back and raising her chin. "Just…let's get this over with. You don't have to explain or apologize or compliment me." Ignoring Aedan, she let the harp's magnetic pull drag her in and her pointer finger touched the mahogany wood.

Everything changed.

Autopilot sounds good. Be a little
distant so he doesn't know
    I crushed on him

30

It was getting too hot in Grace's house, especially with my long sleeves. I pushed the French doors open and escaped onto the deck. I could still hear the faint bass of the music coming from the house as I stepped to the railing, wrapping my arms tight around my body to ward off the January in New Jersey chill.

I wiped the one surviving pile of snow from the wooden bench and sat down, taking a deep breath of ice-cold air and automatically dissolving into a coughing fit. How Maeve managed to do that, like, every other page was beyond me. As cold as it was out here, it was so much more uncomfortable in there. Avoiding Dev while trying to look like I was having fun was exhausting. Usually on New Year's Eve, I hung out with the non-A-listers on the family room couch with Alec and all of Grace's other geeky friends, watching a *Lord of the Rings* marathon or something, but this year Grace, Leia, and Em dragged me into the crowd of dancing and pool-playing people in the rec room.

Plus, Grace made me dance with one of the JV football guys who was a dead ringer for Cyril from *Hidden*. I had to get out before I did something silly, like ask him to start some shirtless sword fighting or creepily stare into his eyes to see if he had flecks of silver in the blue. Okay, maybe I *did* have a skewed sense of reality.

Music blasted through the night air and I looked up to see Dev stepping out onto the deck.

"Frak," I said under my breath. Half of my brain wanted to reach up and fix the hair I knew had fallen out of Grace's glittery clips, but the other, Maeve-like half kept my hands glued in place. I forced myself to gaze out over the lake, trying to look like I hadn't noticed him. Maybe he wouldn't see me, maybe he'd stepped outside for just a second—

"Hey, Phoebe."

My heart dropped to my stomach, where acid started immediately devouring it. I turned my head, hoping my hair would brush my shoulder delicately and the clips would catch the moonlight reflecting off of the lake. Grace had put some sparkly powder on my cheeks and glitter on my eyes, so maybe they had that magical moonlight effect you always read about in books. Like Maeve in the Archives, the first time Aedan saw her power manifest in his POV story they had at the back of the book. I tried to let surprise flow onto my face. And tried not to shiver.

"What are you doing out here?"

"I was going to ask you the same thing. Aren't you freezing?"

I forced myself to look warm and pointed at my sleeve. "Winter fashion to the rescue. It's not too bad out here, really."

He crossed his arms and joined me by the railing, but

didn't sit. "I guess Mumbai spoiled me. It feels freaking cold." He visibly shivered and I grinned. Point for me. Maeve would totally be impressed.

His profile in the moonlight made my half-acid-eaten heart skip a beat. It didn't feel cold at that moment. His skin was darker, tanned from India, and his hair had grown a bit longer and swooped over his forehead almost like the hero in an anime. I sucked in a sharp breath and turned my eyes to the lake and the shadow of a pine dipping into the water.

"How was your trip?"

After what felt like a lifetime of sensing his stare, he turned to stare out at the water, too.

"Way too short. I never even had a chance to get over the jet lag." His fingers tapped the wooden railing in time to the music inside the house. "But it was good. I miss the food already." He tilted his head to smile at me again. "My grandmom's cook makes the best chapatis on the planet."

I smiled, letting myself relax a little, and tried to think of what light, conversational thing I should say next. Something I'd overheard two of the cheerleaders say in the kitchen popped into my head.

"Everyone's been saying you were picked to star in a Bollywood movie and wouldn't come back."

His laugh did funny things to my stomach. "One of those things is kind of true. My uncle got me into a song-and-dance scene in one of the movies they were filming while I was there."

"You'll have to let me and Em know when it comes out.

We'll do a big screening of the movie and tell everyone we know the star."

Dev laughed again, raking his hand through his hair. His sleeve rode up and I saw goosebumps all down his arm.

"I doubt anyone will be impressed when they see me dancing." He looked over at the crowded family room through the glass doors. "But before we both die of cold, let's go in. I can show off my film-worthy dance skills."

Although I was so tempted to take his outstretched hand and head inside, the Maeve-y part of me remained frozen in place. She'd be too proud to jump at an opportunity to look like some lovesick hanger-on.

I shook my head. "I'm okay. It's stuffy in there." I drew up my back meter-stick straight, just like Maeve carried herself when she wore this dress. Like her, I could pretend to be as cold and distant as any of the Seelie high court.

"Oh." He dropped his hand and a frown replaced his grin. "Are you sure?"

I nodded a little too enthusiastically. "I like it out here." Even though my toes were totally numb and my fingers were about to fall off. I had to think warm thoughts. Like Aedan-and-Maeve-making-out kind of thoughts. But that made my eyes start flickering down to Dev's lips. I focused on a bundle of pine needles on the bench next to me.

"Well, when you're finally freezing, I'll be inside." He gave me a crooked grin and then pushed off from the railing. My acid-corroded heart skipped a beat and went back to being tortured somewhere in my stomach. I held my breath until he left the deck, then let it out in a white poofy cloud. I finally let my body dissolve into shivers.

There was no way Dev could read anything into what I'd said or done. Goodbye, silly Phoebe, with her socks and crushing on a guy who probably didn't even like her. Somehow, I'd managed to pull off acting like a perfect model of distant-yet-friendly, like one of the Otherworld fae. Maeve would be proud.

The countdown started on TV and I slid into place between Grace and Em as everyone in the room started yelling the numbers along with the announcer. Dev was on the other side of the room with some of the other theatre people, and he flashed me a smile as he joined us all in saying, "Six!"

I had successfully avoided him all night, dancing a few more times with the Cyril lookalike, always keeping my hands full with food or helping Grace out with something when he came around. When I handed him one of the slices of veggie stromboli, I maneuvered the plate so our hands barely touched. It had been exhausting to keep up that amped version of my normal personal-space bubble for hours.

Em squeezed my hand and yelled, "Three!" into my ear, and I stopped looking at him and went back to the screen. The camera flashed to an image of the crowd on the RiverRink also counting down and I grinned as I caught a flash of a red scarf and red-orange tipped hair in the corner of the TV. And then fireworks filled the screen.

"Happy New Year!"

Grace and Leia started making out, Em was working on a totally new definition of public display of affection with Wilhelm, and I was the really out-of-place fifth wheel in the middle of them all. I looked up at Dev and his smile touched his eyes, shining in the dim lights. My apparently still-intact heart jolted with electricity and I started making my way towards him until Lexie made me feel like my life was on permanent, hellish repeat.

Lexie poked Dev on his shoulder and he turned around to look at her. Her wide grin as she reached up to twine her fingers around his neck and the electricity I'd felt seconds before fizzled, ice replacing it. As she pulled him down towards her, I turned and ran to the quiet of the geek/movie room.

"Feebs, you're just in time to see Legolas do that kick-ass shooting arrows while sliding down a rope thing," Alec said as he made room for me on the couch. "Maybe you can take notes?"

"Awesome," I said with fake enthusiasm. I pulled my legs under myself and gave Alec a tiny shove. "Happy New Year."

He shoved me back without turning away from the screen. "Yup."

31

Em dropped her bag on the seat next to me and perched on the armrest, practically glowing. "I'm so glad you finally listened to reason."

I looked around us at the empty auditorium—except for me and Em, everyone else was already on stage or backstage, preparing for rehearsal. Em had parked us in the second row, close enough that I could hear the thunk of the dancers' feet as they warmed up.

"It was either this or getting an extra shift inventorying yarn for the shop."

"Who says I don't bring excitement into your life?" She poked me in the arm, still grinning as wide as the stage. "I'm glad I rate higher than cashmere."

"And quivut." At the confused tilt of her head, I added. "That's a good thing."

She shook her head in a 'let's tolerate the silly yarn girl' kind of way, as if I never had to deal with her doing the same with ancient actor names. "Right. I'll take your word for it."

"So, what's on the schedule for today?"

"Well, first, Dev's not coming to rehearsal, so you can wipe that suspicious look off your face. It's been two months.

You really need to get over it." She poked me in the arm and screwed up her nose like she was about to stick her tongue out at me. "We're running through some of the songs and marks for *Think of Me, Angel of Music*, and the Lottie scene."

I ignored her Dev comments and focused on pulling up all my *Phantom* knowledge. "Ooooh. So, basically, all Em all the time."

"And Christian, who's playing Raoul, and Lissa." Em bounced off the armrest and paced excitedly in the row in front of me. "I can't wait. They were doing some stage repairs all October, so they had us audition in the gym. This is the first time I'm going to get to sing *Think of Me* on an actual stage. Do you remember when we went to New York to watch it freshman year?"

"After Osoba said we were going to do an Andrew Lloyd Weber medley and your mom decided we needed 'inspiration?' Yes." That had been the best trip ever. Em and I felt so adult going into New York alone on the bus, grabbing dinner at a parental unit-approved pizza shop, and then walking into the Majestic Theater, trying so hard to look like native New Yorkers.

"That night, I promised myself that someday I'd play Christine. And now," she bounced up and down happily, enough that her curls were bouncing with her. "It's not Broadway, but it'll be good practice for it."

I grinned. "So, where's Wilhelm for your *Think of Me* debut?"

She waved her hand dismissively. "He's got some foreign

exchange student thing, and that's totally fine because I think he's not a big musical fan. But," she grabbed my hands and made me bounce with her, "I'm so glad you're here for this. You're probably the only person who understands why I love this musical so much."

The student director, a senior I didn't recognize, hopped up onto the stage and clapped his hands. "Okay, guys, let's get started. Em, Lissa needs to get out of here early, so we're going a little out of order to run through *Angel of Music* first, okay?"

"Got it." Em turned and waved at me before hurrying on stage.

"Sing pretty," I called after her, then snuggled deeper into my seat, flipping on my booklight. The last time I'd sat in on a musical theatre rehearsal, there was a lot of chatting and moving people around and directors fixing little things between takes or scenes or whatever actor-y people called it. I could dive into *Concealed*, the latest *Hidden House* novella and probably not miss a thing.

I bounced between watching rehearsal and reading, but the moment Em softly started singing the first notes of her solo, I dropped my book into my lap and focused entirely on her. She was always different on stage, transformed from my pushy best friend into whatever character she was playing. This time, her posture was straight, like she was wearing a corset. Within a few notes of the song, she morphed from timid Christine to Christine taking over the stage, her voice traveling to the furthest ends of the auditorium.

Someone slid into the row, sitting two seats down from me. I froze the second I realized it was Kris. "I didn't know Em was such a good singer."

Em, with a range most people in the school choir would kill for, ran through a series of notes that brought chills over me. I nodded instead of answering and breaking the spell she had put over the whole auditorium.

As soon as the song was over and the director was working on fixing something with her, I took a deep breath and said, "Yeah, she's going to take over Hollywood and Broadway someday."

Kris looked back up at the stage and studied Em for a second before shaking his head and turning back to me. "So, if she's that good, why is she wasting her time here in Lambertfield instead of building a career?"

"Because her parents would kill her. And because she's convinced ninety percent of the time, child actors end up as total train wrecks."

"Good point."

We sat in silence for a few minutes and I stared at my book, unable to get past the first sentence on the screen. I couldn't remember any good Marissa moments to imitate that really fit the moment. If only I had Em's ability to shift seamlessly into character. I tried skimming down the page, but a novella about a girl trapped in the mirrorworld who turned evil probably wasn't the best research material.

The boy's eyes widen as he sees me for the first time and the terror in his face is easy to read. If I don't turn his head quickly, convince him to trust me, he'll likely drop the drape back onto the mirror and run away like all the others who have seen me.

"So, I'm guessing you're here because of Em?" Kris only glanced up from his phone for a second, then went back to what looked like a long text.

I imitated him, keeping my eyes on the novella while talking. "She talked me into it. I love *Phantom*, anyway, so it wasn't hard. You?"

"Student council let out early. Matt skipped because he had to be here and he's my ride home." Matt, Student Council VP and Kris' best friend. I should have realized that was why he'd take time to be at something like this.

"Oh." How eloquent. I scrambled to remember something that could help, but my mind was completely filled with Camilla's story. I wished he'd go to the bathroom or *anything* so I could check my notebook for something flirty or cute to say or do.

An innocent smile curls over my lips and I drop my eyelashes oh so slightly to project the illusion of a perfectly demure young Victorian lady. "Oh, please don't go. I need your help." I keep my voice soft and musical. "I am an angel and I've been trapped in this mirror by demons. Won't you save me?"

I hold back a grin as his hand freezes midway through covering the mirror and, instead, pulls the mourning drape back completely. Success. If there is one thing boys cannot resist, it is saving a lady in danger. Now, to get him to touch the mirror...

I jumped back to the last two paragraphs. Yes, Camilla was evil, but she was successful, at least with Victorian boys.

I hid the smile that threatened to come out, as a Camilla-worthy plan formed.

Em finished her third run-through of the Lottie scene and I glanced over at Kris to make sure he wasn't too deep into whatever he'd been doing on his phone. Taking a deep breath and channeling Camilla—*be delicate and helpless*—I stood up like I was about to applaud Em's performance and quickly let my knees buckle, pretending to reach for anything solid around me. "Oh, no," I said in as shaky a voice as I could manage, soft enough not to mess with rehearsal, but loud enough for Kris to hear me.

Or maybe not loud enough. Without Kris jumping to my aid and catching me like I'd expected him to, my hip slammed hard against my armrest and I stumbled, barely catching the back of one of the chairs in the row in front of me before I could hit the floor. The sharp yank ran up my bow arm to my shoulder and I prayed that I didn't tear or pull anything.

Kris finally reached out and grabbed my arm to steady me and help me sit back in my seat. "Whoa, are you okay?"

I forced a weak laugh, sucking back pain and the temptation to rub at my sore hip or rotate my shoulder. "I guess I stood up too fast." That had been as far from graceful and Camilla-like as possible. I dropped my eyes, not so I could be demure and Victorian, but so he couldn't see the utter mortification that had to be written all over my face. "Thanks for asking." I pushed my hair out of my eyes and wished I could actually disappear into a mirror.

A dandelion yellow sweater-covered arm swept into my line of sight, knocking Kris' hand away. "C'mon, Feebs. Rehearsal's over and we need to go before Dad decides he's tired of waiting and that I should catch the late bus to 'build character' or something. Let's go." Em hadn't even bothered to put on her coat and tugged so hard at my sore arm I almost cried out.

"Give me a minute." I straightened myself out, giving Kris my best "don't mind my crazy friend" twisted-lip smile before her grip tightened and she started dragging me up the auditorium aisle. I managed a weak wave at Kris on the way out.

Em shrugged on her coat once we were in the hallway, shaking her head at me the whole time. "I saw the whole thing while we were finishing up. You so did that on purpose."

I rotated my arm a few times, thankful that the ache had faded away before putting on my own coat. No permanent damage, thank goodness. "No, I didn't."

Em narrowed her eyes, going so far as to wag a finger at me like I was a two year old caught sneaking out of time out. "Please don't ever do that again. You're just going to perpetuate antiquated gender stereotypes."

"I was imitating Camilla, who was from the late eighteen hundreds, so, success?" I said, weakly.

She made a huffing sound. "I need to burn that notebook of yours. And, FYI, you need to work on your acting skills."

Her last dig hurt. "My acting is perfectly fine."

"Uh-huh." Em laid the back of her hand against her forehead and swayed like she'd just come off the tilt-a-whirl. "Oh, Kris, evil leprechauns have taken away my sense of balance and I need your spaghetti-limp politician arms to catch me before I fall into a magical mirror."

"Em…" I shot a nervous glance around the hallway, but thankfully, we were the only ones there.

"That's what you looked like back there." She twirled happily around me, obviously holding back a laugh from the way she was pressing her lips together.

"No, I didn't." At her level stare, I heaved a saintly sigh and started dragging *her* towards the front door.

"Well, at least I'm happy to see you're moving on from moping about Dev. We just need to find someone—anyone —better than Kris for you to crush on."

I ignored her last comment. "Changing the subject, your singing was amazing today."

She wrapped an arm around my shoulders as we walked. "Thanks. I still have a lot of work to do to hit some of those notes, though. But, watch out Broadway, when I do."

As Em chatted about octaves and stage directions, I mentally made a note to keep Camilla out of my notebook. I should have known from the world of bookish karma that nothing good would come out of imitating one of the bad guys.

32

"Phoebe?"

"Hmm?" I looked up from *Shanghai Summer* and sandwich to see Em frowning at me as she unpacked her own lunch.

"So, first, I swear I didn't plan this," she said, her words flowing together faster than usual.

"O-kay…" I said, taking a bite of my sandwich and waiting for Em to launch into an overly dramatized play-by-play of a beaker blowing up in Chemistry lab or something.

She unconsciously popped the lid of her salad Tupperware open and closed over and over in typical worried-Em fashion. "I tried to convince him we could do this right before rehearsal, but he didn't think we'd have enough time…" Em looked over her shoulder at the lunch line, then turned back to frown at me.

I shrugged, cutting her off before she could keep apologizing for something that really wasn't a big deal. "We can watch *Mystical* tomorrow if you need to do something with Wilhelm," I offered. It wouldn't be the first time one of us had to reschedule watching our favorite tv show together.

She squinted at me confusedly. "Huh? Wilhelm? No, I

was talking about Dev."

I froze. "Dev?" Alec and Grace looked over at us on that and Grace shook her head at Em, frowning.

"We need to run our lines together before rehearsal tonight. So, he's going to sit here today. I'm so sorry." Em's expression was part sympathetic, part guilt. "Really sorry."

My heart dropped into my stomach—Dev had stopped coming regularly to our lunch table back in January, around the time I was avoiding everyone by eating in the band room. I forced a bland expression and another shrug as I looked from Em to Alec and Grace, who had stopped midconversation, too. "It's okay. We're in class together. I'm fine. You guys act like I'm super delicate or something."

But, as I said that, the crowd parted like something out of a movie and Dev broke through, balancing a tray that he slid right next to my lunch bag. "Hey, Phoebe, Em, guys."

I quickly dropped my head and focused on my book, mumbling a hi before turning the page. I started taking a mental inventory of my outfit—glasses, a sweater and skirt just like Marissa's in the *Hidden* goodbye scene, and bright red lipstick that matched the sweater—then remembered I didn't care how I looked around him.

"Hi, everyone." Lexie's voice made me look up again to see her hovering right over me. She shoved her own tray in the nonexistent space between my lunch and Dev's and squeezed herself onto the bench between us, forcing me to scoot over so I was perilously balancing on the edge.

I don't care how I look around Dev, I repeated silently

to myself, dipping my nose even deeper into my book. Especially since Lexie had Velcro-ed herself to Dev since January. Next to her cute, casual model-y look, my outfit and lipstick suddenly felt like I was trying too hard. I blinked at the page and frowned when I realized I'd read the same sentence for the fifth time. Flipping back a page, I started again, but I just couldn't concentrate on Lian's story with the conversation around me. Lexie laughed and I held back a cringe.

I looked up just in time to see Em, Alec, and Grace share a quick series of worried looks before Grace nodded at both of them and said, "I'm going to the bathroom. Phoebe, you're coming with me, right?" She stood up, gently reached over to close my book, and pulled me to standing.

Alec snorted. "I will never understand why you girls need company when you go to the bathroom."

Dev stopped midline and laughed. "Right? I have a sister and I still can't figure that out."

"Ha, ha. You guys are cute," Em said sarcastically. "Dev, focus. We only have ten minutes before lunch ends."

Grace grabbed my sweater sleeve and pulled me out of the lunchroom and into the thankfully empty girl's bathroom. As soon as we stepped inside, she turned to face me, her lips set in a frown. "Hey, are you okay?"

I opened my mouth, closed it, then started again, saying carefully, "I'm fine." I didn't want my friends to think I was this weak, silly girl who couldn't handle being around a guy she had—"had" in the past-tense—crushed on.

Grace made a humming sound, then looked away from me to check her eyeliner in the mirror. "That's good, then. I personally wanted to kick Lexie for being so rude back there," she said casually. She studied me in the mirror, her brow furrowing as she moved her attention from my face to the rest of me. "What are you wearing?"

I tugged at my bright red sweater, loving that the wide neckline fell a little off my shoulder in a totally non-dress code appropriate but so perfectly Marissa-y way. Still, I had no problem defending my style instead of talking about Dev and Lexie. "It's really warm. And cute, right?"

She stopped, tilted her head, and twisted her lips in a "you've got to be kidding me" expression. "It's way too baggy for you. I swear, it's amazing how you have this magical ability to knit things that are absolutely perfect for anyone and then turn around and forget everything you know the second you step in a store. For my sake, can we at least try to acknowledge basic fit rules exist?"

"It's really funny how seriously you're taking this stylist thing. You'd think I was asking for help in chemistry or something."

Grace laughed, circling me and tugging at the sweater like she was trying to make it fit me better. "I like fixing things. Fashion's a puzzle, like everything else, and it's fun finding pieces that fit perfectly together and fit the person wearing them." She then turned to fluffing my hair, and her expression grew serious again. "Are you sure you're okay?" she asked softly. She stopped fluffing and rested her hands on my shoulders.

"I said I'm fine." I waved my hand like I was waving away her concerns. I just needed some time away from Dev and Lexie to clear my head, that was all. I hadn't had a break in ages from the reminders of my complete and utter fail. "In fact," an idea flashed into my brain and I said it before I could change my mind, "I'm so fine because I've decided I'm signing up to help at sixth grade camp. Coach thinks it'll be a good experience for me." *If I go to camp, I'm away for the week.*

"You're not just doing this to get away from things, are you? You do realize Dev's still going to be here when you come back. You can't use camp as a place to hide."

I put on my most insulted look. "I'm not going to camp to hide. It sounds like a lot of fun. I like kids and s'mores and stuff."

"I know we weren't friends back then, but if I remember right, you hated camp. Didn't you fake sick and spend the whole time reading in your cabin?"

"I was eleven."

"And you're really so excited about it that nothing else bothers you?" She did the whole analytical stare thing again. "Did you just finish a book set at camp or something?"

"No." I didn't add that I had finished one about a month ago. Or that Julien was up at the top of my list as my favorite camp book boyfriend.

"Because you know those things are idealized, right? Real life has spiders and kids who like to put spiders in their counselors' beds."

"Just because I like to read doesn't mean I let fictional characters dictate my life." Grace looked pointedly at the sweater and I tilted up my chin defiantly.

Grace pulled a piece of lint off my sleeve. "Fine. Just really think about why you're doing this before you actually sign up, okay?" She checked her reflection one last time, then looked me straight in the eye and said, "If you need to stay here the rest of lunch, I'll cover for you and take your things to class."

I smiled a wavery smile at her. "Thanks."

33

"My neck is killing me," I hissed at Alec. At every single one of Em's plays or musicals, Alec always insisted on us sitting practically front row and far left. But that meant I was praying for act one of "Phantom of the Rock Café" to be over so I could turn my head to the left again.

"Shh. It's more fun this way, because you could watch the drama on- and off-stage," he whispered back. "Now, shut up. Em's about to start that scene where she has to make out with Christian, and I can't wait to watch Wilhelm turn all Hulk in the wings when he sees that."

Em wandered out onto the stage, which was set up like a brownstone rooftop in Philadelphia, down to the William Penn statue painted into the backdrop skyline. Her costume was pretty and sparkly, making her look like she was made of starlight. Christian swept onto the set, the preppy investment banker version of Raoul to Em's backup singer Christine, and they broke into *All I Ask of You.*

I saw Dev standing in the wings, waiting for his entrance. For a second, I forgot my pretend-I never-crushed-on-him pact and smiled at his costume. Instead of an opera cape, he was wearing a cool long-sleeved vintage tee, and instead of a mask, emo-style bangs covered one half of his face.

Grace seemed to notice where I was looking and nudged me, whispering. "What do you think of guyliner?"

"Stupid," Alec said, overhearing, while at the same time I chimed in,

"Hot on the right guy." And this rocker zombie version of Dev was definitely, unquestionably right.

And then my heart sunk back into my shoes and I was slapped back into I'm-an-idiot land as Lexie, dressed all in black, came up alongside him. She said something to him, then reached up to fix his hair in a way that was so much more intimate than anything a normal stage manager would do. Just before he stepped on stage, she stretched up and kissed him on the cheek. I couldn't watch anymore as she pushed Dev onto the stage, the two of them looking so much like Pine Central's power couple. Romeo and Juliet in zombie makeup.

I shut my eyes, digging my nails into the upholstery of my seat. Apparently, two and a half months of casual non-crushworthy contact wasn't enough to make my crush go away. But it was hard to just sit there and not react, especially when he started to sing.

I wasn't the kind of girl who fell for musicians, but it wasn't fair that Dev had a beautiful singing voice that did *things* to the surface of my skin. I opened my eyes, and there was Lexie again in the wings, staring at Dev like he was an advanced reader copy of the last book in a series.

"Bathroom," I whispered to Grace. I abruptly stood and

made my way out of the theatre. I'd deal with the possibility of Em killing me later.

Before I knew it, I was back sitting on the floor in the language hallway. I buried my face into my knees and tried to ignore all of the hurt that hit me full-force, filling every pore. Taking a deep breath that helped break up some of the tension in my stomach, I promised myself I wasn't going to ever repeat this scene again.

"You okay?"

I followed a pair of green and black oxfords up until I saw a familiar face. "Kris?" Any intelligent response flew out of my brain and I floundered for something to say. In my fantasy world, he'd just start spouting Aedan-like things at me and I'd respond with Maeve-ish answers, but instead my brain decided to register that the commercial sweater he was wearing got the Icelandic patterns all wrong.

"Yes," I said, then scrambled to my feet and tried not to look like I'd just been sitting in the hallway like, well, like a loser. "I mean, yes, I'm fine." He kept staring and I added, "I just couldn't deal with any more of the changes they made to the musical. I needed a break." I tried to push my hair back nonchalantly like Maeve would, but my fingers caught in the curls and I had to shake my hand free.

He smiled at me as if it were something he did every day, like we were in an alternate universe fanfiction of my life. "I know the feeling. Not to mention I had enough of these songs the million times I heard it in practice. Do you want to hang out in the library until right before the end?

I've got the code to open up the tech cabinet." He pointed his thumb over his shoulder at the library doors, which were conveniently located right in front of us. "I can pull out two tablets."

My eyes grew wide and my heartbeat sped up the tiniest bit. The parts of me that didn't want to go back into the theater to see more of the Dev and Lexie show and that wanted to bask in the amazingness that was Kris screamed at me to say yes. But the responsible part of me fought back.

"That sounds amazing, but I really should go back inside. Alec picked some seats right in front and Em will notice if I'm not there." The words tripped reluctantly off my tongue, leaving the tiniest bit of a bitter taste.

To my disappointment, Kris didn't look too upset. "That sucks. Next time, you need to sit in the back row like the rest of us cool kids so you can avoid actually watching these things like we do." A brilliant smile spread across his features, lighting them up.

Ohmigosh. I tried not to break into a little happy dance over his offer and instead tried to return that smile, even though I was seriously contemplating taking back my first answer. "You're so right. Thanks for offering."

"Sure." He turned in the direction of the library. "Have fun in there. Don't get hit by a chandelier or anything."

"Right." I watched him walk away, the hall lights catching the faint golden highlights in his hair, and slumped against the wall again.

I was such an idiot.

Aedan seemed to relax a little bit. "Good." He raked his hand through his hair. "Tomorrow, you will need to act like you did down in the tunnels," his tone sounded apologetic, "Otherwise, Connaught and the others may suspect something."

Act like she was his little human servant-with-benefits? Her body said yes and beat down the part of her brain screaming about self-respect. "That's okay," Maeve tried to sound casual, like he had told her she needed to buy a new pair of shoes for the mission or something. "I think we did a pretty good job acting today." She almost choked on the 'acting' part. She couldn't believe all of those gentle, guiding touches, the way he kept grazing her hair with his lips, could have all been acting. Those few moments had convinced her that he felt something for her. But now she questioned even that. If he wasn't so damn unreadable...

He nodded at her. "It's better that way. It's safest if they keep thinking you're just an enspelled human." His hand grazed hers for a hint of a second before he returned to tapping the table and watching.

That touch had been intentional. Frustration bubbled up in her and she pushed her teacup away. Maeve stood, a little bit of satisfaction rising up at the surprise in his face for her abruptness. "I'm heading back. I'm tired and the chaperones will probably do a check soon." Before he could say anything, she turned on

Oh My God. Was Dev doing this to me???
Or maybe that's how he's with all girls??

my heel and tried to make herself disappear into the pub crowd without looking back. Granmom always said that smart women knew how to make great entrances and exits. Let him wonder about how she felt, too.

At least i'm good at that

34

"You're doing it again."

I slammed my locker door shut and looked at Em. "Doing what?"

"Eye-stalking Kris." She nodded towards Kris' locker, where he was talking with a bunch of his friends.

"Eye-stalking? Is that even a word?" I leaned against my closed locker and watched as Kris did the same against his. I could practically melt into the metal and stay that way forever. "I love that he's got this whole Victorian-Edwardian thing going on with his hair." The only thing the moment needed was for Kris to look my way so our eyes could meet. Then, I'd just have to drop my eyes, shyly, and look up again, catching his attention again. Then, he'd push off his locker, make his way across the hallway, and…

"You make me ashamed to be a girl." Em grabbed my arm and started dragging me towards my homeroom, popping me straight out of my daydream. "You've been even more obsessed with him since January."

I tried to shrug free, but that girl had an insane grip. "Have not. I've always thought he was cute."

"Again, unobtainable fictional romance."

I stopped midstep and pinned Em down with a withering glare. "You mean like Dev and your plan to get us together?"

Em rolled her eyes and broke her grip on my arm. "Please, that was not fictional. The two of you were just too chicken shit to actually admit you liked each other. You know, Kris only noticed you after your makeover—"

"Which was your idea," I reminded her. "And, by the way, thanks for that." I straightened the fairy-tale-like top Grace had convinced me to buy and fluffed my still-perfect hair.

She ignored me and kept talking. "—while Dev always looks like he just got a starring role on Broadway every time you walk into a room, no matter what you're wearing." I tried to break in, but she stuck her hand up in the air to stop me. "It's the truth, whether you like it or not. Don't blame the messenger."

"Whatever. Just don't diss the objects of my affection." I paused at the door of my homeroom and glanced one last time over at Kris. He seemed to finally sense my eyes on him and looked up to give me one of his gorgeous smiles. Real, not like those "I have to pretend to like you" smiles he usually gave to people he didn't know during election season.

My heart started doing jumping jacks and I ducked behind the door with a wave at Em. "See you at lunch."

Em shook her head one last time and hurried off to her own homeroom. I wove between the desks to my seat and dropped into it, pulling out *Hiding*. *Found* was coming out in a week and I wanted to reread some of my favorite parts to prep for the last book in the series. Plus, I wanted that smile still fresh in my head while reading a little more Cyril goodness.

Even though I babied my books, the broken spine of my hardback fell open to the mirrorfall scene and I dove in. I read straight through the Pledge of Allegiance and roll. When Ms. Marin handed a few of us an orange paper, I just slipped it in the back of my book so it stuck out like a flag and vaguely registered that the paper said something about the sixth grade camp info session in Mr. Cooper's classroom I had to attend instead of first period.

I feel a cloud of cold engulf me, colder than anything I've ever felt before. My veins freeze, my breath comes out like dry ice shoved into my lungs. And for the first time since all of this started, I scream.

The bell rang and I stood up, propping my book up in one hand and maneuvering out of the classroom without breaking my attention from the book. Being able to walk and read without bumping into things was a major skill I had developed.

I pull my body up off the floor and find myself in a place that's familiar and still not. Like I am in a mirror image of somewhere I know. Instead of a familiar greyish tinge, this place is alive, the vibrant colors of the wood and wallpaper and rugs tugging at my memory. Then, it dawns on me. I'm in the mirror world, the place I saw through the house mirrors. "That bastard."

I flipped the page, dodging a freshman and turning

down the history hallway instead of my usual route. If I read fast enough, I could probably get in another two pages before the bell.

I reach out for the giant gilt Victorian mirror hanging in front of me—my room, or at least a silvery flipped version of it, fills the frame, but when my hands touch the glass, I can't get through. I splay my palms flat and push. Nothing. "Damnit, Damnit, Damnit."

A hand touches my shoulder and I whip around, freezing at the sight of a pair of familiar blue-grey eyes set in a healthily colored face.

"Cyril," I breathe, and my heartbeat is so loud I'm sure it can be heard even through the mirror. "Please, please tell me this is a dream."

He frowns and I notice for the first time the faint purpling on his cheek. "I tried to stop him before he could trap—"

"So, you're counseling, too?" Dev's voice broke through my reading bubble and my head shot up, a mini heart attack happening in my chest. I hadn't even noticed him next to me. I threw him a confused look and he waved an orange flyer at me. "For camp? You're carrying one of these."

I stared at him dumbly for a second, still half in Marissa's world.

Say something, my brain prompted and I sputtered out a barely coherent, "Uh-hrmmm." I slid the ponytail holder off my wrist and shoved it in the book. My brain turned on again and I snapped the cover shut. There was no way I could let him see the absolutely swoon-tastic first kiss between Marissa and Cyril, made especially hot because of all the insane sexual tension from a book and a half of not touching, and her fear of being trapped. Dev seeing that wouldn't be embarrassing at all, never. I pulled the book protectively to my chest. Hopefully, the bright new blush Grace forced on me this morning hid my reddening cheeks.

He didn't seem to notice my momentary breakdown. "That's great. I wasn't going to do it, but Em mentioned to Mr. MacKenzie that I was a scout and he talked me into counseling. Something about how a lot of their senior class first choices had to drop out because of some career fair thing and he had to go with a few junior second picks. He didn't want to leave the counseling to just you and a bunch of delinquents."

I finally snapped all the way back to the non-book world, bringing with me a little bit of Marissa's sass. "Great, so he's still sticking me with a bunch of delinquents."

We reached Mr. Cooper's World History classroom and Dev gestured for me to walk in first. I loved this room. It was the only classroom in the school built auditorium-style, with the seats stepping down to Cooper's desk and the board. When I came here as a freshman, I loved how it made me feel like I was in a college class instead of honors world history.

I stayed one step ahead of Dev in this weird, ever-expanding personal space dance I'd been doing since January. I hesitated, then picked a seat in one of the center rows. Dev followed me, dropping into the seat next to mine. I had to keep reminding myself not to read into anything, and that this was just Dev being his normal, friendly self. He would do the same to Em or any of the other girls in school.

Dev propped his feet up on the back of the seat in front of him. "At least I'm a requested delinquent. Beggars can't be choosers, bookworm." I sat my book on the armrest while digging in my bag for a pen, and he picked it up. "What are you reading now?"

Fear shot through me. I tried to pull it out of his hands, but he twisted so I'd practically have to crawl onto his lap to take the book back.

"*Hiding*. You wouldn't like it, it's nothing like the *Sentinel* series." It wasn't like I'd never recommend this series to a guy, but my brain kept bouncing back to what I knew was after that bookmark.

Dev flipped over the dust cover-less hardcover and studied the spine. "I dunno, you have pretty good taste in books." Then, his fingers moved to the edge of the cover. Even without the help of my makeshift bookmark, I knew right to where the book would fall open. When you reread a scene a million times, the permanent crease in the binding is impossible to fix.

I fought to keep my tone light, not like I was trying to stave off imminent disaster. "No, really, this has no action or anything. It's not your type of book." I prayed that it would open to another scene, any other scene.

His eyes scanned the page and I fought to keep myself from sinking through the wood laminate of the chair in shame as his lips quirked up into a wide grin.

"No action, huh?" He propped the book up, reading from it in a voice that made me want to move to a different country where the sound couldn't dance across my skin. "'His lips whisper along my jawline and I gasp just before they skim my cheek and brush against mine. I melt into his arms, my hands reaching...'" Dev looked up at me, not even bothering to hide his amusement. "Phoebe Martins, I didn't know you were into," he searched for the word, "scandalous books."

Forget landing in his lap—I lunged, but he held me back with one hand while holding the book out of my reach with his other hand. He read for another second, then turned to look at me with smirk.

"Wow. This author needs a thesaurus. She used 'sigh' three times in the same paragraph." He wiggled the book at me while making a tsking sound. "Definitely looks like a lot of 'action' to me."

"Oh, shut up," I mumbled, this time succeeding in prying my book from his hands and shoving it none-too-gently into my bag. "I read *Sentinel Twenty*. That's no different than the scene between Sentinel and Guide." I narrowed my eyes at him like Marissa when she convinced Dan to stop the exorcism, but that didn't make the amused look on his face go away.

"I'm pretty sure there wasn't a part where Guide pressed against Sentinel, '*feeling every inch of him*.'" He said with air quotes. "What do *you* think that means, exactly?"

Damn, he *had* seen that line. I ducked my head and

hoped my hair would swing forward to hide my burning cheeks, but instead ended up pretending I was picking at something on my jeans when it didn't. "I…" Thankfully, at that moment, Mr. Cooper and a few teachers I didn't recognize stood up at the front of the room and called for us to quiet down. Saved by the teachers.

"I'm sure all of you know by now that you have been selected to be counselors at the sixth grade camp in a little over a month. This camp offers a wonderful chance to prepare these now fifth graders for their transition to sixth grade and middle school in the fall." Mr. Cooper looked around the auditorium and I took the time to do the same. Counting Dev and me, there were about twenty of us. Some of the glitterati sat near the front and outdoor club members were parked in a clump near the middle, sharing a bag of what was probably granola. All juniors, and half of them I wouldn't trust to watch each other, much less groups of eleven year olds. "Thank you all for offering to be role models for five days. We've already spoken with all of your teachers to ensure that you will be able to make up the course work from the week you will be missing." A groan came from some of the people in the lower rows. "All of you knew that was part of the bargain when you signed up, right?"

One of the heads up front looked familiar and, as he turned to say something to the person behind him, I caught Kris' profile. Dev and my attempts to avoid him combined with the only other swoonworthy guy in the school? This was bad.

Dev leaned onto our shared armrest. "'*Strong hands running down my back,*'" he said out of the corner of his mouth. Damn, the jerk had some sort of photographic memory.

I sunk lower into my seat, sneaking a glance to the front of the classroom. If Kris heard that, I would melt into a puddle of one-hundred-percent mortified goo. "Shh, they'll hear you. Delinquent." Our row shook with his silent laughter.

Mr. Cooper ignored the drama playing up in our rows, looking instead at the groaners. "Obviously, you should know that this isn't an excuse to slack off from school for a week. You will each be responsible for a cabin of about eight to twelve students and will be paired with a cabin of the opposite sex for meals and events. You and your partner counselor will also be asked to run the camp team-building challenges throughout the week and to assist in some of the camp activities based on your skill sets and certifications. For example, Marcus will man the rock climbing wall," one of the guys up front high-fived another, "and Phoebe," I froze at my name, "is running the archery field."

My stomach turned when every head in the room turned to look at me. This had been a majorly bad idea. Dev nudging me with his elbow didn't help.

"It will be a lot of work, but you can ask anyone who has been a counselor before—it's a very rewarding experience." He started going on about what we'd need to bring and then listed all of the middle school teachers who would be "managing" us during the week, closing with, "Remember, this isn't a chance to party in the woods. I expect you all to do Pine Central proud."

Dev elbowed me again and I shot him a death glare. His teeth practically sparkled, like in a toothpaste commercial. "This is going to be so *rewarding*. Like when Cyril buried his hand in the girl's hair."

Part of me wanted to laugh. The rest of me wished I was safely in Zhdanova's class and had never heard of this camp or Dev or *Hiding*.

35

Reaching out, I touch Dan's elbow with the lightest of touches, pretending to be shy. My lips turn up the tiniest amount that I keep inching up as I talk. "Let's go to the conservatory." Letting my voice grow softer, I add, "Unless you want to hang out in my room for other reasons?" The tips of his ears turn red and he quickly shakes his head. Success. –Marissa, Hidden

"Score! This sleeping bag is rated to negative twenty degrees," Alec said, holding up a thick, bright red roll, tossing it into my shopping cart, basketball-style. His voice echoed down the sleeping bag aisle of the camping supplies store.

I checked the tag and nearly had a heart attack. "Holy cannoli, and it's almost five hundred dollars. My dad said he'd cover reasonable costs." Alec opened his mouth to speak and I cut him off, pulling the bag out of my cart and shoving it back on the shelves. "There is no way this will ever be considered reasonable."

Em was further down the aisle, squinting at a sales sign. "This one is fifty dollars on clearance." Much to Alec's dismay, I maneuvered the cart away from the expensive bags and towards Em. "Oh, and it comes in teal." She pulled one of the bags off of the shelf and handed it to me.

The bag was definitely a pretty shade of teal with a grey

flannel lining. I dug my fingers into the side of the roll and it was gloriously squishy.

"Sold," I said, dropping the bag into my shopping cart.

Alec shook his head. "Teal? You're picking by color? You two would die within seconds on that Survival reality show."

"But at least I'd die in my favorite color." He rolled his eyes at me and I laughed. "You know, if you're so into this stuff, why didn't you sign up?"

"I like survivalist stuff, not keeping a bunch of snot-nosed little kids from killing each other in the woods for a week."

"They're ten and eleven. I think they're probably past the snotty-nose stage at this point," Em said, grabbing a teal camp pillow and throwing it in the cart. "Okay, sleeping bag done. What's next on your list?" We exited the aisle and I started heading towards rows that looked like they had even more camp-ish stuff.

Alec stopped us, waving something he picked up off of an end cap. "Damn, a Swedish fire knife. That would be awesome. You have to get it."

Em snatched it out of his hands and started studying the back of the box. "What does it do?"

"It's a knife, but it also has a Swedish fire steel inside it. You can cut yourself out of bad situations and start a fire." Alec took back the box and pet it like it was the One Ring.

I shook my head and kept pushing the cart forward. "I don't plan on needing to start a fire in the near future."

We were halfway into the next aisle before I saw him

reluctantly put back the box and jog up alongside us. "What if you got lost in the woods and had to fend for yourself?"

"This is Camp Sundew. Not the Arctic or the Serengeti. I'm pretty sure I won't get lost."

He shook his head. "It's your funeral."

"C'mon. I'm sure there are matches there. And when will I ever need to start a fire?" I gave Alec a grin. "And me, with a knife? Bad idea. But thanks, oh guru of camping."

"Somebody called for a camping guru?" A somewhat familiar voice came from behind me.

I turned around slowly, trying not to let any of my surprise show. Kris was leaning against a wall of shelves, carrying one of those camp lanterns. I choked back my initial urge to hide. "Kris?"

He glanced at my friends and full cart. "Getting supplies for camp?"

Something had to be off in the universe—Kris talking to me more than once even though he didn't have to? Marissa would totally use this as an opportunity to set the stage for future flirting success, like the scene in *Hidden* where she tried to distract Dan away from the mirror. I nodded and fortunately, Alec answered while I tried to reassemble my brain and come up with something coherent.

"Trying to. Someone's ignoring all of my legit survival advice."

Okay, Marissa always found some excuse to touch a guy's arm and then play to his strengths. I reached out and tapped the hand Kris was using to hold the lantern.

"Alec thinks I'm going to get lost. Maybe I should get one of those, too, so I don't get stuck somewhere at night?" I felt stupid letting my hand linger a little bit longer than necessary, but I counted to two before pulling my hand back. My fingers still tingled slightly from the contact.

"Nah, I'm just getting this because my flashlight sucks when it comes to lighting up the cabin. I've been camping in that place a million times. The paths are all well marked. It's hard to get lost unless you really want to." He smoothed back his dark hair, confidence practically pouring out of him, looking just like Aedan before a battle.

I looked up at Kris, blinking in what I hoped was a cute way and let a slow smile spread across my face. Marissa would totally let the tiniest bit of breathiness enter her voice at this point. "You'll have to teach me everything you know when you get the chance. I haven't been camping in forever." I copied his stance, trying to do that social mirroring thing Grace had mentioned.

Em made a gagging motion behind Kris, but he didn't notice. A smile spread across his face. "Definitely. It's easy when you've done it a million times." He shrugged. "I wasn't planning on volunteering because this won't even be a challenge, but my pain-in-the-ass little brother is going this year and my parents want me to hold his hand. It'll be nice to have some decent company, instead of hanging with just the football rejects and outdoor club granola people."

"Feebs, we have to go." Em grabbed my arm and started pulling. "I think I'm about to vomit."

I turned to narrow my eyes at her before facing him again. "Um, see you later." I waved in the most Marissa-esque manner I could while tripping after Em and the others. As soon as we were down a different aisle and out of his hearing, I yanked myself free. "What was that about? Kris was actually *talking* to me."

Em let out an exasperated sound. "I can't believe you did it again."

"Did what again?"

"You were acting like…like some airhead and he was eating it up."

I shook my head at her. "I was not acting like an airhead. I was flirting. You should know a lot about that." I looked to Grace for help, but she stepped back, holding up her hands.

"It was pretty bad, Feebs," Alec added, and I threw him a dirty look.

Em nodded. "I could practically see his ego expanding."

I took a deep breath, my flirty high crashing down around me. Leave it to my friends to ruin what was one of the best moments of my junior year. I grabbed the cart handle and started pushing it towards the checkout. "Let's stop talking about this, okay? I don't want to argue."

I looked over my shoulder at Kris, who was disappearing into the hiking boot aisle, and he turned around just in time to wink at me. I hid my grin and picked up my pace. Maybe camp with Kris wouldn't be so bad, after all.

Ignoring Cyril is physically painful, but I push through the feelings. We both agreed that this is the best way to keep sane. The impossibility of being in love with someone whose very touch could trap me in a mirror, or cause him to possess me, really gives us no other choice. But it still hurts every time I see his reflection in the house mirror.

"How was school?" He asks in a guarded 'friend' tone when I crash into my bedroom and throw my backpack onto my desk chair. *I can do that*

I shift from foot to foot. Some girls break up with guys and only have to deal with them in the occasional class. Me, I have a ghostly ex-boyfriend trapped in my bedroom mirror. Thank God I took the bathroom mirror down, even though Cyril is way too Victorian to watch me change or anything. I grab an elastic off my dresser and yank my hair into a high ponytail. "Good." I settle for the one word answer. Less chance of saying anything awkward-inducing. *Or at camp*

"That's...good to hear," he says, sounding as lame as me. His eyes are guarded and I just want to reach into that mirror and touch his cheek, or push back his hair, or—

I close my eyes and turn to grab my phone, taking a deep breath in the process. "I'm going to go study in the conservatory." The only mirror-free room in the house, other than my bathroom.

"Unless you need me for anything…" I trail off and wait. The uncomfortable tension in the room could choke a cat.

Cyril shakes his head maybe a little too hard. "No, I will be perfectly fine. Go study."

I nod and escape with the tiniest of waves. By the time I reach the sunny conservatory, I can finally breathe again. I stare at the fainting couch mom had put in the corner and wonder if I can turn this mirror-free place into a bedroom.

welcome to my life

36

"Isn't it nice to think that tomorrow is a new day with new ways to screw up in it?"—Kaylie, *Cradled on the Waves*

"I'm sorry, but no knives. Trust me, there won't be any chance that you'll end up stranded in the middle of the woods and will have to do 'survivalist things.'" One of the teachers told a student as I passed. "We're going to Burlington County, not the Himalayas."

I choked back a laugh and kept dragging my sleeping bag behind me until I reached the first bus, where we were supposed to meet our 'managing teacher.' A really young-looking blonde with short hair looked up from her tablet and smiled at me. "You must be Phoebe." I blinked and she gestured at my bags before holding out her hand. I tentatively shook it, feeling weird the whole time. Teachers didn't do things like shake hands. "The bow bag gave it away. We're really excited to be able to have an archery module this year." Yeah, this one was probably straight out of college. "I'm Mrs. Forrester and I'll be advising you and the rest of the counselors. For the basics, I mean."

I didn't know how to respond to that or if I even had to, so I just nodded. "Okay." I hitched my bow bag even more securely on my shoulder and stepped back, almost bumping into someone.

"Watch it!" Came the voice from behind me and I turned, an apology on the tip of my tongue. One of Grace's cheerleader friends, Cassie, squinted at me sleepily and shook her head. "Oh, Phoebe, it's you." She yawned. "It's too early to have to watch out for people trying to step on me."

"Sorry." I smiled sheepishly while moving sideways into an empty spot. "It's too early for my brain to work."

"You're telling me." Dev joined us and my stupid, traitorous heart stopped beating for a second. Even in pajama pants with his hair sticking up all over the place in messy spikes, he looked hot. I blinked and tried to focus instead on his ratty grey duffel bag and the Echelon Cricket Club logo on the side. He must have seen me staring. "Sport of champions. It's my dad's bag. I suck at batting and bowling." I just kept staring, feeling a bit dumb.

"Cricket, like in *Alice in Wonderland*?" Cassie asked. She gave my foot a nudge.

God, was I *that* obvious? "No, that was croquet," I said, shifting my focus to her gratefully. Grace had good taste in teammates.

I was saved from having to say anything when Mrs. Forrester blew a little whistle straight out of *The Sound of Music* to get our attention. "Counselors, now that you're all here, just some quick basics. If you check out the packets we sent you, there should be a number on the top of the front page. That's your cabin number." I pulled the green folder out of my bag and flipped the corner down until the big number eight was visible. I breathed a sigh of relief. If the numbering meant anything, at least my cabin wouldn't be the first for anything. While we shuffled through our packets, she handed out bags labeled with our names. I opened mine and pulled out a yellow polo shirt with Lambertfield Middle School logo stamped on the spot where there was usually a pocket.

Mrs. Forrester cleared her throat to get our attention again. At least she wasn't going to whistle at us all the time. "These are your uniforms. There should be three shirts in there, and there are laundry facilities at the camp. Whether or not you clean them is up to you, but you have to wear the shirts during all daytime activities at the camp. Also, a few ground rules. You're here to help the students. No partying in the woods. If your significant other is here, no making out or whatever you kids do nowadays in the woods. First, poison ivy is awful if it gets *there* and second, we *will* call your parents if we catch you." That got a snicker from some of the group. "Also, if you have a problem camper, you are to come to me for advice."

I unzipped my hoodie and pulled one of the shirts over my henley before shrugging back into my jacket. May mornings in New Jersey were still pretty cold.

I saw movement out of the corner of my eye and turned my head, sucking in a breath as Dev, apparently heedless of the chill, pulled off his own shirt and replaced it with the polo. I sucked back a surprised gasp. He was fast, but not so fast that I didn't get a full, unobstructed view of his bare chest for what were the longest few seconds of my life. I pulled my hoodie around my face to hide my burning cheeks.

Cassie grabbed my arm and pulled me over to a red-and-orange suitcase. "Can you help me stuff these in here? I barely got it closed this morning," she said loudly. She gave me a sympathetic smile before bending over and unzipping the bag. "You're so red," she whispered, stating the obvious. "I thought you might want an out."

"Thank you," I said, softly.

"I've been there," she said without looking up. "Ex-boyfriend or crush?"

"Does ex-crush who thinks I just like him as a friend count?" I held the suitcase lid down while she tried to zip it shut. She hadn't been exaggerating about it being overstuffed. Out of the corner of my eye, I saw Kris hurrying our way, a younger version of himself in tow. I ducked my head so my hair covered my face. It was too early to even think of being cute and flirty. "And here comes my current crush."

Cassie looked up, screwing up her nose like a skunk had just walked by. "You mean Mr. 'The Football Team Is a Bunch of Rejects?'" One look at me and she smoothed her features back into a comforting smile. "Ugh. Think of the bright side. Chances are you and Dev aren't co-counselors, which means you won't see him most of the time. And maybe you and Kris might be partnered."

I looked over at Dev again, who was comparing his

folder with some of the other guys. A burning feeling seared me down to my toes. I quickly tried to shift that gaze and feeling over to Kris. "That would be fantastic."

37

By the time my sleeping bag and duffel were unloaded from the bottom of the bus, most of the counselors were already arranging on the far side of the parking lot. After passing the wall of teachers trying to organize all of the sixth graders, I looked up and my heart sunk. Kris was holding up a piece of paper with a big number two written on it while chatting with one of the girls from the outdoor club who had to be his co-counselor. Shoving my disappointment to the back of my mind, I kept walking, eyes scanning for my number.

Dev stood under the number eight taped to the side of the camp parking lot fence.

If this were a perfect world, I would have been able to break into frustrated tears then and there and no one would notice. I almost turned around to run back to the safety of the bus. Instead, I sucked in a deep breath and drew myself up, trying to look graceful and unconcerned as I swung my sleeping bag and dropped it against the fence. That thing was freakishly heavy. "This isn't your number, is it?" That came out before I could stop it. I bit the inside of my cheek before I could say anything else.

His expression was frustratingly unreadable. "You're

eight, too?" I nodded and he stepped aside to make room for me. "I guess we're partners."

"I guess so." The universe had a sick, sick sense of humor. I faked a smile to cover up the churning in my stomach and stood next to him with just enough space between us that I didn't risk brushing up against any part of his body. "Go team eight?" I said halfheartedly, leaning against the wooden boards.

"Ha, yeah. We'll make a great team. Band geeks unite."

I rolled my head against the fence to look at him. "I don't think it would instill a lot of hope in our campers if they heard you say that." He laughed and a little of the tension seeped out of me. At least he didn't seem to notice I was freaking out inside.

Breathe. Deal. It was easy enough to politely avoid him at school, but here…not happening. I was a big girl and if Maeve could work alongside Aedan, I could counsel a few kids and shoot some arrows. I let my eyes slide over to Dev, who was checking his camp papers with an intensity that made the whole breathing thing stop working again. Easier said than done.

While we waited for all of the kids to get sorted, I pulled out my cellphone, which was picking up barely a bar of signal, and started texting with my screen angled away from Dev.

You will never guess who my partner is at camp.

Em's response was fast, as if she'd been waiting. *Dev.* No question mark. A sick realization dawned in me.

I frowned at the screen. *How did you know?* I held my breath, waiting for her answer. Something simple like 'lucky guess' or 'He already texted me.'

Instead, *I let Cooper know that you two would make a great team. You can thank me later.*

WDSFJIEWHFE!

Huh?

I'm going to kill you when I get home. I shoved my phone into my pocket and ignored the ping of three or four texts that followed. Great. Set up by my best friend. For five days. In the woods. Without real showers. At the same camp as Kris. This was going to be about as fun as the presidential fitness test in gym class.

Dev looked over at me with that same odd expression. Maybe not so weird, considering I was the one ignoring my buzzing and ringing jacket. He opened his mouth to say something, but the rush of ten and eleven year olds coming our way stopped him. There was no way this was going to work. No way.

"Okay. Dish." Cassie said, coming up beside me, her bag bouncing on the bumpy dirt path to the mess hall.

I looked up at her for half a second before focusing again on the ground. Between my sleeping bag throwing off my balance and tree roots, my odds of falling were high. "Dish about what?"

"This ex-crush thing of yours. Bad luck with the group assignment, by the way."

That was the understatement of the millennia. Thankfully, Dev and my group were all the way at the front, yelling some kind of campy song. "Yeah."

"So, if you don't mind telling me, why is Dev an ex-crush?" She plucked a dead leaf off a blueberry bush and shook it at me like an old lady wagging her finger disapprovingly. "And please don't try to keep me out of the loop. I'll get it out of you whether you want to tell me or not."

As much as I appreciated her save earlier, I didn't feel like baring my heart to someone I barely knew. "He just wasn't interested in me, that's all. There isn't really a story to tell."

"That sucks." She pat my arm and added, "If this is really hard for you, we could ask to switch our assignments. I'm sure the teachers would be cool with it."

"No, that's okay." If Marissa could deal with Cyril every day despite her broken heart, I could be Dev's co-counselor, build fires, and sing Kumbaya. "I'll be fine."

"If you change your mind, let me know."

"Thanks." We were almost at the mess hall and hearing range of the rest of the group, so I picked up speed and prayed I wouldn't step in a hole and fall face-flat in front of everyone. Last second, I stopped in front of the mess hall steps and said, "You won't tell anyone about this, right?"

"Never." She propped her suitcase along the side of the building and reached over to give me a quick little one-armed hug. "Just say the word and I'll switch. I can already tell half the kids in my cabin are going to be a pain, anyway." She glanced up at the mess hall door and whispered out of the corner of her mouth, "Don't look now, but it looks like your co-counselor is looking for you." She then waved and bounced up the steps. "See you inside."

I tried my hardest not to look at the mess hall windows or door and busied myself finding a place for my duffel and sleeping bag that wouldn't make them disappear in the mountain of look-alike campy stuff.

"C'mon, Phoebe, you're the last one. Team eight is waiting for you!" Dev's voice came clear through the screen door.

Marissa pulled herself up off the ground and pushed her hair—and random drops of viper blood—out of her face. She had to get to the mirror. Ignoring the part of herself that wanted to curl up in a little ball and hide from the vipers, she nodded at Cyril. "I'm ready."

I took a deep breath and gave myself an extra second to adjust my bow bag strap on my shoulder before nodding and heading for the steps. This wasn't the Otherland, full of goblins, or the mirror world. I didn't need Cassie's help. I could do this. "Be right there."

38

The cabin was one of those basic wooden frame things with screen walls and rows of bunks lining the walls. A closed-in area opposite the door looked just big enough for a few people to change without flashing the world. It was rustic, and not in a good way.

I threw my bags onto the bed closest to the doorway and turned to look at my campers. Eleven girls, almost all of them with these super-pretty names that had to have been trendy when they were born. Two Bethanys, a Lilliana, a Miranda, a Giselle, and a few other names I couldn't even remember. And they were all staring at me. Dev had kept the group of both boys and girls going with a steady stream of questions, but now that I was alone with them I had no idea what to say. I couldn't be afraid of a bunch of eleven year olds.

I took a deep breath and clasped my hands to hide my shakiness. This wasn't any different than the classes I taught at Oh, Knit!, just with younger people and no yarn.

"We have until lunch to settle in, so I'd like to start with some rules." A few of the girls groaned and I waited for them to quiet down before I spoke again. "I'm not your mom or your teacher. It wasn't too long ago that I was a camper, too, and I know you're all definitely old enough to know when you're not supposed to do something. Honestly, if you do anything stupid and get sent home, I really don't care. It's not like I'll get anything on my permanent record about being a sucky camp counselor." That made some of the girls look at me with surprise. My hands and breathing steadied and I smiled at them. "If you want to stay up all night talking, take the bunks towards the back of the cabin. I don't care if you don't sleep as long as you're not too loud. The teachers drive around in the camp golf cart to check on all the cabins throughout the night, so when you hear it, make sure to shut off your flashlights and go quiet until a little while after they pass. Otherwise, we'll all get written up."

"That's…good to know." One of the girls—Genevieve, I think—said, slowly.

"Since I remember being a camper, I also remember playing truth-or-dare. I don't care what your dares are, but I really suggest thinking twice before coming up with something like mooning the boy's cabins. It's really, really not worth it." Memories of running over to the cabins and chickening out last minute, only to get in trouble with the teachers, anyway, came flooding back and I held back a laugh. "Trust me." That got a few giggles and whispered comments and I pushed on while I still had momentum. "I'm taking the bunk next to the door because I don't need any of you sneaking out in the middle of the night." I dropped onto the bunk and looked up at them. "And that's about it. Any questions?"

The redhead raised her hand. "Is Dev your boyfriend?"

I blinked at her, caught off-guard. She was like a little demonic Anne of Green Gables. Perky and pushy at the same time. "No." After a beat, I looked around the rest of the group. "Any questions about camp?"

"He totally checked you out when you bent over to pick up your bags." Redhead threw herself onto a bunk and propped her chin in her hands. "I think he's cute."

Bethany Number One shook her head. "Diana, you think any older guy is cute."

"Not true. It's just that the guys our age are so immature."

I dropped my head into my hands and spoke into my palms. "Okay, just...pick your bunks and set up your sleeping bags. We need to leave for the mess hall soon."

"I think we broke her," came a whisper from a far corner of the cabin.

Lilliana actually giggled in response. "Nah, it's totally heartbreak from unrequited love."

I ignored that and started to untie my sleeping bag. A tall shadow fell over me. "Wait, you're reading *Cradled on the Waves?*" Bethany Number Two picked up the book on my bunk and I nodded absently.

Her eyes grew wide. "Did you get to the part where Kaylie and Evan play together on the cliffs?"

That got my attention. I stopped and looked straight at her, excitement at finding a fellow reader making me grin. "Ohmigosh yes. That's my favorite part. Especially when their music starts going in time to the waves?"

BethanyTwo clutched the book to her chest and fake swooned. "That's my favorite, too. I want to move to Canada now."

I nodded enthusiastically. Finally, someone else said what I was thinking. "A little cottage on PEI?"

She flipped to where my bookmark was sitting and seemed to be checking out how far I was in the book. "South shore, right on the cliffs." A dimple appeared in her cheek when she smiled. "Anyone who likes Emma Sanderson is awesome." She then gently put down my book and went back to where the other girls were taking turns checking out and complaining about the changing/sink cubby thing.

I had the best campers ever.

39

In the distance, I heard splashing and screaming, but here on the dock, I was safe from overturning canoes and water wars. I turned the page in my book and paused midchapter to close my eyes and soak in the warm sunlight. Mrs. Forrester let me beg off of canoeing with the excuse that I was afraid of getting hurt and being unable to teach archery the rest of the week. While Dev and the rest of the counselors and campers were out getting soaked, I was dry, warm, and immersed in *Cradled on the Waves'* world of violins and gorgeous seascapes. The earthy scent of cedar water and the smell of pine filled my lungs.

I lay my book down and sat up. The launch was on the opposite shore of the lake and most of the canoes hadn't been able to venture too far past the center. On this shore, the water was mirror-still, reflecting the pines that dipped over it and dotted the shore around me. This was a picture-perfect postcard spot for the Pine Barrens. I slipped off my shoes and dipped my toes into the tea-colored water, pulling them back out right away as the cold hit me with a shock. Another canoe overturned with a splash and I was so glad not to be out there.

I eased my feet into the water and pulled my book back into my lap. In the book, Kaylie was doing the same thing as me, hanging out on a bridge, her feet dangling over the edge into a brook.

Kaylie turned the page of Aunt Ilse's worn copy of Emily Climbs *and shivered as a little breeze kicked up around her. July in Fire Bay was definitely a lot cooler than back home.*

Within seconds, I was there again. The barrens faded, their sandy soil replaced by the rust-colored earth of Prince Edward Island.

She was so deep into the book and the brook and sunlight that only the softest notes of a song drifting towards her on the wind made her aware someone else had joined her on the bridge. The singer crescendoed the tiniest bit when he got to the part in Star of the County Down *that described a pretty, brown-haired girl, and Kaylie's heartbeat sped up at the familiar voice.*

I shivered along with her. A tingle of anticipation ran up my spine—it had to be Evan, and he definitely was singing about Kaylie. My toes curled in the water and I leaned forward, my lips moving as I whispered the song lyrics aloud with him.

A sprig of purple lupine tickled her shoulder, and when she turned to take it, Evan was smiling down at her. He didn't stop singing, and instead, crouched down next to Kaylie, so close she could feel his breath on her cheek. He lowered his volume until he was practically whispering the third verse, where the man in the story gave up his roving ways for Rose McCann.

On the word 'heart,' his eyes met hers, but she quickly dropped her gaze.

My heart practically burst from possibly one of the most

romantic entrances in book history and I wanted to smack Kaylie for being so oblivious to Evan's hints.

The spark of cold in my toes turned to warmth as he leaned closer…

Then a splash of water hit me right in the face and destroyed the magic of the moment. I looked up with a death glare, my eyes meeting Dev's. He maneuvered his rowboat right up to my dock. "Wake up, Phoebe," he said, his grin as wide as the canoes on the lake behind him.

I indignantly wiped at my face with my sleeve and started waving my book in the air to try to dry the pages. "I was awake." I pushed a soaked strand of hair out of my face. "And now I'm wet. Thanks."

"You're welcome."

"Aren't you supposed to be over there, making sure no one drowns?" I waved my book in the direction of the canoes and away from me. "Translation: Go away so I can go back to my book." *And forget about you*, my brain added much to my dismay.

"Just thought I'd check in. I don't want those delicate archer arms getting hurt if you doze off and fall into the lake." Dev dug his oars through the water to move his boat back and forth and I couldn't help but notice the way his arm muscles bunched with the movement.

I focused on my poor book, instead. "Oh, shut up." Crud, the pages were definitely going to dry wrinkled. I tried holding up only the individual pages and blowing on them.

"Nice excuse, by the way."

I tried to arch an eyebrow at him. "Whatever. If I got hurt, would you be able to run the 'first ever archery module' at this camp?" When he didn't say anything, I folded my arms in a way that was supposed to look superior. "I didn't think so."

"Jump in. I'll row and you won't even have to lift an über-useful finger."

"Pass." Why wouldn't he just get the hint and go away? "I'm good here with my book."

"You always beg out of stuff." He squinted his eyes at me in another one of those looks that I couldn't read, just like in the parking lot earlier. "You make me think that you like being apart from the rest of us up in your ivory, book-filled tower. Like you're too good for everything."

That stung. I took a deep breath and ignored how my breath shook. "Maybe I am." A splash across the lake made us both turn to see the tail end of an overturning canoe. "I think that's your cue."

"Damnit." He gave me one last glance and, with a frustrated sound, backed his boat away from the dock and rowed at top speed towards the canoe.

I lay down and rolled over, burying my face in the wet pages of my book. All I wanted was to act like I wasn't crushing on him, not to totally alienate him. I turned his words over in my mind. *Like you're too good for everything.* Was that what he really thought of me?

I blinked to fight off the tears that were threatening to well up in my eyes and pulled back enough to see the pages clearly. I could be snobby and distant, like Kaylie, if I had to. Dev's laugh carried across the lake and I fought to keep from looking up. It was better this way.

I shut my book and hurried back to the cabin. Before the girls could get back, I pulled my notebook out of its hiding place in my duffel, opening it to a fresh page. I poked my tongue out of the corner of my mouth just like Kaylie did when she was thinking through a problem and grabbed a pen. Flipping through *Cradled on the Waves*, I found just the right passage and got to work.

"Sorry I'm late. I had to help pull some girl out of a rut back on Whelan Road. She was definitely from away—" at that, he looked straight at Kaylie and grinned, then turned back to Uncle Matt, "—and would have completely torn her axle out the way she was going."

Uncle Matt let out a big laugh that echoed through the small kitchen. "Let me guess—trying to drive over that big tree root near McIntyres'?"

"Yup. It looks like the rut got worse after the storm last night." Evan then turned that grin back on her, sticking out his hand, red dirt still crusted under his fingernails. "I didn't get a chance to introduce myself," he said, pointedly. "I'm Evan, nice to meet you."

Kaylie schooled her features into a look of disinterested politeness. "Kaylie." One word, no need for embellishments or "pleased to meet you"s. Even though he was decent enough not to embarrass her in front of her uncle about the car thing, she hadn't missed his emphasis on "from away."

"Kaylie's my niece from Connecticut." Uncle Matt said, giving the soup one more stir before turning off the stovetop and joining us. "She'll be helping at the ceilidhs this summer."

Evan's eyebrows jumped up and he looked back at Kaylie

like he was seeing her in a new light. "So you're the violinist Mr. McClellan's been talking so much about? Looks like we might have a lot in common."

"Evan's the best fiddler on the island," Uncle Matt told her, pride in his voice. "He's been bringing crowds to our ceilidhs since he was around ten?" He glanced over at Evan, who confirmed the age with a nod.

Like a fiddler had so much in common with a concert violinist. "Right. I just can't wait to trade tips." She opened her mouth to say something, paused, thinking it might be a little too much, then said it anyway. "I'm working on Paganini's Concerto number five. What are you working on?" she asked in her most conversational tone. Years of cutthroat junior state orchestra tryouts and practices meant she could rock a distant but never overtly rude way of talking. Back home, it was to avoid getting torn apart by some of the other violinists. Here, it was to get back at smug farm boy fiddlers from who seemed to be always laughing at her.

"Oh, I'm just working out some new stuff for the show, nothing as easy as that," Evan countered with an easy smile. "I can't wait to introduce you to some real challenging music. You'll be playing like a true islander in no time."

Kaylie narrowed her eyes at him. "Oh, I'm just dying to dive into Turkey in the straw." She winked at Uncle Matt, then looked towards the dining room. "Excuse me, I'm going to go see if Aunt Ilse needs any help." She swept out of the room with a little wave, tossing her hair over her shoulder like she hadn't even heard his last comment. Podunk farm boys from podunk islands were aggravating.

40

I held the red plastic cup gingerly in my hands and as far away from my body as possible. Ms. Forrester had given us counselors a few hours off while the campers had to sit through a zoologist talking about bats. I didn't know which option was worse—the dark woods and smell of the beer in my hands or the thought of petting a flying rodent.

Someone plucked the cup out of my hand, replacing it with a different one. "It's seltzer water," Cassie said, coming into my line of sight as she dropped my old cup behind a fallen log. "I don't drink, either. The guys are cool with it," she added, probably at the surprise that had to be all over my face. "With that stupid reveille so early tomorrow morning, I don't know how any of them can do it, anyway."

I shifted my weight from side to side, my feet sinking into the soft sand. "Aren't we going to get in trouble? We're supposed to hang out in our cabins or on the docks…" I let my voice drift off. This place, far down a barely used trail, definitely didn't count as one of the acceptable spots the teachers had listed for us.

"Relax, they're too busy with the kids. Trust me, we'll be out of here before anyone comes to check on us." She gestured with her cup at the trees around us. "Every group of counselors has been coming back here on the first night for years. My brother did, when he counseled two years ago."

I took a sip of the seltzer and tried to look relaxed. "Sorry, I'm just not really used to rule breaking. Em calls me a super holy virgin," I confessed.

Cassie giggled. "'Super holy virgin?' You guys are too cute. We should hang out sometime when we get back to civilization." She squeezed my arm and started making her way back towards the circle of flashlights near the keg. "I'll talk to you later. I've gotta get back to Mike. Besides, I don't want to be a third wheel." She winked and tilted her chin at something over my shoulder.

"Huh?" I turned around to find Kris right behind me, the moonlight reflecting off his hair and features making him look even more like a paranormal book hero than usual. I mentally flailed for a minute before my catalogue of bookish flirting started working on disaster control. *Hold the cup to your lips. Smile a slow smile.* A quick review of my outfit concluded that my jeans and hoodie weren't *too* awful. *Speak.* "Oh, hi, Kris."

He smiled. At me. "I'm glad you're here. The guys by the keg started talking about football again. Like they have nothing better to talk about. At least there's one person in this place I can hang out with."

I took a seat on the fallen log, watching to see if he would follow. My heart gave a nervous lurch when he actually did. "How is your cabin?"

"I already had one kid mouth off to me today. You'd think eleven year olds would at least have some respect for us. My parents owe me." He bumped me with his shoulder. "You?"

I thought about our afternoon icebreaker with the campers. "They're pretty awesome. One of the campers is even reading the same book as me."

"Oh, yeah, you read that teen stuff, right? I grew out of those things when I left middle school."

I bit back my automatic defensive response. So we didn't have the same taste in books. "There are a few really good ones."

He shrugged. "You're probably right. I'm just into more literary things, you know? Like when we read *Catcher in the Rye* last year. That's probably my favorite book."

"Sorry, but I couldn't stand Holden's whining. Even if his sister did have an awesome name." I tried to do a quirky half-smile, and hoped that it looked cute and not like I was having a stroke.

He stared at me blankly for a second, then let out a short laugh. "Oh, yeah. Phoebe. Cute." He took a long drink from his beer and shrugged.

An awkward pause followed and I searched the trees for inspiration about something, anything to say. *Talk about him,* the Marissa voice told me. "You said you go camping a lot?"

"I do, but it's nothing like this. You guys are getting it easy with the cabins and bunk beds. I usually sleep in a tent, and once, we made our own lean-tos." I opened my mouth to respond, but he pushed on, "In the middle of winter. I don't know how you and Jacobs got to teach orienteering and firemaking while I got trailbuilding. He probably doesn't know a flint from a lighter."

Something about what he said irked me. "Dev's supposed to be really good at camping, too." Nowhere was it acceptable to totally contradict the guy you're trying to flirt with when he talks about the guy you're not supposed to like, but it was as if the impulsive part of me just didn't care.

"Sorry, I know you guys are friends, but he doesn't ever seem to take anything seriously except his music stuff."

"He does. I—" I stopped myself. Why was I defending Dev, anyway? I bit my lip to keep from talking.

Kris turned to face me and looked me in the eye. "I'm different. I know what I want and go after it. I've been watching how you've changed yourself this year, and I think you're the same as me." He looked and sounded so *confident*.

Not like me. My palms were sweaty, but when he took my hand, there wasn't any of the electric nervousness they kept talking about in books. I didn't feel a jolt like when Dev accidentally brushed past me in the cafeteria the other day, nearly making me drop my lunch tray.

Kris leaned in, his shoulder brushing mine. "We've only hung out a few times, but I know you like me. You're smart, a lot smarter than most of the people in our class." He reached up to touch my cheek with his free hand.

He was really close. I had to tilt my head up a little bit to see his face and was only able to focus on his nose.

Anything Marissa-like flew out of my head. "I'm not that smart. I mean, we have a really smart class. Everyone's so talented in their own way and--" I was babbling. Badly. But his hand felt weird on my face. And as long as I kept talking, he couldn't kiss me. This was like something straight out of a book and all I wanted to do was bolt out of there.

Marissa always felt like there was an irresistible force drawing her closer and closer to Cyril. Her skin would be all tingles and her heart would feel too small for her chest.

Maeve would feel so warm when Aedan was close, it was like her skin was on fire—in a good way. He'd touch her hand and shocks would travels straight up her arm and down her spine.

I felt...neither of those things.

He stuck a finger against my lips. "You're too nice to everyone, also. It's cute."

He bent forward. Oh, God, he really was going to kiss me. Butterflies—no, ravenous clothes moths—took over my stomach. Did I even like him enough? I did a mental inventory of my hands, dropped my cup, and awkwardly put my free hand on his arm, just like Marissa did in the Mirrorfall scene. His chin brushed my cheek, the stubble pricking at my skin. Was he old enough for stubble? Why didn't anyone tell me that it would feel like someone was trying to scrape your skin off with a wire brush? His eyes met mine, like he was asking for permission to kiss me.

I tried to find the gold in his eyes that reminded me of Aedan, but that wasn't enough to make me feel the same wound-up anticipation as when I read about Aedan looking into Maeve's eyes. But maybe we just needed to start kissing and all the feelings would start rushing in—like when Nya and Lito first kissed in *Other Side*. I gave the tiniest of nods and then his lips were on mine. There weren't any fireworks. My heart didn't jump into my throat and I definitely didn't have the urge to pull him closer, like Maeve and Aedan in the cave scene. In fact, it was kind of soggy. And sandpapery. And incredibly uncomfortable. I tried closing my eyes, but that didn't help. My neck hurt from tilting up to meet him.

But Kris seemed to like it. His hands slipped into my hair and he pressed his lips harder against mine. And when he tried to slip his tongue into my mouth, I pulled away as quickly as possible.

"We, um, probably shouldn't be doing this." I resisted the urge to wipe at my lips. Maybe the books were wrong. Maybe all first kisses were miserably awkward. Those clothes moths were having a party in my stomach like they'd just found my best cashmere sweater.

He took my hands into his. "I doubt any of the teachers will say anything. We're some of Pine Central's best students. We can get away with anything." This close, he didn't look so much like my mental picture of Aedan. Not enough gold in his eyes and I couldn't help but notice how much that confident smile of his actually irked me.

He leaned in to kiss me again and I arched my back away from him, like my body was doing what my apparently limited language skills couldn't.

"It's not the teachers. It's just that…"

"She's my girlfriend." Dev came out of the woods with an expression on his face that was a cross between wanting to strangle Kris and disappointment in me. "Phoebe, I thought you said you loved me." With the hood of his sweatshirt up and shoulders back, he looked like an avenging warrior, the tiniest bit like Aedan in the *Glittering* battle in Dublin scene.

Kris jumped away from me like I'd suddenly caught on fire. "Whoa, I didn't know, Jacobs. I'm not the kind of guy to mess around with other guy's girlfriends. She didn't say anything. Honest."

I stared at Dev, half-confused and half-relieved. The tornado had landed me in Oz and everything was topsy-turvy. The corner of Dev's lips quirked up the tiniest amount and everything settled into some semblance of sense. "Dev. I—" I was an awful actress, but adrenaline and confusion melded together into something I hoped was realistic. "—I can explain."

"And I'm getting out of here," Kris said, just before reaching out to squeeze my arm. "If you break up with him and need a shoulder to cry on, I'm here." The confidence slipped back onto his face and he headed back towards the keg like nothing had happened. As soon as he was gone, I collapsed onto the log and let the utter mortification I'd been holding back wash over me. How much had Dev seen?

The log shifted as Dev sat next to me. "Nothing ever bruises that guy's ego, does it?" I didn't answer and he pressed on. "You looked really uncomfortable, like you needed an out. I hope that was okay."

I pulled my face from my hands. "I…yes, thank you. I thought I liked Kris, but the more I got to know him…" *And there was no spark*, I added silently. "I didn't expect—" I broke off again and took a moment to compose myself into a little less embarrassing of a state. "You two could have gotten into a fight."

Dev let out a laugh that had a darker edge to it. "Nah. I know Kris really well. We've been scouts together since we were little kids. He doesn't like being in situations where he doesn't have the upper hand. Nothing fazes the guy." It was easy to tell from his tone that he didn't like Kris at all.

"Even *I* believed you were going to rip his head off for a minute there." I couldn't seem to get a smile to go onto my face, so I settled for a half-cringe smile thing.

It was impossible to see his eyes from the way he tilted his head in the hoodie. "I'm a good actor."

I moved my hands to my lap, weaving my fingers together and apart. "Thanks for looking out for me," I said softly.

"You're my co-counselor. It's my job," he said, but the joking in his voice was tempered with something low and comforting.

Afraid of what my face would reveal, I tilted my head back to look at the stars. Dev didn't push, and we just sat there in silence.

He pulled her tight against him, his arms twined around her waist. She felt the fingers of his hand through the thin silk of her dress.

Gold light wrapped around them, so bright that she had to close her eyes to keep it from blinding her. He bent over and his lips brushed her ear, sending shivers down her spine.

"Don't speak if you can help it when we're in the court. I'll speak for you. And don't let them see you watching them." The gold faded and they were in a hallway straight out of a fairytale picture book. As her eyes adjusted to the darkness, she could make out a gold paneled ceiling and Celtic knot-work tapestries on the stone walls that would make the Book of Kells jealous.

Everything that wasn't stone was some shade of gold or green. It was beautiful.

Maeve took in a deep breath and was about to say something when Aedan's arms tightened around her. She blinked and saw another man coming towards them, dressed in Leprechaun green and brown.

Like Aedan, he was tall, handsome, and built to be a warrior. But the predatory glint in his eye and the almost-sneer on his lips were a definite sign that he was nothing like her protector.

"Aedan, good to see you with a conquest. Two centuries without companionship—we were starting to worry about you." He stepped close to them, a challenge.

"Times and people change, Connaught."

Connaught ran a finger down her cheek and she tried not to flinch.

"Are you sure you know what to do with her?" He continued downwards, his fingers running through her hair and only millimeters from her body. It felt like a predator prepping to eat her. "This one is lovely. If you change your mind, I'll take her."

Aedan stiffened, but his voice was smooth. "She's mine." He grabbed her arm and whipped her around to face him, capturing her cheek with one hand. Eyes burning equal parts passion and apology, he bent over, kissing her fiercely, possessively. She held back a squeak of surprise and relaxed into his kiss. He made her burn. EEEeeeeEEEEeeee. Swoon!

Molten gold rushed through her veins.

This is the most perfect kiss ever. The dress, the cave, Aedan...

41

My first co-counseling module with Dev was the most uncomfortable morning of my life. Neither of us spoke about the night before or what he'd said on the docks, but we had to work together. Theoretically. I could barely make eye contact with him. I grabbed the box of compasses and he gravitated to the fire pits, so we had silently sorted ourselves into two unrelated teams within seconds of getting to the field.

It started out the same way for the archery module as we silently pulled the targets, bows, and arrows out of the storage hut and set up the field. I saw him watching me out of the corner of my eye and matching my setup. But as I took a few test shots with my competition bow, his expression grew serious and he made his way over to me.

Dev cleared his throat, staring down at an arrow he pulled out of the bucket. "Phoebe, I'm sorry about what I said yesterday on the docks. I didn't mean to upset you." His fingers pulled at the fletching and I was convinced he would destroy that poor arrow. "You know I was just trying to get you to join the fun, right?" I nodded ever so slightly and he stuck out his hand. "Truce?"

I completely failed at not letting a smile slip while shaking his hand. "You saved me from totally embarrassing myself with Kris. I owe you an apology for dragging you into that. Truce, as long as you don't try to force me onto another boat."

"Believe me, I don't want to bring down the Wrath of Phoebe onto myself." Dev picked up and twirled one of the learner recurve bows and pointed it at me. "Can I get a refresher? I haven't touched one of these since the mod in gym last year."

I gently set my bow down on its stand, the teal riser and Niamh's gold autograph shining in the sunlight. "Okay." My hands fluttered in the air around the bow and his hands, not quite touching either. "Show me what you remember. Try to hit the target."

"Easy enough." Dev grabbed the arrow he had been abusing out of the bucket and slid it onto the arrow rest.

I watched him nock the arrow and cringed. "Wait." When he squinted questioningly at me, I reached out to un-nock and rotate it into the right position. "The different color feather faces out."

"Oh, yeah. Forgot that." He stared intensely at the target and started pulling back on the bowstring.

"Elbow level." I reached over and put my hand on his elbow, gently pressing down as he pulled his arm into position. I was deep into teacher mode but still noticed how his arm muscles moved and the energy that seemed to radiate through my fingers. My voice lowered to a soft whisper.

"Anchor at your jaw." I tapped the top of his hand and guided it down, my hand brushing his cheek by mistake. I pulled away quickly and moved my hand back to his elbow, glad he couldn't see my face. "Pick a spot on your arrow or your bow to aim. Breathe." I felt his arm respond and my brain catalogued the fact that we were now both breathing at the same time. "And release."

I stepped away from him, keeping my eyes on the arrow. It was definitely off-center, but at least it hit the target. Behind me, I heard Dev reach for another arrow out of the bucket. "That was awesome. Can I try again?"

"Go for it." I turned and busied myself with counting all of the bows we had laid out at the stations. He did *not* need to see how much that lesson had thrown me off. If I tried to shoot right now, my shot would probably be as bad as his.

"Is this right?" I heard him call out to me.

I turned and took in his awful position. Dev seemed to have forgotten everything I'd just corrected. "Not really." I took a deep breath to steel myself and tried to look professional as I walked back to him. "Elbow?" Dev dropped his elbow, but it was still way up over his shoulder. I tried to force an annoyed sigh and positioned myself alongside him again. From here, I could smell the spicy-soapy Dev smell and our breathing was once again back in sync. Time slowed. I swore he could feel my heartbeat through my fingertips. I was in trouble.

Once his elbow was in the right position, I gently pushed down his shoulder and leaned in a little to gauge his aim. The hair around his ear moved with my breath as I said, "Okay, now."

He releascd the arrow and right away his aim was much better than the last time.

Dev dropped his bow and jumped away from me. "Shit." He rubbed at a welt quickly reddening on his arm and looked at me apologetically. "Sorry."

I tapped at my arm guard. "It's my fault. I should have made you wear an arm guard." Happy to have an excuse to step back a little bit more, I almost backtracked all the way to the table where we'd laid out the equipment and pointed at the target. "But at least you got a bull's-eye for it." I watched as he glanced up and seemed to forget his arm in a nanosecond.

Dev walked over to the target and poked at the arrow sticking out of the side of the yellow circle. "Huh. Watch out, zombies. I'm ready to shoot you back to hell." He wiggled the arrow free.

"Yeah, not that ready. And am I the only one who isn't into *Perfect Zombieism?*"

"Yes." The kids from group three started filtering into the clearing and he walked back over to where I stood. "So, why do you get to wear all that stuff and we don't?" He gestured at my chest guard.

I tugged self-consciously at the giant black triangle that covered my left boob. "Because I'm doing this every day for a few hours? If you start demonstrating, I'll lend you mine."

He put up his hands in a stop motion and shook his

head. "No way, the demos are all yours."

"It's all about relaxing and becoming one with the bow," I said, giving him what I hoped was a quirky-but-only-friendly smile. Something about being on familiar territory seemed to make me bolder than usual. I was like Maeve here, and I didn't even have to try.

He bumped me playfully with his side. "You're, like, Zen-Master Archer Phoebe," he said softly as the campers started gathering in a horseshoe shape around us.

A feeling, like when Maeve first picked up her bow and landed every shot perfectly bubbled up in me. I clipped my quiver onto my jeans and winked at him.

"Okay, guys, who wants to shoot some arrows?"

I winked at him. Ohmigod, I was an idiot. He'd totally guess and I'd go back to being ego-fodder for a guy who had a girlfriend and definitely wasn't interested in me. I buried my face in my sleeping bag and wondered if polyfill was thick enough to properly suffocate me.

"Phoebe?" I rolled my head sideways to one of my campers shining a flashlight in my face. "Aren't you going to change?"

I blinked at the light and reached out to push the flashlight away. When the spots faded, I made out wild curls a lot like Em's.

"Giselle?" The form nodded and I sat up. "Yeah. Give me a second. I'm trying to climb out of the pits of my own stupidity."

"O-kay." Giselle backed up and twirled her flashlight so it illuminated the cabin like a disco ball. "What happened?"

Bethany Two slid onto my bunk, surreptitiously glancing over at where my book lay open on the windowsill. "We heard the archery thing was pretty awesome, so it can't be that."

Damn, they were attracting a crowd. "Nothing, really. I was just being dramatic." I shook my head and reached into my duffle to pull out a wool sweater and fleece hoodie.

"I'm glad you're not fighting with Dev anymore. He's cool, even though he was an ass for splashing you on the dock." I almost choked at angelic little Lily saying "ass." "We're pretty lucky to have the best counselors in this place."

I popped my head through the neck hole of my sweater and pat my static-y hair back to semi-flat. "Now I know you guys want something."

Bethany One shook her head. "Nah. We talked to the other girl cabins. Their counselors treat them like kids, yell at them, and Mary's cabin had to cover for their counselor because she snuck out last night to go make out with her boyfriend."

"We like you because you talk to us like we're adults," Eliana added. She finished dressing and looked like she'd been eaten by a marshmallow.

"I think you might be a little overdressed," I pointed out to her in my most adult voice.

She shook her head and pointed at the little backpack she had slung over everything. "Layers, baby. All of this stuff squishes to, like, sock size. I'd rather keep stripping down than freeze my tuchus off in the middle of the woods." She raised an eyebrow at some of the looks she got. "Laugh all you want now, but you all'll be begging to borrow a layer after an hour out there."

Genevieve poked Eliana in the side and the jacket material engulfed about half of her hand. "You can't possibly think Tanner will think this is cute."

"Cute isn't about what you wear, it's about who you are." Eliana flipped her hair over her shoulder with an attitude that made me grin. Em would love her.

I checked the clock on the far wall. My poor phone languished practically signal-less along with all of the others in the cabin.

"Enough about cuteness. We've got about two minutes to finish getting changed."

Redhead blinked at me from where she was fixing her ponytail in front of a small mirror someone had hung from one of the top bunks. "You know, if you put on a little bit of lipgloss, it might get Dev's attention. And then it'll be like in the *Music Camp* movie." She clutched her hands to her chest and made a swoony face.

And...I was back to regretting that I was such an "approachable" counselor. "Um, that's okay..." I wracked my brain for her name.

"Diana." Bethany Two mouthed at me and I smiled at her thankfully.

"...Diana. But believe me, there's no dramatic high

school romance here. Life isn't like movies or books," *Unfortunately*, I silently added, patting *Cradled on the Waves* before standing up. "Okay, we're going to be late if we don't get going right now."

42

"Tonight, we're going on a trust walk." Mrs. Forrester stood with one of the other teachers on one of the docks, holding a bag full of brightly colored fabric strips. "There will be a lot of group projects next year. You need to learn how to trust your classmates." A groan could be heard from some of the campers and I suppressed a grin. I remembered this exercise. "I need you to pair up in teams of two and your counselors will hand out a blindfold to each team." She gestured for Dev and me to come forward and gave us each a handful of those fabric strips. "We'll be watching to make sure no one cheats."

We finished handing out the blindfolds to our campers and I turned to give the extras to Mrs. Forrester. She took all of them except for one. "You two also need a blindfold."

I exchanged a glance with Dev, whose frown mirrored mine. "Aren't we supposed to make sure the kids don't walk each other into trees or something?"

"There aren't that many people in this group. Mr. Hamm and I can take care of that part. And you'll get a chance to try this, too. It's a fun experience."

Fun? I mouthed at Dev, who made a face when Mrs.

Forrester's back was to us.

"Besides," Forrester continued, nudging us into line behind the already blindfolded and laughing campers, "it's not like the two of you should worry. You don't seem to have trust issues." She moved on to the front of the line, pausing along the way to check blindfolds.

"I doubt they're making the other counselors do this," I said, twisting the blindfold.

"Probably because we're special." Dev took the blindfold from me and balanced it in his hand. He bounced on his heels while looking into dark forest path ahead of us. "Ladies first?"

"Thanks," I said, dryly. I turned around and he slipped the blindfold over my eyes. His fingers gently moved through my hair to keep it from getting tied into the fabric and I hoped he didn't hear the catch in my breath. The heat from his body left as he stepped away and, for a second, a little bit of panic rose up in me. My hands reflexively went up to the edge of the blindfold. "Frak. I don't think I like this."

And then the heat returned, one hand grabbing mine and bringing it down to my waist and an arm wrapped around me so that another hand was on my opposite shoulder. "It's okay. I got you."

"I swear to God, Dev, if you walk me into a tree, I'll guide you straight into the lake on your turn."

"If I make it a small tree, will you make it a stream instead?" He laughed close to my ear and I turned in the direction of his heat and his voice to give him a piece of my mind.

But Mrs. Forrester's voice kept me from answering. "Okay, campers and counselors," at "counselors," I could hear the giggles of a few of the girls from my cabin. "No cheating with the blindfolds. The purpose of this game is to learn to trust your fellow classmates. Blindfoldees, follow the lead you're given. Guides, remember—your turn is next. We're going halfway around the lake for the first group and then we're switching and finishing up right back here with the second group."

"Around the lake?" I asked softly in the general Dev direction. "That's a lot of walking." I did *not* like the thought of not having control for that long.

Dev leaned so close that his breath tickled my ear. My heartbeat picked up just a notch. "Don't you trust me?"

I had to pause and gave myself a second—now I understood what Maeve must have felt when Aedan brought her through the Otherland entrance. Goosebumps prickled at my skin even though I wasn't cold at all.. I choked out my next words. "Says the guy who walked the entire clarinet section into the color guard during Carmina Burana practice."

"Okay, campers, let's go!"

Dev's fingers tightened a and he started moving us forward. "That was a joke."

"I'm so glad I'm not a marcher." I stumbled as the path changed to soft sugar sand and Dev quickly righted me.

"With smooth moves like that, I'm glad you're not a marcher, too."

"Shut up." And he did. For a few minutes, I was

surrounded by darkness. I could hear the campers ahead, but, except for the occasional yell from one of the boys, they were hushed as well, all soft whispers. My skin tingled from the pressure of Dev's touch as he guided me around obstacles in our path.

"See, not so bad."

"Says you."

"C'mon. This has to beat hanging out in the corner of the mess hall with your knitting or a book."

I almost stopped to give him an incredulous look, then realized that he wouldn't be able to see it, anyway. "Um, no."

"What's it about?"

"The knitting?" I asked, and he used our conjoined hands to jab me in the side. "It's a pair of Celtic knot cabled arm warmers—" he jabbed again and I laughed. "Okay, but you're going to think that the book is boring and girly."

"I promise not to laugh. It has to be good if you're so into it."

"Oh, it totally is. It's about this girl whose parents send her up to Canada to help out her uncle for the summer. She plays violin at this ceilidh," I was careful to pronounce it kay-lee, like in the author's guide at the front of the book, "—um, like a celtic singing-and-story-and-sometimes-dancing show that they put on for the tourists all summer long. And she doesn't want to be there because it's not cool like NYC. But then she meets this guy…"

"Big surprise."

I elbowed him, "Who is this awesome fiddler but wants

to be a potato farmer..."

"Because that's really glamorous."

"And she gets offered a seat in an August music intensive back home. Right now she's torn between staying on the Island for the rest of the summer or going to the intensive." Dev gave my arm a squeeze and I moved to the right under his guidance.

He didn't miss a beat. "Why is she torn?"

"Because she thinks she's falling for the guy."

"Who wants to be a potato farmer."

I laughed. "Yeah. You know, not everyone can be a Bollywood star."

"Tree root." Dev's arms tightened around me and, before I could really trip, he half-lifted me over something that had caught on the toe of my Keds. He then continued like nothing had happened. "And I didn't star. I was a background dancer. Which, by the way, still beats potato farmer."

I tried to make a dismissive gesture with my free hand. "Whatever. You can keep telling yourself that." I took a deep breath and the earthy-pine scented air steadied me. "You know what I love the most about this book?"

"What?"

"The author isn't a musician, but she gets it. That magical feeling you have when you're playing and everything falls together and you're nothing but the music."

He squeezed my shoulder and hand, but this time it wasn't to get me around an obstacle. "That really *is* an awesome feeling. I love that someone else gets it."

We walked silently for a minute, the campers fading away and it was just me and Dev walking through this pine-scented darkness. Just as I was about to say something, Mrs. Forrester's voice broke through and shattered the spell. "Good job, guides. Blindfoldees, you can take off your blindfolds now."

I reached up to slip off the blindfold. With the few lanterns surrounding the clearing, it was dark enough for my eyes to adjust almost immediately, focusing first on Dev and then shifting quickly to the moonlight reflections of the pines in the lake behind him.

"No trees, as promised," he said, and I blinked back to his face.

"That must have been really hard for you," I shot back teasingly. Dev let go of my arm and hand and suddenly, the night's chill washed over me.

"Before we switch and finish the rest of the trip around the lake, we have a mini science experiment for all of you." The campers groaned and Forrester waited until they quieted down before continuing. "Tonight, we're going to learn about triboluminescence."

"Cool," Dev said under his breath.

I tilted my head at him and mouthed "Geek" before turning back to face Mrs. Forrester. That was a new addition from the trust walk when we were sixth graders.

"Triboluminescence is what causes things to spark when you crush them, releasing extra electrons. You'll cover that in your science classes next year, but for now, we're going to watch triboluminescence in action."

Mr. Hamm started walking through us, handing out candies as he spoke. "All sugar-based candies triboluminesce when you bite into them, but the wintergreen flavoring makes for a very visible spark because it's fluorescent." He shook his head at one of the boys who was about to pop the candy in his mouth. "Don't eat these until we tell you to, because you'll need to watch your partner if you want to see chemistry in action." He gave me and Dev each a little white mint and moved on until everyone had a piece of candy.

"Everyone have their mints?" At the nods from all of us, Forrester said, "We're turning off the lanterns. I need you to face your partners and wait for my signal to bite down on the candy. This is going to be the only time that eating with your mouth open is acceptable, by the way."

I turned slowly to face Dev and the words "chemistry in action" ran through my head again at the way his moonlit profile made me feel like I had a chemical reaction going on in my heart and lungs. His eyes locked with mine before his attention slipped to a spot closer to my ear. He reached out, his hand almost brushing my cheek, and I froze, like Maeve on Midwinter night. He pulled a pine needle out of my hair and twirled the needle between his fingers before letting it flutter to the ground. Dev seemed as breathless as me.

He has a girlfriend, the little voice in my head reminded me.

The last lantern clicked off, turning the clearing into a giant shadow. Some of the girls giggled and I heard a friendly scuffle behind me.

"Okay," Mr. Hamm said, his voice effectively silencing the group. "On the count of three, bite into your mints. One," I took the mint between my fingers and watched as Dev did the same with his. "Two." I brought the mint up to my lips, seriously regretting turning down the lipgloss advice as Dev's gaze dropped to my lips. "Three." I watched as blue light sparked from Dev's mouth and the cold around us disappeared as I watched his lips move. His hand accidentally brushed mine in the dark.

Sparks flew. Oh, hell, sparks *flew*.

43

There was nothing like sneaking out after breakfast and moving around a camp parking lot trying to get a signal on my cell phone to kill the magic left over from the trust walk. I squinted at the number of bars on my phone and sat on a stump at the edge of the lot.

"You're breaking up again." Em's voice was static-y but her annoyance was clear.

I stood and watched the bars jump up. "Sorry. Camp Sundew hasn't moved into the twenty-first century. Better?"

"Much. So, you were saying?" She switched to speakerphone on her end and the sound of her closet squeaking open came through the line.

"You were right. Kris was…" I searched for the right words, "not as wonderful as I thought he would be. It was like he only liked me because I matched some sort of checklist for him after Grace's makeover."

"I told you. Fictional romance. Too bad you didn't figure it out when half the junior class told you he was a jerk."

I couldn't help but correct her. As much as I didn't want to think about the whole conversation and kiss, I still couldn't think of Kris as bad as Em and the others described.

"He's not a jerk. He's just really, really focused on what he wants."

A dismissive sound came over the phone. At least, I thought it was a dismissive sound and not Em choking on something.

"And doesn't care about what anyone else wants unless it matches up with his plans."

"It *was* awful, especially when Dev had to save me." I played with the hem of my polo. Today, I had stylishly accessorized it with a red bandana belt. "Between that and the trust walk thing, I don't think I can do this co-counseling thing anymore. Last night was torture."

"It sounded pretty awesome to me. Dev swooped in and got you out of a bad situation. Then, you guys held hands and wandered through the woods in the moonlight."

The force of my eye roll had to be heard over the phone. Leave it to Em to turn a trust exercise into something it wasn't. "Blindfolded."

"Whatever turns you on."

"You're not taking this seriously. It's a lot easier to think of Dev as just a friend when I'm not with him practically twenty-four hours a day and when I don't have to watch him make sparks in the dark." I tugged at my bun, feeling a few of the looser pieces slip out. Hello, disheveled Phoebe.

I could hear her giggles over the line. "You know, it would be a little easier to take you seriously if you didn't say stuff like that. It's just too easy to tease you. At least you're not here, feeling the wrath of Osoba."

"I'll take Osoba over suffocating under the weight of pretending this totally unrequited crush doesn't exist. It's so romantic in books, but in real life it totally sucks."

"I knew it!" A high-pitched squeal erupted behind me and ice washed through me as I turned slowly to find Diana and Eliana standing on the edge of the closest parking space. "You do like him!" Diana grabbed my free hand and swung it happily.

I could barely keep my phone to my ear. "What the hell is going on?" Em asked with her special blend of pissy annoyance.

"This is awesome," Eliana said, giving a little twirl. "Like Romeo and Juliet. But not."

I tried to stare the two of them into silence. "Two of the girls from my cabin just found me."

A groan came from the other side of the phone line. "That's not good, is it?"

I shook my head out of habit. "Not particularly. Not if I don't want Dev to find out."

"Oh, we won't tell him," Diana looked up at me angelically, big eyes and all.

Apparently, my death glare was broken. "I gotta go. I'll call you when I can." I eyed the two campers and hoped they wouldn't rush off before I could talk to them. "Text me about the interpreter audition? I want to know how it went." She'd been preparing for days for the audition and it killed me that I wasn't there to cheer her on this time.

"Spoiler alert: I got it. I'll tell you all about ficus and

corsets and people who were in the Philadelphia Female Anti-Slavery Society later, when you don't have to deal with little monsters."

"That's awesome," I said, cringing at how distracted I sounded.

"Yes, it is. But that's nineteenth-century, and you have some twenty-first century eavesdroppers. Go. Good luck with that mess."

"Thanks," I said, clicked off my phone, and pocketed it before regarding the two campers. "Please just pretend you never heard this. Please?"

Eliana reached up and tugged a few more strands out of my bun so they brushed my cheek. "That's a lot better. Dev looked like he liked it when your hair was down yesterday."

"Huh?"

Diana answered that one. "At the walk. He played with your hair."

I blinked at both of them, running through my memories of the night. "No, he pulled a pine needle out of it."

"Keep telling yourself that," Diana said. "You definitely need our help if you want to get him to ask you out."

"I don't want anything like that." I dropped my hands from my hips and tried a calming breath. "I have to go set up for orienteering, Go back and eat some more scrambled eggs or something and don't worry about this Dev thing."

"But—" Eliana didn't seem too happy.

I tried to look both of them in the eye and settled for ping-ponging between them with my best serious face.

"Please? This is something personal that I need to deal with on my own."

Diana crossed her arms and actually made a pouty face. That girl had conniving angel down pat. "Fine, but when you need help, we'll be here."

I put one hand on each girls' shoulders and started guiding them back towards the mess hall.

"Thanks," I said, trying my best to sound appreciative. "I'll remember that."

Dev was already preparing the stones and sticks for the fire pits when I arrived at our clearing. I dropped my bag of compasses on the table and tried to look nonchalant as I collapsed onto the bench and started shuffling through the packets we'd be handing the kids.

He looked up with a sleepy smile. "Where did you disappear to during breakfast? That table was pretty hard to handle on my own."

I cringed, then pulled my phone out of my pocket and waved it at him. "Sorry, I actually found a signal and was checking in with Em."

"Afraid she'll send a search and rescue team if she didn't hear from you for more than a day?"

"Something like that." I shrugged. "Besides, it couldn't have been that bad. We definitely won the counselor lottery with our campers. They're not a lot of trouble."

"Right, maybe all your girls aren't." He stood and sat

on the bench next to me and I tried not to notice how hyperaware I'd become of the little bit of air between our arms and legs, my skin buzzing where we were practically touching. "Tanner was acting up last night, so I threatened to kick him out of the cabin. When he called my bluff, I took all his things and threw them out the front door. He tried sleeping outside for about half an hour before coming inside and promising he'd behave."

I covered my mouth to hide my smile. "What if he hadn't done that?"

Dev shrugged. His fingers picked at a frayed spot on the knee of his jeans. "I'm sure Forrester would have understood." I gave him a look that said I wasn't as sure as he was. He reached over and pulled the packets out of my hands. "So, as payback, how about I take the easy orienteering part this morning and you get down and dirty with the fire building?" he asked, pulling out one of the maps and rotating it to find up.

I reached over and positioned the map for him, careful to grab the sides opposite from his hands. "That would be fair, except for the tiny fact I have no idea how to build a fire."

"It wasn't in any of the books you've read?" I locked him in a death glare and he stood up, grabbing my arm and pulling me with him. "Just kidding. Part of the reason why they asked me to be a counselor is because I'm a scout and the king of outdoorsyness." He knelt in front of one of the supply piles and gestured for me to join him. "We have a few minutes. Come learn, little padawan."

"I still can't picture you as a scout." I folded my legs under myself and sat as far from him as I could while still being within reach of the fire pit site.

He didn't look up from his task of shredding some bark and dry pine needles, but a little dimple appeared in his cheek.

"Mom and Dad like it because it looks good on college applications. I like it because I get to occasionally blow stuff up." His eyes met mine, like he was checking to see if I was smiling. He reached out with a handful of the shredded stuff. "This is kindling. We're going to use a bow and drill setup to get some embers going in here."

"I once read a book where the character used a tinderbox to—" I stopped and bit my lip to keep from spouting any more utter book geekishness. Part of me wished I'd had that tinderbox and, like Scarlet in *The Bear's Daughter*, could show off by making a fire in seconds.

"I knew it. What haven't you read about?" He handed me a few sticks and a rock. One of those things looked like a mini-version of a rough bow. "No tinderboxes. You have to work for your fire here."

"Okay, Yoda. Teach me," I said and he failed miserably at hiding his surprise. *Touche*, geek checkmate. He probably hadn't expected me to get the padawan reference. "I'll try my best to learn."

"'There is no try. Just do.'" He put the sticks, rock, and bow together in a setup and then came around to cup his hands around mine to teach me the motions. His chest pressed against my back and his chin almost rested on my shoulder. "If people in ancient times could do this, so can you."

Having Dev this close was actually painful. My heart beat erratically and my fingers moved clumsily, almost dropping the rock/stick setup. Scarlet wouldn't even blink at a guy when she was focused on a task, but combining my total lack of skill with the unshakeable *awareness* of Dev behind me made my hands useless. Even with his help, I didn't get much more than a little bit of smoke and embers that would blow out the second I tried to make them grow into a flame.

"Try again." Dev's breath brushed my cheek, starting a different sort of fire across my skin. I fought the irrational urge to turn towards him and, frustrated with his closeness and the whole fire thing, dropped everything and pulled away until I was back standing by the compasses.

I crossed my arms to hide how my hands were shaking. "I guess I'm not as good as people in ancient times. I'll stick to modern technologies like matches."

"And bows and compasses?" He shot back. He looked disappointed in me. "You don't seem like the type to just give up on things, Phoebe."

I shrugged, adopting a Maeve-like nonchalance. "I guess you don't know me that well." The first campers started coming down the path from the mess hall and I picked up one of the compasses. This group was made up of our kids, and some of the girls from my cabin were whispering amongst themselves, looking from me to Dev with frowns. I ignored them and turned back to my co-counselor. "I guess I'm back on orienteering."

Dev stared at me for an uncomfortable moment before shaking his head and turning to greet the campers. "Who here wants to learn how to set stuff on fire?"

While the girls were out swimming, I dug through my duffel, pushing aside sweaters and extra socks until my fingers curled around the familiar edges of my notebook. I'd almost chucked it into the lake after my disastrous kiss with Kris, but couldn't do it, and was thankful I hadn't. I needed every page of bookish advice I could get if I wanted to survive the rest of camp.

I flipped through, looking for the strongest Maeve and Marissa excerpts I'd pasted inside, and started reading. I'd be a warrior—unafraid, strong, and beautiful and completely immune to any of my old feelings for Dev.

Aedan's lecture the minute she arrived in the training hall was unexpected. "If you want to learn how to fight, you have to get dirty. This will not be like fighting with your bow or magic. You need to be willing to drive a sword into your opponent's stomach and get covered in his blood. You have to know you can die the instant you step foot on the battlefield."

She narrowed her eyes at him in her best bored-warrior look and twirled the gold-colored sword, trying not to show how heavy it really felt. For an archer, she'd expected to at least have gained a little more upper body strength. "I'm the Harper. You might remember that I fought a horde of goblins and saved both our worlds. I think I can handle a little bit of hand-to-hand combat."

Moving faster than she could react, Aedan twirled his sword to pin hers down against the floor. A heartbeat and he was just inches from her face, the point of his *sgian* shimmering millimeters from her carotid artery.

"Can you?" he asked, a hint of an impish grin breaking his formerly stern look.

Maeve shoved aside the little voice in her stupid brain telling her to kiss him and, instead, pulled back from his blade. As Aedan's grin grew wider, heat replaced her breathlessness from a few seconds before. "You made your point. This isn't training, this is you stoking your stupid Leprechaun warrior ego at my expense.

Definitely have to practice this "bored warrior" thing.

I'll get Colm to teach me, instead. He'll train me properly." She grabbed her coat and stalked towards the door. "I'm out of here."

Out of the corner of her eye, she caught Aedan coming at her again with his sword, and she instinctively swung around and blocked his blow, her arms vibrating with the force of the impact. Adrenaline took over and she pulled a page from his book, stepping close so she could disengage her sword and deliver a not-too-gentle tap to his waist while he tried to adjust his reach. "What the hell, Aedan?"

"Interesting. You're a natural, just like with the bow." He stepped back, nodding to concede the point, but his smile was full blown. "Now you're learning."

She blew air through her lips and tried to slow her insane heartbeat. "If making the Harper die of a heart attack was part of your lesson plan, congrats, you almost did. I *can't* learn if you don't teach me the rules and just mess around."

His expression grew dead serious. "Rules are good and honorable. But, sometimes, to survive, you need to break them. If it's a choice between you and your opponent, be as ruthless as your part-goblin blood will allow. And you need to forget that fear exists."

"Having my Leprechaun warrior jerk of a soon-to-be exboyfriend come at me with weaponry isn't going to help get rid of any fear, you know."

He kept going as if she hadn't said anything. "Fear will paralyse you. You doubt yourself, you'll die."

"Cheery."

"I'll teach you the rules, but I will *also* teach you reality. <u>If you only train to the rules, you'll be tied to the rules. And then you will die."</u>

"Got it. I get scared, I die. I follow the rules, I die. Any more lectures around that theme, or are you going to stop talking and teach me?"

"Never doubt yourself. Others will, and you need to prove them wrong." With that, he sheathed his sword and turned towards the exit. "We'll practice again tomorrow. I suggest you wear a lot of padding."

No fear. Got it.

44

"Group eight, welcome to the low ropes course." Mr. Hamm stood at the center of a pair of ropes that were attached to one tree on one end and then spread into a wide V where they attached to two trees on the other side. "Just like the trust walk, the purpose of the course is to learn teamwork."

"I'm starting to see a theme," one of the boys from Dev's cabin muttered with a barely audible groan and Dev made a shh-ing sign at him.

Ms. Forrester looked up from checking the ropes and nodded. "Yes, there is a theme, Nathan." She stood and wiped her hands on her cargo pants. "Teamwork is important, and the first exercise is going to teach you how to work with a partner to get to your goal." She pointed to the ropes. "This is called the wild V. In this exercise, you'll need to partner up with someone close to your height. You'll start at this end," she pointed to the tree with both ropes attached, "and, working with each other for balance, you will try to go as far as possible without falling off the ropes."

"You need to find a partner who is about your size. Try to partner with someone you really don't know as well." As the kids scrambled to grab their friends, Mr. Hamm walked through the group and mixed up the pairs, to the groans of the whole group. Once he was satisfied with the pairs, he stepped back into the middle of the V. "Who wants to go first to demonstrate for the rest of the group?"

"What about Phoebe and Dev?" Eliana grabbed my and Dev's hands and started pulling us forward. "I think they should demonstrate for us."

"No, that's okay." I shot a death glare at Eliana. "These exercises are for you guys. We already did this back when we were going into sixth grade." I looked over at Dev for help, but he just shrugged.

"Which is why you'll be perfect demonstrators," Diana said, reaching over to poke her partner's arm until he nodded in reluctant agreement. "See? Even Mark agrees."

Mr. Hamm nodded thoughtfully and gestured for Dev and me to come to the front with him. "That's actually a great idea."

Ms. Forrester gestured at us to get moving towards the narrow end of the rope V. "Don't worry, Mr. Hamm and I will talk you through the whole thing. And you'll have spotters." She nodded at the four kids Mr. Hamm was organizing around the ropes.

"Why don't you say anything to try and get us out of this?" I whispered to Dev as we made our way to the tree. "You're good at convincing teachers about anything."

"It sounds like fun." Dev looked over at me with an amused grin. "Or don't you trust me?"

"I don't trust trust exercises that involve being off the

ground, even if it's only a little bit off the ground."

"You're not instilling confidence in the campers," Dev pointed out, nodding over at my cabin and how they were watching us with wide eyes and huge grins. Little stinking mini-Em wannabes.

"Believe me, my campers don't need help when it comes to confidence."

Eliana made a whooping sound and Dev snorted. He nodded at me, conceding how right I was.

"Ready?"

"Not really." Maeve would hop onto the rope like it was nothing—heck, she'd probably find a way to do this whole ropes course on her own in a way that would make Aedan marvel yet again at her skills. But Maeve was actually athletic. Meanwhile, there was a massive chance I'd break my ankle. I climbed up onto the rope, hugging the tree with my left arm to keep my balance. "Remember, you're the coordinated one." *Forget that fear exists.*

"You're the one with insane hand-eye coordination." Dev jumped onto his rope and took my right hand like he was pulling me into a dance. My chest pressed against his and it really was like we were dancing. "It's okay. I got you," he said, and his breath tickled my cheek in a way that made a shiver run through my whole body.

Suddenly, breaking my leg or trying to be like Maeve flew to the back of my mind and I had to work on breathing, instead.

"On three, let go of the tree, grab my hand, and start

shuffling down the rope." He tested his balance and wobbled, swinging his body as he tried to balance. "Whoa." He let go of my hand and tumbled off the rope, but thanks to my death-grip on the trunk and his instinctive grab at my waist to keep me upright, I stayed on my rope. "Sorry, lost my balance," he said, sounding out of breath. He brushed up close against me, setting every one of my nerves on fire as he stepped back onto his rope and got back into position.

One of the campers let off a wolf-whistle as he took my hand again, and I heard Diana say, "I think he just touched her butt."

That made me look up at Dev, whose face was growing redder by the second. "I didn't, um, did I?" he asked, haltingly.

I wanted the ground under us to turn into quicksand so I could jump in and disappear. "No…no, you didn't." Ms. Forrester was saying something about balance and planks and working together but neither of us was paying her any attention.

His entire body shifted with a relieved exhale. "Good. Because…" he broke off and cleared his throat before putting on his serious game-face. "Okay, let's get this over with. On three? One, two," and with his three, I let go of the tree and fumbled for his other hand as we wobbled like we were trying to balance on jelly.

"Lean into each other," Mr. Hamm called out.

I choked back a laugh. If we leaned any closer, the kids would have even more stuff to giggle about.

"Lock your arms and keep moving," Ms. Forrester added as she joined Mr. Hamm in the center of the V to catch us in case we fell.

I fought the urge to lean back and away from the buzz that ran across my skin he closer I came to Dev and forced myself to lean into him while pushing against his hands. Dev kept his eyes trained on the ground while I split my attention between his face and his feet.

The thirty seconds of moving down the rope took a lifetime. Before we got to the point where we were leaning at over forty-five degree angles to each other, Dev stepped off his rope. He held his grip steady until I was back on solid ground, then quickly let go of my hands. "Let's stop while we're ahead," he said.

"Good idea."

"See? Easy, right?" Ms. Forrester didn't seem to notice our awkward shuffling and, without waiting for a response, turned to the campers. "Now, it's your turn. Any volunteers?"

Mr. Hamm clapped Dev on the shoulder and nodded at me as he passed us. "Good job. Take a break, you two. We've got them from here."

"Thanks." I picked my way over to a fallen log behind the rope tree and sat, trying to ignore the possibility of crawly things on it. The log was the perfect spot to watch my campers without getting sucked into another demonstration.

Dev followed, looking down at me with a quirky smile. "See? I told you it would be okay. We make a good team."

Something in my chest warmed at that last line, but I

tried not to let it show on my face. "Except for the whole falling thing."

"I was the one that fell, not you. You're better at a lot of things than you think you are."

I picked at a mushroom-y thing growing out of the log. Hopefully it wasn't something poisonous that would go through my skin and kill me on the spot. "Not fire making."

"We can work on that," he said.

"Or I can just carry around matches all the time in case I'm ever stranded in the wilderness without," a flirty line popped into my head, reminding me to be more like Marissa, and I threw caution to the wind and said it before I could chicken out, "a big strong scout like you." I fake-batted my eyelashes, and put my hand to my chest in a mock-swoon. Marissa always threw those kind of harmless, cute, funny lines to Dan after they became just friends. Friends could totally flirt-joke with each other.

"Ha. Nice." He sat down next to me with only an arm's breadth of space between us and propped his elbows on his knees. "I actually used to suck at wilderness things, if you'd believe it."

"You?

"Don't let my perfect veneer of confidence fool you." He shrugged, then continued, "This is going to sound stupid, but I had to trick myself into believing I could actually do things like build fires." He looked down at his hands, his fingers picking apart a piece of bark, his lips turned up the tiniest bit. "One thing I'm really good at is acting."

I rocked on the log, curious to see where this was going to go. "Now you're starting to sound like Em."

He twisted his nose in faux-disapproval until I made a zipping motion across my lips. "I decided that maybe I could try acting like I knew what I was doing. I wasn't Dev-the-guy-who-couldn't-hike. I was Dev-the-outdoor-guru. And after a little bit, it actually worked." The bark fluttered in pieces from his hands down to the ground. "It doesn't work for everything, like calculus, but it helps. I'm not so afraid of messing up, you know?"

Me-as-Marissa leaned sideways and bumped him gently with my shoulder. "Actually, I do."

He tilted his head to smile at me and I smiled back, forgetting about rope courses and possibly poisonous mushrooms and Lexies for a few moments.

"Dev, I'm sorry, I know I told you to take a break, but can you help spot these two?" Ms. Forrester's voice broke the silence between us, and Dev popped up to standing so quickly, it jarred me back into reality.

"Sure, Ms. Forrester, on my way." Dev looked over his shoulder at me and said, "Be right back. Don't let any strange counselors take my spot," before bounding off to help with two of the tallest kids in the group.

"I...won't," I said, lamely, but he was already hard at work smiling and charming the campers. He definitely didn't hear me.

45

Flames licked the night sky as Dev and some of the teachers added more logs to the giant bonfire. I had a front-row seat, which meant that my face was starting to feel hot and I had to duck flying embers every time another log was added to the pile. At least it kept me from creepily staring at Dev.

"I cannot wait for this week to be over," Cassie said as she slid onto the rough log next to me. "The only bright spot to this entire thing is that Mike's also counseling here and he switched so we could be co-counselors."

Her sudden appearance and rapid speech gave me whiplash. "Mike?" I asked dumbly.

Cassie laughed like I had asked her who the president of the United States was. "Mike Lyons? You know, our football team's fullback? My boyfriend. The guy I mentioned the first night?"

"Oh, yeah."

"Every time I want to strangle one of these brats, he talks me down. God, I have a cabin full of terrors."

"Really?" I looked over at the group of girls a few logs over comparing the gimp lanyards they'd made during break that afternoon. None of them looked menacing. "They seem pretty nice."

"That's because they're in public." She waved away some of the smoke that came our way with a cough. "They pranked one of the girls the other night so badly, I spent half the night cleaning up shaving cream from her bunk. And that one over there," she pointed at a girl wearing a daisy crown, "is a mouth-breather. Oh my gosh, I just had to leave the other night to go hang out with Mike because I couldn't take her breathing anymore."

"You don't have a girl named Mary in your cabin, do you?" I asked, remembering what Bethany One had said the other night.

"That's the mouth-breather. Why?"

"I think she's friends with some of the girls in my cabin."

"Do you want to take her?" She asked with a contagious grin.

"Sorry, I'm all out of bunks."

"Earplugs for the rest of this camp it is, then."

Thinking about what my campers said about the other counselors, I said, slowly, "Have you tried talking to them on the same level as, like, me or Mike?"

"You mean act like I'm their friend? Because that doesn't exactly scream 'responsible camp counselor.'"

I almost said, *Neither does leaving the cabin to be with your boyfriend and expecting them to cover for you,* but I bit back that reply. Cassie was too nice to deserve snark. "No, I mean don't talk to them like they're kids. I think, maybe, if you treat them like kids, they'll only act like little kids."

"You're starting to sound like Grace." At my surprised head-tilt, she added, "You know, giving calm, logical advice that assumes the whole rest of the world is logical, including me?" She tossed a piece of bark in the direction of the campfire and turned back to face me, propping her hands onto her knees in a listening pose. "Anyway, I'm tired of talking about campers. How's the ex-crush thing working out for you? It kind-of sucks that you were stuck with him."

I glanced back at my campers, some of whom were avidly listening in. Diana gave me an almost cartoonish wink before going back to talking with one of the boys from Dev's cabin. "Yeah, it does."

"And Kris?"

This time, I tried not to look at the girls. I didn't need them getting involved in yet another one of my personal dramas. Instead, I picked out his familiar dark hair on the other side of the fire pit. "I'm so over him."

"That bad, huh?" When I didn't give any details, she patted my arm in a way I guessed was supposed to be sympathetic. "It's better that way. Anyone who hates us athletes isn't even worth talking to. Anyway, I have to get back to my cabin before they set themselves on fire or something, but I wanted to check on you. Party in the woods later tonight? We can get away from the kids. I promise it will be more awesome than last time," she paused, waiting for my answer.

"Um, maybe?" *Not*, I added silently. But, instead, I smiled as she waved and bounced off to the other side of the horseshoe of log seats.

"You're not going to leave us to go party, are you?" Bethany One crept over from her bench and took Cassie's vacated seat.

"Right, like I'd ask you guys to promise me you won't sneak out, and then go do that myself." Plus, I didn't need a repeat of the first night.

"And you're a geek," Eliana added, making it sound like it was a good thing.

"I guess."

We were then hushed by one of the teachers, who started lecturing us with a history/geography lesson about the Pine Barrens. Just as the kids started shifting around in boredom, he broke into a story about the most famous occupant, the thirteenth Leeds child, "better known as the Jersey Devil."

Like every other kid from the area, I had grown up on stories of the Jersey Devil. As the teachers and some of the counselors took turns telling different stories, I curled my arms happily around my knees, basking in the familiar tales. The crackle and pop of the bonfire accompanied the storytellers' hushed voices and turned the pines and oaks surrounding us into shadowy outlines. Even the lake was mirror-still. The perfect setting for a horned monster to swoop in.

A familiar silhouette replaced Mr. Hamm. Dev was in his element, his very stature transforming as he took center stage in front of the bonfire. A delicious shiver ran over my skin as his voice carried over us, low and creepy.

"Every seven years, when a blue mist rises off of the

lake, the Jersey Devil comes searching for his next victim." Every head turned towards the lake, where the moonlight made the fog rising off of it look a pale, pale blue. Whispers started working through the crowd. Dev continued with a serious expression. "The last time a camper disappeared from the Barrens without a trace was on a night just like this one. *Seven years ago.*" Bethany One's nails dug into my palm. "Tonight, as we gather around the bonfire, watch your backs. Because the Jersey Devil is wandering and hungry for his next kill. *Beware.*"

On those words, bodies leapt out of the woods and Bethany One, along with most of the campers, let off a deafening scream. My own heart jumped into my throat and I had to take deep breaths to make my heart rate go back to normal. When the light from the bonfire revealed some of the counselors standing around us draped in black tablecloths, the kids started laughing. The other male counselors surrounded Dev, making gruesome faces accentuated by sticking flashlights under their chins. With a final cackle and a bunch of moans, Dev and the other guys slunk back into the shadows until it was just the bonfire and silence.

After an appropriately creepy period of time, Mrs. Forrester asked us to break back into our cabin groups to move to the smaller fires in the field behind us to roast marshmallows. While Dev was busy lighting the fires—*with matches*, my brain noted—I herded our cabins over to one. Unlike in high school, the girls and boys automatically separated like oil and water, the boys taking the far side of the fire and three-quarters of the marshmallows.

My cabin crowded around me, wielding their roasting twigs like stakes. Genevieve, who was usually one of the quieter ones, stepped forward and put her hands on her hips. "Enough with this secrecy. Half of the people in our cabin think they know what's going on with you and Dev. Why don't you set the record straight for once and for all?"

"Because it's my private life?" At their defiant looks, I sighed. I was facing a wall of pure pre-teen stubbornness. "If I tell you, will you stop bothering me?"

"Depends on what you tell us," Diana said, but when Giselle elbowed her in the side, she screwed up her lip and nodded.

Checking out of the corner of my eye to make sure Dev was still busy doing bonfire-y stuff, I tore open the bag of marshmallows and started handing them to the girls as I spoke.

"Start toasting marshmallows so it doesn't look weird while I'm talking." Some of the girls waved away the marsh-mallows, grabbing doughnut holes from the box behind us and started toasting those instead. "Oooooh-kay, whatever floats your boat. Anyway..." I closed my eyes for a second. I couldn't believe I was going to do this. "Once upon a time, there was a geeky book nerd." The boys from Dev's cabin started making torches out of their marshmallows and I spoke faster. He'd be back any minute now, or I'd have to rush one of the boys to the first aid station. Either way, I didn't have much time. "This nerd also happened to be a knitter who taught knitting classes to pay for her yarn and book addictions. She was very happy crushing on cute guys who looked like book characters, until her best friend messed it all up."

"I like crushing on book hotties like Evan," Bethany Two said softly around a mouthful of marshmallow. I smiled at her and nodded. I loved my mini-me book nerd camper.

"Her friend had to ruin her perfect bookish happiness by telling her that a non-book-boyfriend-y boy was the perfect love interest for her. And knitterly girl, after much protesting about her shyness, agreed to try to woo him. This knitter tried smiling, being nice, and even acting like her favorite romantically successful book characters, but the boy never asked her out. Instead, he teased her, always asking her to knit him a pair of socks. So, what was a shy, knitterly girl to do?"

"She asked him out?" Genevieve asked, eyes wide.

I tilted my head and gave her a grin. "No. She knit him socks." I said it like it was the most natural thing in the world, though it really did sound ridiculous.

"Ohmigosh, you *are* such a wimp." Came a voice from the group, overlapping with someone else's "What happened?"

"He ended up dating another girl, who was a lot bolder than knitterly girl and actually kept hanging around him instead of knitting and reading books. So, knitterly girl went back to reading books about cute boys and they all lived bookishly ever after. The end."

"Telling fairy tales? Or leprechaun stories?" Dev asked teasingly as he passed us, but he didn't wait for the answer as he rushed over to where his campers were building a multi-marshmallow torch by melting and sticking marshmallows together until they made a giant blob on the end of one of their skewers.

I froze, cold dread washing over me like an early fall wind on Prince Edward Island's cliffs. Giselle took in my expression and shook her head.

"I don't think he heard anything important."

"And what if he did?" Bethany One asked. "Maybe you'll finally get together because of it."

"He has a girlfriend, Bethany," I said tiredly.

"We'll see about that." Lilliana practically skipped over the invisible line the boys and girls had drawn and looked up at Dev while he was busy confiscating the bag of marshmallows. Before I could stop her, she drew up by his elbow and smiled innocently at him. "Dev, do you have a girlfriend?" I dropped onto the closest wooden stump and prayed that no one could see the abject horror that had to be written across my face.

He smiled distractedly at her. "I think you're a little bit young for me, Lilli." He pulled another bag of marshmallows from a hole in one of the log benches. "Where the heck did you guys get all these?" he asked the boys, only to get innocent shrugs.

Lilliana giggled. "I don't want to date you, silly, I'm just curious. All the girls are, because you're really good looking.

The girls at your school have to think you're cute, too." My jaw dropped at how sugary-sweet she made her voice, freakishly innocent and younger sounding.

Dev fell for it. "Sadly, no," he winked at her. "You can tell the other girls that I'm not dating anyone, but I only date tenth graders and up."

"Like Phoebe?" I was going to kill that girl. Strangle her. Or throw her in the lake. Or roast her over the bonfire.

Dev looked across the bonfire at me, but I couldn't see his expression in the light and shadows of the fire.

"Oh, Phoebe is too smart to date a guy like me," he told Lilliana lightly.

I wanted to melt into the sugar sand under my feet as Lilliana turned and gave me a thumbs-up.

46

"Phoebe... Feebs, wake up." An insistent voice broke through my dreams and my eyes shot open. The wood and screen walls around me registered as unfamiliar to my brain, as did the shadowed face that seemed to be hovering just at my side. I started to scream but a hand reached through the screen and covered my mouth. "Feebs, it's me. Calm down."

Oh, right. Dev. And camp. And he had just used my nickname for the first time ever, which my sleepy brain hadn't expected. I pushed his hand away and fumbled for my glasses. No longer blind, I sat up, checking to make sure none of the girls had woken up because of us. When I was satisfied they were still asleep, I turned back towards the window. Dev pulled his arm back through a hole between the screen and the wooden frame. Some protection *that* turned out to be. "What?" I mouthed at him, gesturing to the sleeping cabin and giving him the universal sign for "What the heck?"

"Come out here for a few. I need your help."

I caught his eyes as best I could in this lighting and, after a second's stare-down, sighed. "Give me a minute." I threw a hoodie over my flannel pajamas and slipped my feet into a pair of sneakers. Checking one last time that the girls were all still asleep, I stepped outside.

"Over here." Dev waved from the walking path and I carefully made my way over. Grogginess plus clumsiness plus random pieces of wood and rocks were definitely a bad combination. As I got closer, I could make out his shorts and sweatshirt combo. Even in the middle of the night he looked gorgeous, especially with the shadow of stubble across his chin and tousled hair. Me, on the other hand…

"Nice pajamas."

"Uhm. Yeah. Thanks." I tugged at my Hello Kitty pajama pants with one hand while trying to tame my Bride of Frankenstein hair with the other. All of that, plus my glasses, definitely made me *not* gorgeous. "Why are we out here in the middle of the night?" Where I didn't want to be. He supposedly didn't have a girlfriend, which meant I was pretty much a flat-out reject. Now, I was a Hello Kitty pants-wearing reject.

A wide grin spread across his face.

"We're playing Jersey Devil."

I knew I had just woken up and was still a bit groggy, but that made absolutely no sense. I stared at him with a frown until he continued. "You know, tradition. The counselors always go around the cabins leaving footprints after the bonfire." He held up a stick with a shape at the end that looked like a three-clawed foot. "Mrs. Forrester asked me to do it and I thought you might want in on this."

Right. The stories at the bonfire. So *that* was where the footprints had come from when I was a camper. I opened my mouth to say no—my warm sleeping bag and a chance to not expose him any further to my freakish middle of the night look were definitely tempting, but then he caught my eyes. The smile he gave me made it impossible not to agree. I covered my sigh with a yawn.

"What do you need me to do?" Another yawn, then I pulled myself together. If Maeve could battle a *Gancanagh* in her underwear, I could make a few footprints in my pajamas.

"Awesome. I knew I could count on you." He reached behind a tree and handed me a broom. "Your job is to get rid of our footprints."

"Got it." I took the broom from him with one hand while zipping my hoodie up the rest of the way with the other. "I don't want to ruin our chance to terrify a group of eleven year olds."

"Tradition, Feebs. You can't be a piney kid without having at least one run-in with the Jersey Devil." He yawned, not bothering to cover his mouth. "If we hurry, we can still get an hour or two of sleep before reveille."

"Joy. Let's get this over with." I followed him down the path, my eyes glued to the ground and, occasionally to the back of his bare legs. "Aren't you cold?" I asked. I had slipped my own hands into my sleeves. A cool wind was whipping between the cabins.

He shrugged, "Nah, I'm hot tonight."

My eyes wandered upwards for a second and I suppressed the urge to say, *Yes, you are.* I blinked a few times and forced my eyes back on to the path.

"So, why'd you pick me to help out? Adam or Cassie would love this. They'd probably even figure out ways to put footprints on the cabin roofs or something."

He looked back at me over his shoulder and his teeth shone in the moonlight. "You're my counseling partner. It's my job to bring more excitement into your life."

My heart nearly skipped a beat and I stumbled. Straightening up again, I ducked my head so he couldn't see my red cheeks. "Um, I think we need to work on your reading comprehension skills. I don't think you read the job description right."

"It's an added perk of the job. Counsel some kids, make you take your nose out of those books of yours…"

"I take my nose out of books!" It was hard to sound indignant when speaking in a whisper.

"'Reading comprehension?' Who *says* stuff like that?"

I stuck my nose up in the air to give myself a snobbish appearance. "People who want A's in English."

He poked me with the foot-stick. "Just sweep, book nerd."

We worked in silence for the next few minutes, Dev laying down trails of "footprints" around the cabins, me sweeping away any trace of our non-devil existence. After we finished with the girls' cabins, we started the trek around the lake to the boys' cabins. When we were far enough from any cabin, I tilted my head to stare at the perfectly clear sky above us.

"I love how the stars and the moon are so much brighter

out here. It's like you can practically reach out and touch them," I said, when the tension of the silence between us got to be too much. "I never can tell if the moon's waxing or waning."

"The moon is a liar," he said under his breath. Dev had stopped walking and was also staring at the perfect crescent in the sky.

"Excuse me?" I turned my focus from the sky to his shadowed profile.

"The moon's a liar," he repeated, this time in his regular voice. "You know crescendo and decrescendo, right? Like, the way they work in music?"

I tilted my head and snorted inelegantly, cringing at my faux pas. "No. I've only played flute for seven years."

"Nice sarcasm."

"I learned from Em." I brushed at imaginary lint on my shoulder and fake-polished my nails on my sleeve.

"Why doesn't that surprise me?" He flashed me a grin before tracing the moon's silhouette with his finger. "What letter is the moon making right now? C or D?"

That was a weird question, but I gamely played along. "It looks like a C."

"C, like crescendo. That means the moon is waning. Decrescendo-ing. Because the moon just lied to you."

"Huh."

"So now you know."

He started walking again and I hurried to come up alongside him. Damn his longer legs. "How did you learn that trick?"

Dev gave me a sheepish smile. "Every time I visited my grandparents on their plantation in India, my grandfather would wake me up and drag me out to the fields in the middle of the night to teach me about the stars. He used to be an astronomer." He lifted an open palm to the sky. "The sky there was kind of like this, with no artificial lights to fade it out." This Dev was quiet and serious, almost reverent, while he spoke.

I could just picture little Dev in his pajamas staring at the sky. "It sounds beautiful."

"It is. I love going there—it's kind of magical. It has the biggest, clearest sky on the planet. The poinsettia bushes lining the drive to their house are as tall as you. Butterflies are everywhere. And when the bougainvillea is in bloom, it's like snow is swirling around you as you walk up to the house."

"You should write that down. I'd definitely love to read about that."

"Nah, I'm not good at writing. I'm good at making words and music come to life."

"The acting thing. That's why you and Lexie get along so well."

He faltered a step and tried to cover it up with a cool expression. "And me and Em and all the other theatre geeks."

"Yeah, but aren't you and Lexie closer than you and Em?" I asked, forcing my tone to stay light. I picked up a rock and tossed it into the lake so it made a satisfying plunk. Like my heart in a minute.

"Lexie's cool, but she can get kind of needy. I don't really know why she invited herself over to our lunch table like she did." *Our* lunch table. I froze midway through throwing another rock. Dev's expression smoothed into something that was frustratingly impossible to read again. "Why are we talking about Lexie?"

This time, I shrugged. *Remember, no matter what, you still didn't interest him enough to ask you out,* a little voice warned me. But the tiniest bubble of hope rose up in me. "I'm not sure. C'mon, we have kids to scare." I kept my eyes on the lake so he couldn't really see my face or the tiny smile that threatened to break through. *Maybe he really is just shy.*

Maeve's breath came in short bursts, freezing in little clouds that were barely visible in the twilight. It was impossible for the *Dullahan* to miss her, considering she was standing in the middle of the road, but a primal part of her wanted to hold her breath and hide any sign she was there. With shaking hands, she pulled off her golden torque and closed her eyes as she rubbed its braided surface one last time before slipping it into her bag. The *Dullahan* may have found a way to make himself immune to gold, but she wasn't going to risk turning him away.

The rush of demonic horse's hooves carried on the wind towards her and she widened her stance, pushing back the urge to throw up as she drew her sword. "*Your chances of dying are about ninety-five percent,*" Sibeal's words came back to her, and she tightened her grip on the sword so much that the hilt's leather wrapping cut into her palm, "*but, the good news is, if he beheads you, the energy released by the evil of his blade touching the good of your blood will make everything go boom.*"

Either her powers would destroy him or her blood would. One way or another, she was going to stop him. She was the Harper. Her powers were the stuff of legend, and she'd be damned if her courage didn't live up to those same legends. Maeve pulled back her shoulders and shook off the last of her fear as a dark shadow came into her line of sight.

She was ready.

He was never going to hurt anyone in her or Aedan's worlds ever again.

If Maeve can risk her life
to fight a creepy Irish
headless horseman thing,
I can make it
through anything

47

The energy from the night before still danced across my skin. Dev and I had finished putting out the footprints and he walked me back around the lake. We had fallen into this weirdly comfortable silence that he would sometimes break to point out a constellation. He had even grabbed my hand to steady me when the moonlight wasn't enough to see all the ruts in the path, and hadn't let go until we were close to the girls' cabins. And all of that happened despite the fact that I'd completely forgotten to be Maeve or Marissa or anyone out of my notebook. I hadn't been able to sleep after practically floating back to bed and spent the night flipping through it and taking more notes. There had been something about the easy way that we were able to talk that almost made me feel like it was okay that I forgot for one night, but I wouldn't forget again.

I absently curled and uncurled my fingers, the ghost of his touch still there a few hours later. After working so hard to push him out of my head, now this whole camping thing brought me right back to December. I was in so much trouble.

"Phoebe, are you paying attention?"

I looked up sharply to see Dev gesturing at one of the campers who was trying to position herself on the crawling rope bridge.

"Sorry." I reached out to steady the two ropes that hung in parallel above the small creek and almost jostled the camper still making his way across. Smooth.

That camper climbed off of the bridge and threw a dirty look my way before high-fiving Dev and heading off to join his classmates in the next challenge.

The girl on my bank, watching the whole exchange, looked at me with a little bit of fear before starting to cross. While I was useless and a potential danger to them, Dev was so good with the kids, encouraging them and treating them as if they were the same age as us. The guys fist-bumped him as soon as they reached the other side, the girls blushed and giggled as he reached out and lifted them off of the ropes and onto solid ground. He really was a little bit like Evan from *Cradled*. Actually, a lot, if Evan played clarinet and didn't farm and was Indian instead of Scotch- Canadian. The absolutely perfect love interest.

"Last one!" Dev called out as I steadied the ropes for one of the boys.

"Thank goodness." As soon as the camper was most of the way across the creek, I stood and checked behind me. He was right, no more campers. "What was that supposed to teach them, anyway? How to get muddy?"

Dev glanced up from his clipboard with barely concealed amusement on his face. "Concentration and balance.

It's really not bad. Haven't you ever gone across a two rope bridge before?" In the noon sunlight, his teeth were bright white against his tanned skin, already darker from our days outside.

I looked down. The dirt that had collected on my sneakers became endlessly fascinating. "Uh, no. I got 'sick' when we had to do it in sixth grade and skipped to the next obstacle."

His grin grew wider. "Well, we have a few minutes before they expect us at the mess. Give it a try."

I stared in horror at him. "No."

"I tried archery."

The heat rose again in my cheeks as the memory came rushing back. "Well, that's different. You can't get hurt doing archery."

"Tell that to my arm. That string hurt."

"Wimp."

He bounced the ropes in a way that was probably supposed to make them look inviting. "I know you'll regret it if you don't try. Do it for me?" He waggled his eyebrows in a way that made me want to giggle.

His grey-green eyes caught mine and I sighed. Why was it that I could never say no to this guy?

"Fine." I eyed the bridge warily. The ropes were low, like floppy parallel bars close to water that had mostly churned to a few inches of pure mud at this point. I bent over, getting a closer-than-usual whiff of the earthy decaying plant smell of the creek. "Seriously, Dev, I don't know about this..."

"C'mon. It's easier than starting a fire."

"Ha. Very funny, Nature Boy." But as I spoke, I leaned over until I was almost horizontal to the creek. I arranged myself on top of the ropes the same way we had taught the kids, those two ropes the only things between me and an instant soaking. I closed my eyes and took a deep breath—I was Maeve, strong and beautiful and, just like in Chapter Thirty of *Glittering*, ready to face anything.

"You know, you have to move if you want to make it across the bridge," Dev called out with a chuckle.

"I was just getting my balance." I said before starting to pull myself across the bridge. I got about a yard in before the ropes wobbled under me, and my leg splashed into the creek, water seeping into my sneaker. "Oh, frak!"

"Frak? Do you ever actually curse?"

I looked up at him with a grimace. The water actually felt slimy. "I say frak all the time."

He coughed, but I could tell he was covering up a laugh. "That's not a curse. That's a *Battlestar Galactica* reference."

"Well, frak you."

That time, he did laugh. "You're doing okay. Just wrap that leg back onto the rope and keep going." I looked up. He had crouched down on his side of the creek, his hands held out encouragingly, as if he could pull me across with the sheer force of his will.

I grit my teeth and pulled myself back onto the two ropes. Eleven year olds had gotten across this thing with only a splash or two and I had almost six years on them. I could totally do it. My arms burned as I tried to drag myself forward in the weird froggy-crawly motion Dev had used in his demo. Another half a yard and the ropes unbalanced and twisted again, flipping me over so I landed directly under them, butt-deep in muddy water. A choked, almost laugh-like sound came from the opposite bank, but when I checked, Dev still had that serious, supportive expression on his face.

I was wet and soggy from head to toe. My counselor polo was spattered with mud and clung in an unflattering way to my chest. My one pair of cute jeans was now covered in a layer of mud. I had to be honest with myself—even if Dev could see past my knitting stuff, the geekiness, and the whole book thing, how I looked at this moment was probably just icing on the cake. I should have gotten up, walked away, and tried to preserve a scrap of my dignity, but then a little laugh bubbled up in me. The universe really had a sick sense of humor.

Dev's brows were drawn together in confusion and worry. "Are you okay over there? Do you need me to help you up?"

"No, no..." I laughed, squeezing out words between giggles. The whole situation was ridiculous. "Just hold the ropes steady so I can get back on without flipping over again." Maeve wouldn't have given up, and at this point neither would I.

"Are you sure?"

"Positive." I pulled myself to standing, dissolving into

another round of giggles at the suction-y sound that accompanied dragging my butt up out of the mud. "Like you said, I can do this." I plopped back onto the ropes, the mud making them slippery on top of being wobbly. Keeping my eyes trained on his, I slowly made my way across the creek.

It only took three or four more falls into the mud to get to the other side.

Dev reached out a hand to help me out, pulling me up off of the bridge as if I weighed nothing. "That was...interesting," he said, giving my very muddy form a once-over. "Are you really okay?"

I squeezed water out of my limp and stringy ponytail. "I'm fine. Wet, but—" I plopped onto the ground beside his feet and rolled up the soggy legs of my jeans, cursing at the sight before me. "Oh, frak, these are handknit. And Malabrigo." I tugged at my now stained socks, the colorway unrecognizable under all of the mud and silt.

He sat next to me on the bank. "You wore handknit socks to go camping?"

I shrugged, slipping off my sneaker to assess the rest of the damage. "Normal socks give you blisters and wool gets warmer when it's wet. Plus, I kitchener the toe, which is so much better than the seam on commercial socks..." I trailed off, realizing I was babbling and that he was looking at me strangely again. "Um, yeah, it's a knitter thing. I know it sounds strange..."

"It is," he agreed, but instead of walking away like I thought he would, he reached over and wiped a glob of mud off of my forehead. "You know, you really are unique, Feebs."

My skin tingled where he had touched it, but I pushed that feeling away, trying to focus on not turning into a whimpering puddle of knitterly geek. At least I had that much self-respect.

"Thanks," I said, dryly.

He kicked at my sock-clad foot, not meeting my eyes. "I like unique."

My head shot up. What?

He paused for a moment before continuing, as if he— Dev, the hottie of the entire clarinet section, the guy who could have any girl in the marching band or theatre club— was trying to drum up the guts to say something to me. Sock-knitting, book-reading, hadn't been on a date—like, ever—me.

"Most girls would have stopped the first time that they fell off of that thing. You didn't. That's impressive."

"Lexie wouldn't have fallen at all." I shivered as a stiff breeze blew over us. It wasn't too cold out, but being wet didn't help with staying warm.

He laughed. "What is it with you always bringing up Lexie?" He reached over and started rubbing my arms to help me warm up.

I turned as still as a statue, heat rushing over me. Suddenly, I didn't notice the cold. "I thought you two liked each other." I sucked in a breath.

He finally looked up, his eyes greener than ever as they reflected the barrens around us.

"Phoebe…" he reached over, flicking another blob of mud off my nose where it had settled in the last minute, "I don't like Lexie as anything more than a friend."

"Oh." What would Maeve do? I mentally scanned through my library of heroines and landed on Marissa. What would Marissa do?

Dev kept staring at me, a frown tugging at his lips. "You didn't think that she and I were dating, did you?"

I shook my head, still praying that some Marissa-wisdom would pop into my head. "No, I mean, kind of. I mean, I saw you two on New Years." Oh, hell. Somehow, every plot in the *Hidden House* series had totally flown out of my head. I was so screwed. "You know how Em and I are always trying to keep up with everything going on with all of our friends." And the horrible attempt at butt-saving babble started. "I mean, we're still trying to figure out who Alec's been crushing on, and you should have seen us with Grace and—"

"Got it," he said. His frown grew a little deeper and he stood, holding out his hand to help me. "You need to get cleaned up and I need to get over to the mess to supervise our table."

"Right." I waved his hand away. "I can do this." I pushed myself to standing, my footing a little bit uncertain between my wet sneakers, the mud, and the sand.

Dev reached out to steady me and my arms slipped in his hands, making me fall against him. "Frakin' mud," he choked out but laughed as he tried to straighten me up and slipped again. After another few moments of wobbliness, he dragged us both onto the relatively dry sugar sand.

I couldn't help it. His shirt was now stained with a me-shaped imprint and I pressed a cold, muddy hand against his face and back into his hair with a giggle. I was giddy, an electric buzz running from my stomach and practically shooting out of my fingers and toes. "I think you missed a spot."

He stealth-grabbed a blob of mud from my shirt and squished it into my ponytail. "So did you. Why are we friends when you're so mean to me?" he asked, staring down at me with a faux-serious expression.

I swatted at that serious nose with a muddy finger and giggled so much that my side started to hurt. I was punch-drunk from the falls into the creek, or maybe there was something off about the water. Whichever one, some part of me that I couldn't seem to control took over. Marissa would be proud. I leaned closer, feeling the heat rising off of his body.

"I have no idea. That's okay, when you're a big Bollywood star, you can talk about the mean girl back home who threw mud at you. And did this." With a nudge from my hip, Dev lost his balance on the bank and landed with a splash flat on his butt on the shallow edge of the creek. The wide-eyed, O-mouthed expression on his face as he hit the water made me curl over with even more hiccup-y laughter.

Dev wiped the back of his hand across his face, spreading a streak of mud across his forehead.

"Oh, now that's grounds for payback." Instead of getting up, he swiped a leg under my feet and, with a totally non-Marissa-like screech, I was back in the water and practically on his lap. And while his fall only got him a little wet, I managed to splash another layer of silty mud onto myself.

Scooping up a handful of mud and decayed plant-goo, I scooted closer to him and held it up like a baseball. "You did *not* just do that. You're supposed to be the nice counselor." Even though the water was cold, being this close to him made me feel like I was in a sauna.

Dev bumped my shoulder with his so I had to drop my "weapon" just to keep from getting submerged again. "I like this mud-slinging you. You know, sometimes you make yourself unapproachable. You're always so deep in your own world that it's hard to break in."

I looked up at him and, unbidden, one of Kaylie's lines straight out of *Cradled on the Waves* popped out of my mouth.

"Am I unapproachable now?" Oh my God, I did *not* just say that. It was the mud or the sun or this temporary insanity that dragged me into that book moment.

The corner of his mouth turned up slightly and he swiped some mud under my eyes, warrior-style. But his fingers lingered on my cheek. "Not so much." He tilted his head closer to mine and I froze. This wasn't like anything I've read about or planned. Still, every single molecule in my body took over, anticipating his movement, and I stretched up to meet him. We were a breath away from each other.

"Oh, there you two are. What happened here?" Mr. Hamm's voice broke the silence and I jumped away from

Dev, scrambling ungracefully onto the creek's bank. Flames of embarrassment rushed over me and I tried wiping my face with my wet and muddy sleeve.

Dev, looking a lot more composed than I felt, stood, wiped his hands on a dry part of his shirt and turned to face the teacher. "I goaded Phoebe into trying the bridge and, um, she fell in a few times. And then I fell in when I tried to help her."

Mr. Hamm took in both of our appearances and looked like he was trying not to laugh. "I'm used to seeing a few campers get muddy, but this is a first."

"And a last. I'm not athletic enough for something like this. I'm sticking with archery." I was finally steady enough to walk back over to them. I gave Dev a sidelong glance. He didn't seem flustered at all. Maybe I had just imagined the whole moment between us.

"Good idea. How about you go get cleaned up and I'll get one of the other counselors to help Dev with your table until you get back?" Mr. Hamm frowned at Dev. "You're not too much of a mess."

Dev tugged at his polo. The me-shaped mud was drying and flaking at the edges. "Sure. I'll grab a fresh shirt and jeans on the way over." He nodded at me. "See you in a few, Feebs."

After the two left, I turned and headed for my cabin and the communal camp showers, turning the last few moments over and over in my head. Maybe all of these books full of fictional romances were starting to get to me.

Dev was probably just joking around, like he did with all of his friends.

That still didn't make the goose bumps on my skin go away, or the ghost of his touch on my cheek. I shuffled my way to the showers. I needed to wash away the memory with the mud. Not even bothering to strip off my muddy clothes or sneakers, I stuck myself under the running water.

48

Lunch was half over by the time I reached the mess hall. I grabbed a hobo hamburger and that watered-down stuff we called bug juice and made my way over to our long table, acutely conscious of how I looked. No spare shoes meant that I had to wear my flip-flops until my sneakers dried, oh-so-fashionable with a pair of striped toe socks. My hair dripped down my back, the drying pieces starting to stand out halo-like around my head. And my shorts stood out in a mess hall full of jeans. Grace would have had a heart attack if she saw me right then.

"And the mudwoman returneth," Dev said, sliding over to make room for me next to him.

I pretended I didn't see him move and instead squeezed into a spot next to Bethany Two. I also pretended not to notice the confused look he gave me.

"That stuff took forever to get out of my hair," I said lightly and then bit into my burger. I was not going to act like this whole situation was awkward. Not if I could help it. The almost-kiss was probably all in my head.

Miranda grimaced at me. "We have to do the bridge this afternoon. And I don't like mud."

"Believe me, no one is as clumsy as Phoebe. You'll be fine." Dev told her. His hair still had visible patches of mud in spots and I resisted the urge to reach across the table and smooth a stick-y out piece into place.

"I didn't have anyone to steady the bridge for me on one side. I promise Dev and I will make sure it doesn't wobble on you," I said in a reassuring tone. In a fit of forced silliness, I pat my face dramatically. "Besides, mud does wonders for your complexion, you know."

"You're absolutely radiant, darling," Dev said in a mock British accent before a mini pickle-fight between two of the boys in his cabin had him running to the far end of the table.

I looked at my campers, who had been watching the conversation between Dev and me like it was a tennis match. "I'm so glad I got you guys and not them. At least when you drive me crazy, it doesn't involve food or fire."

Diana smiled over her glass of bug juice. "It's because girls are just so much more sophisticated."

Bethany Two poked me to get my attention. "Phoebe, I peeked at your copy of *Cradled on the Waves* and we're finally on the same part."

At the moment, I wanted to forget the book that was making me so dramatic and making me feel all the screwed-up feels as Kaylie and Evan's conflict and relationship built up in it. But I schooled my expression into a curious one.

"Really? What do you think so far?"

Bethany Two dropped her chin into her hands. "I think

Kaylie needs to stay on PEI with Evan. Maybe forever, if she becomes a permanent foreign exchange student."

"But she doesn't even know how Evan feels. He could just be acting like one of those stereotypical über-helpful and polite Canadian farmboys, eh?" The "eh" sounded weird. Maybe I was too South Jersey to "eh" properly.

She shook her head emphatically. "Oh, come *on*. The way they talked during the performance at the Indian River Festival? No way, he's totally into her. And the way he pushed back that loose strand of her hair at the bridge? That was H. O. T. *Hot.*" Pulling one hand out from under her chin, she fanned herself.

I smiled at her drama. This was my kind of camper. "The hair was in her face. He probably talks like that to every girl on the island."

"So, you really think she's right about wanting go to New York?" She paused and tilted her head. "I mean, we both know she's not going for the music program, because it's pretty obvious that working at the ceilidh and practicing with Evan is making her a better violinist, even if she doesn't know it." Her tongue tripped over ceilidh, pronouncing it "see-le-deh."

"It's kay-lee, like her name," I pointed out. "I think she has no idea how she feels and doesn't want to get played by anyone. Even someone who probably doesn't realize he's playing her," I said softly, willing myself not to look at Dev.

"No way. Evan's too nice to play anyone."

"I think she should stay wherever she is and give this

guy a chance," Dev said, dropping a handful of confiscated pickle slices onto his place as he sat down again.

I looked up sharply, wondered how much he heard, and hoped he didn't think I was projecting or anything. "You have no idea what we're talking about, do you?"

"Potato farmer book?"

"Ugh." He really had a memory like an elephant. "You should be on my side, then. You were the one who said Bollywood backup dancer beat potato farmer." I made little air-quotes as I spoke.

Dev's eyes met mine. "What's this girl afraid of, anyway?"

I didn't break his gaze. "Letting herself fall for him completely and then getting her heart and ego crushed." That came out softer than I had planned.

He let out a frustrated sound. "So, you'd rather have her throw away any chance with this guy because of the tiniest chance she could be reading him wrong?"

"No, she—" Bethany Two tried to break in, but failed.

"If the guy was more transparent and didn't keep leaving her wondering how he felt, she wouldn't be in this situation at all," I said.

Bethany Two tugged at my sleeve, but I brushed her hand away.

His mouth set in a straight line at the challenge. "Maybe she's just too dense to see the signs he keeps throwing at her."

"Maybe putting herself out there is too much to ask for just a few signs," I shot back.

"I bet potato farmer guy has put himself out there a few

times and this girl just blew him off like this hot-and-cold bookworm ice princess."

"She's a violinist, *not* a bookworm, and—"

"Guys? Guys!" Bethany Two's raised voice made us both turn our heads to face her, and that's when I realized that Dev and I were standing and practically nose-to-nose over the table. "It's just a book, you know."

Holy heavens above, half of the mess hall was watching us. Waves of embarrassment washed over me. "It's never just a book," I said under my breath as I sat down again.

"And, anyway, you're both getting the plot wrong. Evan and Kaylie aren't like that."

I surreptitiously looked up at Dev, who was busy twisting and untwisting his napkin. His lips relaxed from that straight line as he checked his watch. "Okay, guys, five minutes 'til the end of lunch. Anyone in the mood to rile up the other teams?"

Our entire table let off a chorus of "yeah"s and yeses except for Bethany Two and some of the other girls from my cabin, who were all watching me with matching smirks. The team cheer was some silly thing Dev had created that the kids loved to yell randomly throughout the day. Other teams tried to match it, resulting in a lot of off-key chanting through all of the activities. Usually, he used it to break up any arguments that might happen between the campers, but this time, he seemed to want to break the intense tension between us that hung in the air like the energy of a pending thunderstorm.

"Awesome. Let's make this loud and proud. Ready?"

Cups and trays rattled as the campers started stomping their feet under the table. "Team eight, team eight, team eight is really great. We're great in the morning, we're great at night, we're better than dynamite!" Thank God most of them were still too innocent to get any possible innuendo from that.

I cringed as the chant set off similar ones throughout the mess hall until I could barely think through all the noise. One-and-a-half more days. And then I could hide from him again.

I clutch at the bundle of lace and flowers in my hand as I make my way up to my room. If Cyril's not going to talk to me in modern terms, I'm going to talk his language. Mirror or not, this thing has dragged on way too long. My hands shake a little too much and some of the hydrangea petals flutter down to the carpet.

Good idea

I push into my room and hold the little bouquet behind my back with one hand while smoothing the skirt of my dress with the other. "Cyril?"

No matter how many times I see him, my heart still does a little flip when he walks into the mirror frame on his side. His eyes grow wide when he sees me, and I grow warm as he looks me up and down in a way that he never does when I'm wearing my normal clothes. "You are dressed very—"

"—old fashioned," I finish for him, resisting the urge to tug at my blouse's high neck or untie the bow at my collar. My black skirt is still short, but from midthigh up, I can probably pass for a girl from his time. I don't know how girls back then kept from overheating, especially when dressed like this around guys like him.

He smiles and nods. "Perhaps. But in my time, you'd never have an empty dance card."

Oooh, maybe this might work at a dance? If anyone actually gets the dance card thing. Which they probably won't, but it might be nice to say, anyway

The smile comes naturally to my face and, like that, my nerves disappear. "Would you be one of the names?" I ask in my flirtiest—but Victorianish—voice.

"Marissa." His tone is guarded and, from the look on his face, I know he's going to jump into his "we can't talk about feelings and stuff" speech.

Before he can, I pull the bouquet out from behind my back and hold it up so he can see all the flowers in it, hours of research on the internet and hours more of babysitting money spent at the florist all rolled into a bundle a little bigger than my fist. "I made something for you." A yellow tulip, red rose, and some lilac are clumped in the center of the bouquet, with hydrangeas circling them. I hope the whole thing says "I'm hopelessly in love with you and I won't give up" and not "did anyone die of consumption today?" *Maybe?*

He freezes on his side of the mirror and I can assume from his expression that I got it right. "You made that?"

I capture his gaze and nod. "It's called a tussie-mussie, right? It took me a little bit to research the right flowers to say what I wanted to. I know I can't *really* give it to you, but I can put it right in front of the mirror for you if you want." My smile falters and I lean forward to tie the bouquet to the mirror frame, my face inches from the silvered surface. "I need you to know how I feel," I whisper.

49

"Sometimes, fear like this can be a gift. It means you're growing beyond any artificial boundaries you thought you had."- Daymeon, *Starbound*

I pressed the pulp into the screen, looking up to check that all of the other campers at my table were doing the same. Most of them watched my movements and tried to imitate the way I dipped my screen and wiggled it in the water to catch the pulp. It wasn't like I knew anything more about papermaking than they did, but I picked it up like it was second nature. My pulp sheets were thin, rectangular, and sort of uniform as I flipped them out onto the felt to dry, unlike the campers' and Dev's clumpy blobs. After the mud thing, a little part of me thrilled at being better than him at something other than archery.

Working the afternoon shift at the rope bridge had been the most uncomfortable five hours of my life. Dev and I didn't talk to each other the whole time beyond what was absolutely necessary, but he was still his awesome, joking self to the kids. Dinner was impossible—we sat on opposite ends of the table. The dark cloud from our sort of-fight still hung heavy in the air, and even the kids seemed to sense it.

Even now, the tension between us was like a too-taut rope. Pairing us up had been the worst idea Em ever had.

I looked up to find Dev studying me from across the room like he was trying to figure something out. For a second, our eyes met and I froze. It was only a heartbeat before he dropped his gaze back to the mound of paper clumping on his screen. Confusion tangled with an intense need to just throw myself at him and I fumbled, dropping my screen into the pan of pulpy water.

I steadied my fingers and dug the screen out of the pan. Forcing myself to sound light, I demonstrated—again — how to dip and float just enough pulp on the surface of the screen to make a perfect sheet.

"And then you just wiggle it really carefully to distribute the pulp, just like the teacher showed us. See?" I set my screen down to drain and stood back to watch everyone else try.

Dev's eyes met mine again and this time I was the one who turned away, acting like I had been focusing on the boy next to him.

"Make sure you hold that screen parallel, Lee." But I felt my ears getting warm.

I gently rolled the surface of my paper, flipped it out, and mechanically went back into the pulp. The watery sludge swirled around my fingers and I pretended to be deep in my work. At the rate I was going, I'd have enough pages for a high fantasy novel.

Why was he always staring at me in that weird, but toe-curling way? Something rose to the surface of my thoughts, like the lighter pieces of pulp, and I didn't push it away.

Maybe those looks of his were like when Aedan was always watching Maeve, while he was trying to figure out if they could actually be together. Maybe he really was about to kiss me at the bridge, and I'd never know. Maybe I really was pushing him away without knowing it, like Maeve pushed away Aedan or Kaylie avoided Evan.

"I'm not an ice princess," I said to myself, earning a weird look from the boy at my elbow.

What if Dev's comments at lunch were him projecting, too?

I had a crazy, scary, maybe-awesome-maybe-awful idea. Was I really strong enough, like Maeve, to put everything on the line?

The friction between us was still thick through orienteering the next morning. Dev didn't joke around like he usually did and we seemed to move in concentric circles around each other—passing but insanely careful not to touch. Afterwards, as I was packing up all of the compasses and maps, I took a deep breath and tried to sound light as I kept my back to him and said,

"I just need to weed through all of the bows and arrows for this afternoon, replace a few strings, put aside anything that's too beaten up to use. You can handle lunch, right?"

"You're not going to eat?" he asked as he reached around me for the small rake he used to cover up all of the fire pits.

"Not hungry. I had a big breakfast." I turned to face

him, but his back was to me. "So, can you? The equipment is really in too bad a shape to get through one more lesson and I don't want anyone getting hurt." I crossed my fingers and hoped he wouldn't argue.

"I'll bring you back a burger," he said, tossing the rake onto the table and grabbing his clipboard. He started walking and added over his shoulder, "No extra pickles, since you don't need the ammunition."

I cracked a smile. "You're the best." As soon as he left, I jumped into action, grabbing my bag of supplies and high-tailing it to the archery field.

I hadn't lied about the condition of the bows and arrows. About a third of the arrows had chipped or damaged shafts, or destroyed fletching and some of the bows desperately needed new strings. I tore through the equipment and repairs faster than I'd ever done anything in my life. That didn't mean I wasn't nervous when I checked the time on the little clock on my clipboard. I really wanted to get this over with so I could enjoy what would potentially be my last afternoon of not feeling like an idiot.

I still had fifteen minutes before Dev was supposed to show up to help set up. Hands shaking, I spread my borrowed supplies on the ground and got to work sewing together the sheets of paper I had made the night before and writing. I was Marissa, figuring out the tussie-mussie. I was Maeve with the clover. I was Kaylie, planning out her song.

I was concentrating so deeply on my writing that I didn't even notice Dev until he was nearly on top of me. With a squeak, I rolled up my work and shoved it in my quiver.

"One burger, ammunition-free." Dev slid a napkin-wrapped burger across the table and, without waiting for my "thanks," headed over to my rack of repaired bows. He twanged a string. "Looks good."

"Yeah." The rest of our setup went the same way, him making one or two word comments and me unable to say anything longer back. By the time the campers arrived, the atmosphere around us was back to charged and tight, like we were engulfed in a ball of coarse Suffolk yarn.

"Do something cool," one of the boys challenged me, like every group had, and I looked over at Dev.

"We're here to teach you basic—" he started his usual spiel about safety and how tricks could wait. But as he was speaking, I nocked an arrow and, in an attempt to repeat what I'd done that day in the school field, whipped around and took a shot. The arrow zipped through the air and hit the blue circle. Not as impressive as a bullseye, but it still elicited a few gasps and "cool"s from the kids.

Dev joined them in staring at me. I shrugged, plucking another arrow out of my quiver—careful not to jostle my papers—and preparing for a proper demonstration. "I thought it might be good to change things up a little bit." I felt the corners of my lips turn up before I turned my attention to the campers and launched into archery 101. His eyes never left me.

Golden series
book 1: Golden
Pg: 443

take a deep breath,
don't be afraid,
and be just like Maeve

A feeling, like the heavy shadow of a wrecking ball, pressed against her skin.

"It's coming," Maeve whispered, the warm wood of the harp practically melting into her palm as she squeezed it.

Aedan looked up, shock clear across his features. "Not yet. You're not ready."

She took a deep breath. Now that the time had arrived, instinct was taking over, telling her what to do. "I'm the Harper. It doesn't matter if I'm ready. I have to stand at the gates or they'll fall. And then everything will be destroyed."

"The Guard will stand at the gates. They can protect both our worlds."

"Right. So they can get crushed first? Aedan, I need to do this. Alone. It's my *job*." The wind kicked up as she stood in the middle of rocks and gorse and moss. Her hair whipped around her like a wild thing, like she belonged in this place. The harp might have been symbolic of her power, but right now, she couldn't imagine being there without it.

Aedan bounded the rocks like they were nothing and pulled her close. "You're never going to be alone." Instead of struggling, she leaned against him and let herself soak in his strength and warmth. His chest rumbled when he spoke, his words vibrating through to her core. "We'll stand together. Legend be damned."

She laughed, but it was a hopeless laugh. That wrecking ball had turned into a bulldozer. Soon. "You and me, it's all like a bad fairytale, isn't it?" Aedan made it sound so possible, like this fantasy could be real, like they could stand against a century of prophecies and rules. She breathed in his scent of sea and clover one last time. "It was always meant to be this way. The Harper is supposed to fight without support from anyone. Not even you." She had to say goodbye, break away, and take her stand. Touching his cheek lightly, she whispered, "We weren't supposed to be together, anyway."

Maeve slipped out of his arms, but his hand wrapped tightly around her harp-hand. His eyes met hers and she couldn't look away.

"Enough of letting stories dictate what I can and cannot do or how either of us can feel." He said. "I want to stay with you. I will support you while you fight to save both our worlds. We will win this fight." He bent forward until his lips brushed hers, so light it could have been a breath except for the fire that rose up in her at his touch. "Please."

What she heard in that "please" undid her. "If the gates fall, save yourself. Go somewhere safe." She turned instinctively towards where the gates should open.

His hand gave hers a squeeze before letting go. "Safety is

nothing without you." He moved behind her, a warm shadow.

"Stubborn."

"Says the redhead."

She laughed and took her position between the worlds, fingers poised over the harp strings while Aedan's arms anchored her firmly in their world. Anticipation and fear coiled up in her, like a harp string tuned too tight. "Let it come."

The clearing in front of the mess hall was filled with hay wagons packed with campers, their voices filling the quickly darkening sky. Even though it wasn't fall, the night was that perfectly crisp kind that was just right for a hayride. Willing myself not to shake, I tugged the sleeves of my merino sweater over my hands and slipped my fingers into the thumbholes before reaching up to grab Dev's hand. Even the few seconds of contact though the wool as he helped me up into the wagon were enough to send tingles up my arm and straight down my spine.

"You look...abnormally nice for the woods," he said before quickly letting go of my hand and turning his attention to locking up the back of the wagon.

I let a tiny smile break through my nerves. I had trolled this Juliet pattern on Ravelry for ages before finally giving in, and knitting it in the Woolbearers rosewood colorway that almost made my hair and eyes look pretty. It was totally a Grace-approved sweater.

"I figured it would be cold out. This is local wool." An evil little Marissa-like part of me was tempted to stick my arm out and ask him if he wanted to pet the sweater, but

I held back and dropped onto a mound of hay at the back of the wagon across from him. My secret project, slipped up my sleeve, dug into my arm and my stomach started churning again.

One positive: if I threw up, at least I could blame it on the hayride.

The campers were wound up and, just as the wagon started moving, hay began flying.

"Whoa. Hay stays in the wagon!" Dev called out, ducking in an unsuccessful attempt to avoid a bundle of hay thrown his way. At the front of the wagon, Cassie and Mike were also trying to keep their campers—and the hay—from flying out into the dark woods around us.

A few more minutes of chaos and then Dev's voice carried over the dark night in an old, ridiculous camp-y song. Silly as it was, his singing reached straight to my bones and settled there, my body humming in time with his words. Dev wasn't one of our musical theatre stars for nothing. As he kept going, the kids started chiming in and the song carried over to the other wagons until the mostly off-key singing took over the quiet of the night. Between verses, Dev looked over at me and gave me a *Why aren't you singing along?* gesture, but I pressed my lips together tightly and shook my head. Em was the singer. I'd just sound like someone was skinning a cat in the middle of the woods.

By the tenth verse of "Henry the Eighth," half of the girls from my cabin had dissolved into giggles and the rest were starting to sound hoarse from trying to yell louder and sound "worse." The wagons pulled up alongside of the firepit and Dev popped open the wagon door, starting the campers on another song as we helped them down. I noticed how almost all of the girls went over to Dev's side. He was grabbing them by the waists and lowering them down to the ground, even though most of them didn't need the help.

Cassie bumped me in the side as she passed me, her free hand glued to Mike's. "Can you and Dev handle straightening out all the mess in here? Mike and I want to squeeze in some quality time," she wiggled her eyebrows at me, "before we have to make nice and sing kumbaya around the campfire."

I glanced over at Dev, who was still busy playing human elevator to all the female campers, and my insides twisted again. No use delaying my deep confession. "Sure."

"Grace was right, you are the best." Cassie winked at me before jumping into Mike's arms in a totally graceful cheerleader move.

When all of the campers were off the wagon, Dev pulled himself back on board and flopped onto a half-destroyed hay bale, rubbing at his arms.

"Who knew almost-sixth graders could be so heavy?" he complained, before looking at me and the empty wagon. "Where are Mike and Cassie?"

"I told them we'd handle clean up." I couldn't meet his eyes and instead focused on picking random pieces of hay from between the wagon's wooden slats. Back in the cabin, I'd gone through my entire notebook one more time to

ISABEL BANDEIRA

absorb as much bookishly romantic knowledge as I could
to be ready for this moment, but it didn't stop my stomach
from turning somersaults.

"Thanks for volunteering me," he said dryly, tilting his
head back against the side of the wagon. "We really need
to work on that selfless impulse of yours. It's making a lot
of work for both of us."

"It's just hay. Besides," I gulped down my nerves and
pulled my secret project out of my sleeve, hands shaking. *I
was Maeve, ready to defend the gates. I was Marissa, sealing
back the demonic spirit.* Sliding next to him in the wagon, I
handed him the folded up bundle of papers. Even though
we still weren't sitting that close, I could feel the heat radi-
ating from his body and all the chilled parts of me were so
tempted to burrow into his warmth.

He looked from the little book to me like opening it
could make laser beams shoot into his eyes. "What's this?"

Another deep breath. *I was Kaylee, baring her soul on a
stage where everyone could see.*

"Just read it," I said as fast as I could, pulling my flashlight out of my back pocket and wiggling it at him.

Dev squinted at the title in the sparse light coming from
the clearing and the moon. "The story of the shy knitting
girl and the mini sock boy?" He looked up at me, brows
furrowed together. "Phoebe—"

"Read it, please?" I whispered, my throat tight. I needed
to get this over with so I could dive under the remaining
hay and wallow in my mortification.

He stared at me for a few heartbeats before nodding silently and taking the flashlight from me.

While waiting, I grabbed a piece of hay and started splitting it with my fingernail. I reached for another and another until I had a pile of stiff strings in my lap. At least it kept my hands busy so he couldn't see them shaking. I snuck a glance at him, but his face was shadowed and his lips were in a straight line, neither smiling nor frowning. Ice shot down my spine. Maybe I should start neatening up the wagon. That way, if he rejected me, I'd have an excuse to keep my back to him.

I started to turn, but Dev's hand on my arm stayed my motion. His eyes were wide and his expression serious. "Is this story about us? You and me?" He gently lay the bound pile of handmade paper on his lap and his thumb traced the rough edges.

My fingers curled around the pile of hay-strings and I nodded, dropping my eyes. This was a stupid, ridiculous idea. He had to think I was some nutty—

"Is it true?" He reached over and gently used two fingers to lift my chin so I had to look him in the eye. It took monumental effort to keep from sucking in my breath. "You like me?"

My brain ran through the possible answers. Marissa would have something snappy and cute. Maeve would say something immensely quotable. I could just quote directly from that part in *Golden* where she confessed her feelings to Aedan. Or—Dev's thumb just barely grazed my chin and cleverness flew out of my head as my heart decided to stop.

"Yes," I breathed. I wasn't Marissa or Maeve. I was Phoebe. I wrote a silly story about the guy I liked. And I was positive he was about to reject me, let me down easy. I braced myself for his answer.

Dev's expression remained serious, but his voice seemed to shake. "I was hoping you'd say yes," he whispered back.

"Really?" Cue pulse running though my whole body, centering on those spots where his fingers touched me.

"Really."

He leaned forward, but I reached out and stopped him with a hand against his chest, as bold as Maeve. If this was my story, I was going to be the one to decide the ending. "And you like me?"

"I've been trying to tell you that for ages, but you kept finding ways to push me away." At my raised eyebrow, he moved his fingers from my chin to my cheek. His other hand came up to pull a piece of hay out of my formerly perfect curls. He squinted at me for a few long seconds, making me wonder if I had pushed too much. "I'd level cities for one of your smiles."

I held back a laugh, the tightness in my chest loosening to make room for the same feeling as finding a book I really wanted on shelves a few days before its release date. "That's from the *Sentinel* series!" Any boy who would quote a romantic line from a bestselling YA novel had me, heart and soul.

"Caught me." In the dark, his pupils had dilated, making

me feel like I could fall and fall into his eyes forever.

"No," I said, dropping my hand and leaning forward until my lips were millimeters from his, just as bold and crazy as any of the characters I admired. "You caught me." We both seemed to move at the same time and I didn't know or cared who closed the distance between us.

Our lips met and it was like the fire Maeve described running through her veins when kissing Aedan, and the energy Marissa felt with Cyril, hit me all at the same time. Our first kiss was tentative and awkward as we tried to figure out where to put our heads and hands and bodies. It was clumsy and definitely not "perfect" like any of my favorite book kisses, but all I wanted to do was pull him closer and never let go. Dev leaned forward and his hand slipped on a patch of hay in the wagon, sending us both tumbling into a mound of hay. He pulled back, using the side of the wagon to prop himself up slightly.

"Sorry." But a silly grin spread across his face and he brushed hair and hay out of my face. "Not as smooth as your book crushes, huh?"

"I don't know. I think I like the real thing better." That earned me an even wider grin and this time when he bent to kiss me, we lined up perfectly. Hay dug into my back through my sweater and jeans and I didn't even notice.

After what seemed like a lifetime of kissing, Dev pulled back, his lips a whisper against my cheek. "We need to get this wagon cleaned up and get to the bonfire before Mr. Hamm comes looking for us again and busts us for PDA."

I groaned, but let him pull me up to sitting with a coaxing kiss...or two or three. "So, what do we do now?" A limp curl hung in front of my nose and I pushed it behind my ear. My hair was probably a rat's nest of tangles, but he didn't seem to notice.

Dev seemed to take a lot of pleasure out of helping me wipe the hay off of where it clung to my sweater and hair.

"Considering what just happened now and everything, does that mean I finally get a real pair of socks?" At the look on my face, he flicked a piece of hay at my nose. "I hear that kitchenered toe thing is amazing."

I tossed a handful of hay in his face, then shrieked as he stuffed a retaliatory bunch down the back of my sweater.

"Goof," I choked out between laughs.

"But a cute goof, right?"

"Bollywood-worthy cuteness." In a move that would make Marissa proud, I reached up and pulled him down for a kiss, breaking away after a few seconds to start working on straightening up the wagon. I turned and smiled at his surprised but happy expression.

This was the best camping trip ever.

The camp was quiet at the moment. In a few hours, we'd be loading up the buses, but now, everything was still. I'd felt electrified all night, the haywagon and the bonfire and our ride back running over and over in my mind. So, when the first hints of sunlight tinged the sky, I climbed out of my bunk, grabbed a sweatshirt and my book, and slipped out of the cabin without waking any of the girls. A bit of reading might calm down my all-too-active brain. I touched my lips with my fingertips and stifled the urge to giggle like a little kid.

I set myself up on the dock, dangling my legs over the edge so the toes of my sneakers just barely skimmed the water's surface. I only had about two chapters left of *Cradled* and I could probably finish them before reveille.

"'Sometimes you need to leave everything you know to find yourself and to learn that life isn't a solo,'" I read aloud to the pines.

"Talking to yourself?" A voice said behind me and I nearly fell off the dock. Dev grabbed my shoulder to steady me. "Sorry, didn't mean to scare you." He joined me on the edge of the dock, letting his hand slide down my arm to capture mine. Even through my sweatshirt, his touch brought goose bumps up on my skin.

I tilted my head to look at him, smiling but wishing I had thought to put in my contacts. "I'm quoting from great literature while communing with nature, and you just interrupted me." A part of me wanted to reach up and kiss him, but the still awkward and tentative part of me held back, waiting for him.

Dev didn't kiss me, just started rubbing the back of my hand with his thumb. His other hand tilted my book so the page faced him, too.

"Is that the book with the whispering lips on the jawline?"

Out came the blush, rushing at warp speed from my roots and down my neck. "No, it's the book about the violinist. And I'm never going to live that down, am I?" His lips turned up in a wicked little smile in response, and I sighed. "Didn't think so."

He bumped me lightly with his arm and squeezed my hand. "You could always take notes…"

Even though laughter was threatening to escape the faux stern set of my lips, I resisted the urge and pretended to go back to my book. It was hard balancing the book and turning pages with just one hand, though, and I resorted to trying to use my nose.

Dev laughed, tapped me on the tip of my nose, and turned my page. "Allow me."

I smiled up at him and felt like my heart was going to burst through my shirt. His face was a silhouette against the sun as it rose over the lake.

"'Oh, keep the world forever at the dawn,'" I said, quoting Kaylie in chapter eight when she quoted Emily quoting Marjorie Pickthall in *Emily's Quest*, which was totally on my to-be-read list. I had to stifle a giggle at the fact that I was quoting a line from a real poem quoted by a fictional character being quoted by another fictional character. Like book geekishness times three.

"I'm down for that." Dev's fingers left my book's page and he reached up to tug a strand of hair out of the loose crown braid I'd slept in. The curly piece bounced in front of my eyes.

Hands occupied, I twisted my lips and unsuccessfully tried to blow it out of my face. "What did you do that for?"

"I'm supposed to push a loose strand of hair out of your face, then let my hand linger on your cheek, or isn't that how, like, every other kissing scene in those books you read goes?" He gently tucked that piece of hair behind my ear and let his fingers slide down to tilt my chin up until my eyes met his. "Well?"

I blinked, my skin hyperaware of his touch and probably short-circuiting my brain a bit. Even while being completely and totally swoon-inducing, he still managed to make me want to laugh.

"Sounds like you've been..." His thumb traced my chin and just barely glanced over my bottom lip. I sucked in a breath and almost forgot what I was going to say, "...taking notes, yourself." I gently lay my book down on the dock, far from any risk of falling in the water. I might have been captivated by Dev's eyes on mine, but this *was* a collector's edition.

That dimple showed up again in his cheek. "I actually rate higher than your book?" His thumb paused again over the corner of my lips.

I reached up around his neck, letting my fingers dig into his hair. "For now. But when the last *Hidden House* book comes out, you're gonna have some serious competition."

"We'll see about that." He was close enough that everything was out of focus but his eyes, which took on a little bit of a gold-green glint in the soft morning light. My focus dropped to his lips, which quirked up—he noticed. He moved and his mouth was millimeters from mine. "I plan on making you forget all those book boyfriends of yours."

His breath tickled my lips and, heart pounding, I inched a tiny bit closer so mine just brushed his as I spoke.

"Good luck trying." And then gravity took over and there was no space between us.

Dev pulled back, dropping a quick peck on the corner of my mouth. "I think I love the woods. It took getting you covered in mud and hay to admit you liked me."

I put my hand on his chest before he could come in for another kiss. "What about later today?" I tried not to let that oh-so-real fear creep into my words, and just aimed for a very light Marissa-like tone. I let my other hand trail along the neckline of his sweatshirt and I marveled at how he froze and his eyes grew brighter at my touch.

"Huh?"

"Well, we're not going to be co-counselors anymore. You don't have to bring excitement into my life, or whatever the job description said, after we step off that bus." Being this flirty with him felt funny and yet right.

Amusement flickered across his face. "I'm sure I read about this being a long-term position." He played with that loose strand of hair again, tugging the curl straight and watching it bounce back into a limp spiral. "Besides, maybe I'll start getting As in English. The perks of dating you definitely outweigh all of your book nerdiness."

He didn't say the right thing, the perfect, bookish love-interest answer, but it was still wonderful and real. Relief flowed through me and my smile grew into a cheek-achingly wide grin.

"Look who's talking, theatre geek."

"So, how does that story of the shy knitter and the mini sock boy end?" His fingers trailed down my cheek before slipping away and wrapping around the edge of the dock.

Turning my head to look across the lake, I shrugged. "Would it be too predictable to say I hope they're going to live happily ever after?" I held my breath, waiting for his answer. I didn't want to scare him away.

Dev began swinging his legs and every tiny contact of his leg against mine sent tingles across my skin. "Well, I'm still aiming for a sequel, maybe a trilogy. Definitely something truly epic." He grinned when I looked skeptically back at him. "What?"

"Sequels have too much drama. And usually have cliff-hangers." I started swinging my legs in time with his, like a metronome for our matching heartbeats. "I have a love-hate relationship with cliffhangers."

"How about a trilogy with our own weird drama-free kind of epic?" He leaned forward until his nose bumped mine and added, "I'm aiming for bestseller status with this one." He kissed me softly, so lightly, before sitting back and waiting for my response.

I reached for his hand and squeezed, leaning against him and letting him wrap his free arm around me. "'Oh, keep the world forever at the dawn,'" I said again, and his arm pulled me a little bit closer.

52

Pine Central's cafeteria was louder than usual, but I barely noticed. I absently dipped my grilled cheese stick into my tomato soup and flipped the page, careful not to get grease on *Northern Light*'s crisp, new pages. Aurora had just entered the home of the leader of the *Huldufólk* and was about to see Gideon again. A whoop a few tables away as the hockey guys did...something...just became background noise.

"I don't know why she even bothers to sit with us." Em's hand waved in front of my face and broke my concentration. "Seriously, Feebs?"

I swatted at her hand and turned a little so my book was propped on the corner of the table. "Shh. it's getting really good," I said, wishing I could stick a "do not disturb" sign on the back of my shirt.

A hand clamped on her shoulder and the light in her rose up to twine with the darkness seeping off of his hand. It was funny how the darkness used to feel ominous and now felt wonderful, like a caress.

"Weirdo."

"Shh." Any scene with Gideon in it was worth missing out on the latest lunch gossip.

His other hand brushed gently against her back to turn her so she was partly facing him. "Yes, she may be new, but Aurora has been a fast study." Those almost unnaturally blue eyes met hers.

A hand softly brushed my arm and I looked up into naturally hazel eyes that were a brownish-green at the moment. Dev slipped onto the bench between me and Em, managing to squeeze two trays of food onto the already crowded table. Between his massive lunch and Alec's, it was amazing the cafeteria didn't run out of food. "Sorry I'm late, MacKenzie wanted tips for a teacher flash mob at graduation this year."

I smiled up at him, pointed at the page, and gave him the one-second gesture before turning back to the book.

"Let's go talk," Gideon whispered and gave my arm a tug.

I resisted his pull for a second, two seconds, but his shadows twined with my light and by second three, I was following him. He had less to lose if I became trapped—in fact, life would be better for him, but, still, he'd worked so hard to teach me how to talk to these leaders. He wouldn't trip me up in the last minute.

We stepped through the doorway into a short, narrow hallway leading to a staircase. "Aurora, what I said earlier, about how I feel—" he said softly making me freeze midstep. I turned to look at him, but he was staring straight ahead. "—it was only because I didn't want Hallur to use me and my feelings against you—"

My heartbeat sped up in time with Aurora's. This was it—Gideon's confession. Tingles flowed over my skin.

"Just a tip, Phoebe," Em said, reaching over and closing

the book on my fingers, "Normal people don't ignore their boyfriends for books."

I leaned against Dev and book tingles were replaced with real-life warmth. "He's okay with it."

Dev's chest shook with laughter. "I know there's no point in getting between you and," he craned his neck to see my book's cover, "what's the paranormal creature of the week?"

"Besides," I said, ignoring his comment and swatting at his hand with my book when he tried to swipe a bite of my grilled cheese, "Normalcy is overrated."

He avoided the book and grabbed a grilled cheese, anyway, scrunching his nose in a "so there" look before taking a bite. "Definitely overrated."

Alec finished his cheesesteak, balled up the wrapper, and tossed it so it hit Dev's shoulder. "Can you two please stop being so…couple-ish? Em's been gloating since you came back from camp last week and it's starting to get old."

Grace looked up from her chemistry notebook, eyebrows arched and lips pressed together with the corners just barely turned up.

"Only starting?" She met my eyes, letting a little amusement slip through.

"I have a high tolerance for Em hyperbole," Alec said, ducking the wrapper that Dev threw back at him.

"Mmmhmm," Em said, studying him with a mock thoughtful look. "Watch out, Alec . I'm on a roll. Maybe I'll find someone for you, next."

"If you do, I'll tell your dad about Wilhelm."

"Really? Wait until your parents hear about the microwave experiment that destroyed their season 4 *Enterprise* DVDs," Em said pointedly.

While they argued, Dev put an arm around me and I snuggled against him as I opened my book again. "So, Feebs," he started, and I reached up to put a finger against his lips.

"Just one more page."

ACKNOWLEDGEMENTS

Even though I've dreamed of writing the acknowledgements for my first book since I was old enough to hold a pen, I never thought it would be this hard to write. Maybe because I'm afraid of missing someone (like Maria in *The Sound of Music,* I'm convinced I'm going to write "Well, God bless what's-his-name" and post-printing, I'll be the one yelling, "Kurt! That's the one I left out. God bless Kurt!" in a book-store…) So, first, to the person I'll inevitably forget: God bless what's-your-name.

Carrie Howland, you are a super-agent. I couldn't have made it through these past two years without your support and guidance. Thanks for loving *Bookishly,* putting up with my non-stop texts and loooong emails, and for always making me smile. The next time I'm in NYC, I totally owe you an ice cream!

To my amazing editors Patricia Riley and Asja Parrish: your book-making magic is beyond compare. Thank you so, so much for championing and believing in this book. From our first chat, I knew I'd love working—and being friends—with both of you. I fangirled you on our first call and I'm still fangirling you today. I owe you both a massive hug.

Thank you to Karen Hughes, Michael Short, Mark Karis, and everyone at Spencer Hill and Midpoint who gave me such a beautiful book. (BOOKS! BOOKS EVERYWHERE!!!!) And Meredith Maresco—I'm so glad that you're not only *Bookishly's* publicist, but also, from my first photobomb in your Meg Cabot picture at BEA to all the book squeeeeing we've done together, my friend.

To my CPs, friends, and book angels: Veronica Bartles, Stephanie Pajonas, and Deena Graves. *Bookishly* was a wee baby mess of a manuscript when you first saw it and you helped make it into what it is today. I can't put into words how lucky I am to have you, but to borrow a phrase from Veronica: "I'm so thankful"—I couldn't have done this without you. Thanks to Marnee, Kim, Travis, Megan, Nori, and Jodi for beta reading this book. Sending tons of happy book karma your way!

Kissy scenes are my Kryptonite, and without Madeline Martin, they would have all looked like: "and they kissed. And then they stopped kissing." I'm sure everyone reading this is thankful you made sure that didn't happen. Thank you so much for that and for your support and advice, Twitter Twin!!!! To Erica Cameron and Liza Wiemer for calming me down when the whirlwind of publishing had me feeling like Dorothy on the way to Oz. And to all of my author and blogger friends on Twitter, thank you for always knowing exactly what to say when I needed it the most.

While researching archery for this book, I fell down the archery rabbit hole and fell head over heels in love with the sport. Coach Cindy Gilbert-Bevilacqua and Coach Dawn Altomonte, thank you not only for looking over the archery scenes to make sure I didn't have Phoebe "notching" her hand at her forehead to start "shooting arrows into things," but for also for being the amazing coaches you are and for feeding my love of archery. And to everyone at Middletown Archery, you blow me away with your skill and talent—thank you for welcoming me into your world.

A long time ago, I had received bad advice that made me give up on writing. It took a lot of people—whether they knew it or not—to inspire me to try again. This book exists because of you. Thank you to the 'Celsies—especially James Heaney and Emily Potter, for reminding me of how much I loved writing and for teaching me so much about building engaging narratives. I look up to all of you as the incredibly talented writers you are. To Amy Plum, your book *DIE FOR ME* and meeting you at your signing in Tuxedo Park is what really inspired me to actually try to write my own book (and thank you for sharing your incredibly swoonworthy fictional dead boys with the world). And to Meg Cabot, whose blog-y advice helped me jump from fanfiction to my own fiction—meeting you not long after meeting Amy inspired me to keep going and push past the dreaded "elephant butt" middle section of my first real manuscript. Both of you might not read this, but I have to thank you, anyway.

To all the R&Divas, especially Lori Dombrowski, Erika Corbin, Yolanda Shepard, and Chris Herrmann—the four of you were my go-tos for every drama and doubt as I tried to make it through writing and queries and publishing. Thanks for all the after-work and lunch cubicle chats, advice, and endless reads and re-reads of my awful queries, drafts, and bios.

I'm so lucky to be a part of the kidlit writing community, where many people give so much of their time to help support others. Thank you, Brenda Drake, for Pitch Madness and to Summer Heacock and Dee Romito for picking *Bookishly* for Team Fizzee. To the Eastern PA SCBWI region, especially the advisors, organizers, faculty, and fellow writers at the annual Poconos retreat at the Highlights Foundation. Those cabins contain a lot of book-making magic.

To Phoebe-cat. Without you, Phoebe-not-a-cat wouldn't have a name. I owe you some extra fancy dry food.

Nela and Susie—you are the Trixies to my Phoebe and the Phoebes to my Trixie, and two of my most favorite people in the world. Thank you both for all of the support and love. To Joey and Dennis, who put up with a crazy writer sister-in-law but are never afraid to chip in when I need help—thank you. And, of course, to little Joey and Sara—shh, TiTi is making a book, but she'll make a tunnel/read you a book/play with you later because you're her favoritest first nephew and first niece.

Last, but not least, to Mom and Dad, who gave me a loving and supportive home, lots of good food (aka: writer fuel), and who put up with a lot of *"Can this wait? I'm writing"* over the years. (Dad, you were 100% right—I can be an engineer and a writer!) I love you both so much.

ABOUT THE AUTHOR

Author photo by Rachel McCalley

Growing up, Isabel Bandeira split her time between summers surrounded by cathedrals, castles, and ancient tombs in Portugal and the rest of the year hanging around the lakes and trees of Southern New Jersey, which only fed her fairy-tale and nature obsessions. In her day job, she's a Mechanical Engineer and tones down her love of all things glittery while designing medical devices, but it all comes out in her writing. The rest of the time, you'll find her reading, at the dance studio, or working on her jumps and spins at the ice rink.

Isabel lives in South Jersey with her little black cat, too much yarn, and a closetful of vintage hats. She is represented by Carrie Howland of Donadio and Olson, Inc.

31901056912266

CPSIA information can be obtained at www.ICGtesting.com
Printed in the USA
LVOW07s0247261215

R10392100001B/R103921PG467761LVX1B/5/P